the *Buoyant Letters* of *Mimsy Bell*

the Buoyant Letters of Mimsy Bell

LAUREL DODGE

Littoral Books
Portland, Maine

Cover art from Fire on Water *by printmaker Deborah Kozak*
Cover design and book design by Lori Harley

ISBN: 979-8-9878057-4-9

Littoral Books
Portland, Maine
www.littoralbooks.com

To my husband, Ben,
for his unwavering love and
support. Thank you
for always believing in me
and my writing.

Dear Gerald,

The water into which I release this letter is not the same water in which you slipped away, though the river remains the same: sinuous, deceptive, violent. Cursed though she is, people still come from all directions to bob along on floats, ride her rapids, and dance and drink themselves insensate on her beaches as if she were tame. It's said she takes three lives per year, a debt for a wrong done many years ago. The year of your death she took only two. I'd like to think you were so alive you counted for more than one, that your sacrifice spared another.

Sixty years ago, the water ran like silk under our canoe. Your paddle on the left, mine on the right. You were heavier by a few pounds, so you took the stern even though I was better at steering through the boulders. Those boulders remain in place. The river's done her best to bury a few, but then she digs them up again. They never travel, not like the millions of other stones she incessantly sorts, always by size, from the smallest clay particles, to silt, sand, granules, pebbles, and finally the cobbles. The boulders, they wait, immobile, frozen beneath the surface, as they did the day she took you from me.

Sixty years ago, her banks were flushed with crimson cardinal flower and a delicate white flower I never found in any field guide. You'd stripped to the waist, and my eyes soaked in the strength of your body like nourishment. We heard the wood thrush beguiling us with his magical flute. We smiled and kissed and made love in a bed of pine needles, our bodies reflected in the water. You and I and the river, all the right ones together.

Today, I watch the young people in their canoes pass by banks covered with trillium and lady slipper. They wear bikinis and board shorts, their bodies mostly naked in the sun. The air is fresh, so clean their city lungs are drinking it in like ambrosia. Brown-headed cowbirds sing with a watery burbling, serenading the lovers who laugh too loudly, drink too much, and make out with all the wrong partners.

Your face was rapturous after we made love; that is what I remember from the best day of my life. Your eyes were empty after you hit the boulder; that is what I remember from the worst day of my life. Two days that were one. If only I had the luxury of remembering the first and forgetting the second. Sometimes, on the road with the band, I hoped that the next hit or toke would be the one that erased that sector of my brain, but drugs never offer such kindnesses.

After you died, I gave up my home. You slipped away. I turned away. Away from friends, neighbors, the nets my family threw out to break my fall. The young people nowadays say to find your tribe, as if surrounding yourself with people just like you will insulate you against the big bad world out there. Well, I had a tribe for sixty years. We looked alike, thought alike; our dreams were all the same. But membership was conditional. And when Lawrence died, I no longer met their criteria. The elderly widow of a great musician with no chops of her own was someone to leave behind, an unnecessary burden.

Back here in Menotomy, I am not Mrs. Lawrence Bell. I am baby Maggie who had such terrible colic that her mother had to walk her around and around the gazebo in the town square a hundred times a night until she settled. I am Margaret, the little girl who got her head stuck between the posts of the library railing and howled so fiercely half the town came to witness my release. I am the ten-year-old Meg who stole a licorice whip from the five-and-dime and got beaten with it after the shopkeeper chased her down and snatched it from her guilty hand. And I am the svelte, young, fresh ingénue Mimsy who took up with the wildest boy in town despite the headmaster, the minister, and the sheriff having given me the low-down on your background.

It is comforting to have everyone's provenance in the back of my mind. Who is whose baby, cousin, auntie, business partner, sworn enemy, ex-boyfriend, or secret lover. To know how they fit together.

How they've rooted and branched out since their families first settled here, two-hundred-and-fifty years ago, or for some like me, returning just last week. The human landscape is at a scale that makes sense. They are all neighbors and there are not so many of them that I can't keep track. And the physical landscape hasn't changed, I can walk upon the same roads and paths I knew when I was a girl. And even before I could walk, my mind imprinted on these woods and fields, their mountain backdrops, and on that damn river.

I traded this community for a tribe because I couldn't handle all the reminders of you. I am old enough to know better now, just shy of eighty-one. I aim to make peace with the river. I want to return to being who I was when I was with you. I want to be buried at home, and I think there is just enough time left to weave myself back into the fabric of this town, so that they can legitimately lay me to rest in its soil.

I've collected antique bottles ever since we dug around in that old dump in the woods and unearthed that one I fancied so, the dark cobalt blue. The ones in my collection are all different, mostly patent medicine, some sarsaparilla, some sulfur bitters, all from antique shops. One day I found myself ordering corks to fit. I suspect they are seaworthy now, or riverworthy, as that is what I need them to be. I often wondered if I'd let go of the canoe and followed the roiling waters to the sea if I might have found you there. Maybe these letters will.

I've missed you,

Mimsy

~~~~~~~~~~

Dear Gerald,

Early this morning, I called up the Menotomy Cemetery Committee and asked them if there was any room in the Fight Brook Burial Ground. Despite looking half empty, it is closed and has been since 1921. But I have a great-great-great-aunt and uncle, resting in peace under the old oak tree, waiting for me there. I've been on the move, on the road, forever, and soon enough it will be time for a permanent patch of ground to rest my bones. And I prefer it be ground consecrated by kin. Closed or not, I'll try to find a way in. Once in, there I will stay.

To stay in one place seems so appealing. I have so many cities under my belt: New York, Boston, Los Angeles, Detroit, Dallas, Chicago, Memphis. Reno. Rolling in under cover of darkness with the band, met by screaming crowds, seeking oblivion in someone's arms, doing the whole thing again three hundred miles down the highway. We were vagabonds, a band of famous and anonymous drifters. Our sound brought thousands of people together and not one of them ever had a glimpse of who we really were. Thousands of shows and we made no permanent connections. Wait, I take part of that back. Lawrence "connected" to one, or two, or three particularly fetching girls every two-night stay, and I with him, but that is a nameless fuck, not an intimacy.

Now, don't fret about my language. Nor about the sex. Things have changed since the 1950s. And just because I am an old lady doesn't mean I am good. I have been bad, very bad, far worse than you. Even the animals know it. As I sit here on the slope of Mt. Tom, two jays are reciting my sins; a cheeky red squirrel, its tiny back legs thumping against the branch, is scolding me; and even the crows atop the pines are taking a vituperative tone. I am getting closer to the river and nature is throwing down the unwelcome mat.

And well she should. I am an environmentalist's nightmare. My flesh has been pickled by so many drugs I ought to walk around with a HAZMAT warning sign around my neck. I abandoned nature completely for decades, traded our lovely soft landscapes for the dirty, sharp edges of nightclubs and stadiums. I've left outdoor concert venues that fans covered from end to end with garbage without feeling an iota of responsibility. I did not procreate, did not contribute a person to the whims of nature's evolutionary playground. I no longer have any connection to the land and from the sound of its emissaries, loudly encouraging me to turn back, nature knows it.

What I had instead were lots and lots of people and lots and lots of fights. Jealous rages, frustrated meltdowns, angry outbursts complete with broken plates. You wouldn't have recognized me back then. I had some rough decades there. The free love '60s and free- to-be-you-and-me '70s, every minute of which I spent stoned or under one band member or another and feeling completely and vastly alone while shoulder to shoulder with my tribe in the middle of two thousand fans. Knowing that I wasn't good enough to be on that stage and taking it out on anyone who looked at me sideways.

It is a long way from the band-shell at the county fair to the Fillmore, but I made it there—if only by virtue of marriage. To be sure, I did play fiddle well enough to impress the judges. You heard me play. I was good. Lawrence heard me the year you died, when I was playing my pain away, and I was even better. He heard me play on a Sunday night; the rest of fair week he romanced me, and when they swept out the band-shell for the last time, I left with him and did not look back. His band was in its infancy then. I was there for every growing pain, every bumped head, every loose tooth. And I was there for the band's growth spurt, Lawrence's meteoric rise, and the real-deal, pot-scented, hippie-guru fame, the stardom.

But no matter how Lawrence and I tried, no matter how brightly he and his bandmates burned, we were atoms, millions of miles apart, profoundly disconnected. In retrospect, I see there was no other way for me to be without you. That one time with you by the river eclipsed a thousand times with him on the road. One perfect moment. I always had that. I don't think my husband ever found it. No, not even with me.

Love,

Mimsy

Dear Gerald,

On my way down to the river today, I saw one of the young cops striding through the hayfield in full uniform with a black lab by his side. I recognized him. His name's Aidan Ward. Heard the river took his partner last year during a rescue. I wanted to stop and give him my condolences, but he was sweeping the field as if searching for a body. I didn't overhear anything during breakfast so I am pretty sure there hasn't been a killing—news like that travels fast in a small town—but the officer seemed intent on his task so I left him to his work.

Gerald, do you recall the thoroughbreds that used to be pastured in that field? Gosh, we must have stolen and returned them twenty or thirty times a summer. You were so bold. Just walked right up to them in the pasture with the bridles you'd snuck out of the barn and exchanged a handful of sugar cubes for their silence. Hours of riding side by side through the forests and meadows. Remember the day we flushed a couple of grouse from the side of the trail and the horses exploded? I thought we were goners, but you quieted the black and I pulled up the bay before they could toss us into the ravine. We always brought them back wet and blowing, but the farmer never caught on.

Other rides were more peaceful. We'd drop the reins and let the horses walk at their own pace. We'd listen to the rush of the wind through the pines or the hushed pitter-pat of young toads hopping away from their big, clumsy hooves. Some rides were unforgettable. Like the day the baby spiders decided to go ballooning. On thousands of gossamer strands of silk that glinted silver in the sunbeams, they were drifting through the air all around us. Little tiny specks of life, hopeful, traveling to new homes. I was enchanted. You were twisting and turning in the saddle like a madman, frantic, brushing the spiderwebs away with both hands. We laughed about it later, but at the time you were not at all amused.

After you died, well, my exploits weren't so romantic. Lying on top of Jockey Cap Mountain for hours, eyes drinking in the impossible blue of the sky, wishing that I was pregnant was the first of them. A shameful wish that would have dishonored my parents, but that is what I wanted. I knew unmarried girls who "got themselves in trouble" were shipped off to relatives, like that Thompson girl, the one who left for Christmas recess and never returned. Even knowing that would be my fate, I hoped for it with every fiber in my being. I wished so hard to retain a part of you that I was truly shocked when my body made it clear I wasn't carrying your child; any chance of it flowing from my body with my blood.

Presently, I am at the end of the road, sitting by the river, ready to send this letter to you. There are no tales of our child to share. My trajectory would have been so different had my wish for a baby been granted. If my family had let me keep her (in my dream it is always a girl) and not insisted she be given away, I would write to you of the baskets full of diapers I washed, how clever she was at math, the many birthday parties we threw, her wedding at the church, her children's weddings. I'd relay stories of the joyful hours I'd spent playing with your grandchildren and great-grandchildren. No band, no drugs, no adventures, just a slightly improper start to a regular woman's life. But we both know a regular life was never in the cards for me.

How I miss you,

Mimsy

~~~~~~~~~

Dear Gerald,

I don't remember them being so thick. In fact, I barely remember them at all. But here they are, clouds upon clouds of them—a ground fog made up entirely of mosquitoes. Already the whine of their evil little wings is inducing madness. Several of their little hypodermic needles are stabbing me in the back of the neck. I am sorry, Gerald, but I will have to finish this letter as quickly as possible or be drained of blood!

I came across Aidan, the young police officer, in Fawcett's Pharmacy yesterday. I found out he's a transplant, moved here two years ago, and I think he's feeling a little lost. I introduced myself. He is too young to know who I am, which is a gift in first meetings. Too often the fame of the band precedes me. I asked him where his dog was. He said it belongs to the family of his late partner and he just takes it out for a run on occasion. I offered my condolences. He spoke bitterly of the river. He has every right to. My own bitterness has lasted sixty years almost to the day.

The great thing about being old is you can just launch into reminiscences and the young have to indulge you. I mentioned that you were never a great favorite of the sheriff, that you stole many things including my heart, and that the river took you when you were only twenty years old. He was surprised when I told him I write letters to you and use the river as my postman. I mentioned that I would be at Hemlock Bridge next Thursday afternoon, on the anniversary of our first date. I didn't quite invite him, but I think he felt invited. I hope he shows up. Occasionally, strong young men get knocked down by their feelings in a particularly bad way. They pride themselves on standing so straight and tall that they refuse to bend with life's circumstances, and instead they break.

But I didn't break, Gerald. For a long time, it felt like I would. My arms would ache at night in their desire to hold you. I wept every morning for months. The smallest reminder would trigger the tears. I railed against God and the universe—still don't trust either of those tricksters. But while I shrugged off the comforts of family and friends, I did not abandon the little things I loved: my music and my sketchbook and the little wildflowers. If anything, I became more obsessed. The changing seasons kept me going outside to look for new flowers, to collect seeds for my garden, and to draw what I found. And the fiddle, well, eventually it took me away from the river's taunting, mocking song, her twists and turns that make it so that no matter which way you travel in this county, you always end up on a bridge crossing her waters. I needed to go then as much as I needed to come back now. And I am glad I am back. Not only do I need to be here, but I am beginning to think here needs me too.

I heard Mackey Wright yelling at that tiny little wife of his when I walked by their house today. You remember his great-grandpa, Old Man Wright, who lived on the farm halfway up Fight Brook Road? Well, the great-grandson doesn't seem quite so upright as his lineage would predict. The girl came out into the dooryard, sat sobbing on the granite steps. Didn't see me though I was only fifteen feet away. Poor little dear. It was all I could do not to run up to her and hug her hard, but Mackey was still tossing stuff around by the sound of it, and people around here are fiercely private, wanting to solve their own problems, even when they know they can't.

I saw plenty of the same among the rich and famous on the road. Strung out, angry, and out-of-control doesn't discriminate by social class. When I was young, I could have used a shoulder for comfort more than once. Later on, there were bandmates who could have used a hand up after one of my intoxicated dressing downs. Now I am old and I am sober and I am kinder, there is nothing stopping me from offering comfort to others.

You know, Gerald, I didn't come home to be a bystander. I came home to be part of this town again. What do you think about me stopping by the Wright's place when it is quiet? John Wright was my great-grand-father, so I have the perfect excuse. That's where my cousins are buried. As we both know, I'm still searching for my final resting place. This one would be under a tall grove of pines with a nice view of Mt. Washington. As my real estate agent tells me, it's all about location, location, location.

So much for the hurried letter! I may be half a pint of blood lighter, but talking to you has lightened my heart in a good way.

Love bites,

Mimsy

Dear Gerald,

You aren't going to believe this! They are knocking down the White Pine Tavern where we used to con that dim-witted busboy into stealing beer for us. He'd hand them out the cellar window. I'd give him one kiss on the cheek per beer. Worked very well as I remember from how very drunk we got. Those were the halcyon days, Gerald. Now, I'm not quite so pretty, and I have to buy my own beer.

Fellas with huge backhoes are having a go at the tavern's façade, swinging those heavy-toothed buckets into the two-hundred-year-old walls, but she's creaking and groaning and fighting back. Those six-inch posts and massive timber-framed beams aren't going down easy. Two other demolition guys are waiting in the dump trucks to receive the broken timbers and cracked boards, but it is clear it will be a slow death, so they're napping while they idle.

You'd think they'd at least have the courtesy to reclaim the old wood, put it back to work decorating some rich guy's summer house so he can have photos taken for the tourist magazines, but no, into the grave it goes. To make room for what? A Dollar General, the type of establishment that gets built in towns too small or too poor to attract a Walmart. Of course, you aren't familiar with any of these names. All I can say is that society gave up on the family business decades ago. And that everyone from sea to shining sea knows Dollar General and Walmart because now there are just a handful of giant corporations, their stores the same in each and every town.

I didn't linger by the construction site. I kept walking lest I give in to the feeling that I should defend our history by throwing stones at the bucket loaders. But my legs aren't as quick in a getaway as they used to be. Bursitis in my left hip slows me down. And with surveillance cameras everywhere, vandalism isn't half so appealing as it once was. But, perhaps as a reward for turning my back on my baser instincts, I rounded the corner just in time to see the giant, stilt-legged, lumbering backside of a bull moose disappear into the fir trees near the stream.

There are fewer and fewer moose each year. People still hunt them, of course. Cars wipe out quite a few. Ticks, thousands of ticks, suck the life right out of them. And then there is the heat, like nothing you or I ever experienced back in the old days, and you know that moose practically wilt in the heat. Soon they'll decide Menotomy is too tropical for their liking and hightail it up to Canada.

After the moose, I didn't expect more entertainment, but this town is plagued with eccentrics. Walking down the opposite side of the road was a young man, probably in his sixties, completely engrossed in a paperback and blind to his surroundings. He stumbled twice over impediments and was constantly drifting to the left. I couldn't help myself, as soon as we were abreast, I shouted over, "You are going to get hit by a car." The man looked up for a moment and said, "Doubtful," then glued his eyes firmly back onto the page. They say you lose your filter as you age, but considering the roadside he walks is littered with beer cans and fallen branches and that speeders and logging trucks careen down it every day at fifty miles per hour, I think I can let my inner busybody out rather than suffer the guilt of not having spoken up when one day I happen across his prone and lifeless body.

Speaking of butting in, I am thinking I should tell Oswald Martin about the fight I heard up at the Wrights'. He's the minister of the Congregational Church now, if you can believe it. But, of course, you can believe it; he was always shepherding people, even as a teen. You know how I used to go steady with him before you and I fastened eyes upon each other? Well, the first and last time I kissed him he fell right off the log we were sitting on and into the river. Came back up soaking wet and started lecturing me about the mind-body dichotomy and the sins of the flesh! Back then I was convinced I'd done something terribly, terribly wrong. Now I think he just got a boner and freaked out. Life on the road might have been tough, but no tougher than life as the chaste minister's wife in this gossipy town would have been. A life of Woodstock, music, and weed vs. parsonage, prayer, and creed. If those were my only options in this life, I'm glad I took the first. But if there had been a "door number three" with you hidden behind it, there is no doubt that's the one I would have chosen.

I wonder what Oswald thought when I took up with you? God, our relationship wouldn't be worth a "tsk, tsk" compared to what went on with the band after you died. There is a reason we find the words "sex" and "drugs" and "rock 'n' roll" together so often. Let's multiply by a hundredfold the shock Oswald suffered when I kissed him. Then multiply that by a thousand to estimate his reaction to our riverside dalliance. And finally, explode that by multiplying it times itself to find out just how bad it would have been if he found out his first girlfriend went on to become a drug-abusing orgy-instigator! I believe sudden death would not be an unexpected consequence of that revelation. Still, as uptight as he was and still is, I think he is in a position to help. I know Mackey's mom was in his fold and so Mackey probably spent a few of his younger Sundays in those pews. Gerald, I will not be able to die properly if I don't do my duty here, so it's off to church I go!

Miss you too much,

Mimsy

Dear Gerald,

My dear, the gossip in this town is not only excessive, it is also immortal. Not one day after I visited Oswald, lips were flapping in the hardware store. The bloviating old coots remembered I'd dated him in high school, remembered I'd left him when I became spellbound by you, and speculated that I was finally going back in for the kill sixty-four years later!

Oswald looked as if he'd had a sudden onset of thyroid disease, his eyes bulging out of his skull, when I opened the door of his office. I have to admit that I intentionally dressed to shock him. Among the perks of being a rock star are all the stage costumes. We played a mix of rock, folk, and psychedelic, so skimpy, fringed outfits were the look of the day. I still have all my clothes from over the years, and due to decades of childlessness, cigarettes, and heroin, I still fit in them.

Oswald got an eyeful. I have a rockin' bod—for an octogenarian—

probably from all that walking I do. And my hair is white and hangs to my waist. Let's just say I don't look like your average short-haired, elastic-waist, buttoned-up New England grandma. After Osgood regained control of his eyes, he stood and greeted me properly. He listened closely and professionally to my story. There were nods of under-standing at appropriate intervals and he said "hmmm" a lot. He shook his head sadly once and cleared his throat twice. But I guess the collar comes with a gag order. Oswald wouldn't tell me a damn thing about the couple. Neither would he open up about what he was going to do, nor did he make a single suggestion as to what I should do. The man is maddening. Well, if he doesn't act quickly I may have to go in for the kill, just not the kind of kill the portly codgers at the hardware store are dreaming up in the privacy of their lonely beds.

Well, I did my best and it's time to head home. That is, if my lonely bed at the inn can be considered home.

Yours,

Mimsy

Dear Gerald,

It's Mimsy. But you knew that. Even the name I go by is of your invention. So taken by the poem *Jabberwocky*, and how it wasn't sappy, dour, or drear like the rest of the poetry we memorized in school, you would recite it aloud at the slightest provocation. And so, from the third line, "*All mimsy were the borogoves*," my nickname was born. Still not quite sure what it means, though it rhymes charmingly with whimsy, something many of my lovers took advantage of in the poems they penned and left on my pillow. I thank you wholeheartedly. "Mimsy" was a gift that fit perfectly, a light raiment. Not heavy boots like Margaret or sudden and full stop like Meg or shapeless like Marge. Not everyone gets the gift of a new name. I hope, in the end, I fulfill its promise.

I wasn't sure Aidan would come. But it was with great relief that I heard tires crunch on gravel. As soon as my ears caught the sound, I smiled. He was quiet when he got out of the car. I motioned for him to sit beside me, inside, on the covered wooden deck. Each of us leaning against one of the two wide, curved trusses that run the length of the bridge. I gave him some paper and a pen. He wrote, left handed, wrist bent, with the paper cocked oddly. He filled up the page quickly, in an untidy scrawl and then folded and creased the paper repeatedly as if making a paper fan. I pulled out a blue bottle from my bag—a really nice one—his partner will love it, and handed it to him. He gave the note a final fold to make it fit and then capped the bottle tight.

We stood side by side and leaned out over the rail. I dropped your letter straight down. I like to see them go under and then bob to the surface. Aidan tossed his. We stood, silent, until she carried both letters out of sight. He took his leave with a "Ma'am" and a nod. "Next year?" I asked. "Yup." Then he proceeded down the rutted washboard of a dirt road and out of sight in the pine and fir.

All yours,

Mimsy in Wonderland

Dear Gerald,

No, in case you've been wondering, I have not found an actual home yet, still living at the Hobblebush Inn, though my real estate agent is working on it. But I did buy a car. I traded in Lawrence's Jag. It was garnering too much attention. I loved the connection it gave me to him, but I'll never fit in driving one of those. People will accuse me of "putting on airs," a catchall insult around here. (Little do they know, hippies don't have airs.) And I am sure the beautiful, useless thing will slide right off the road as soon as the first snowflake hits the ground. I bought a Subaru, a Japanese car. Don't scold! We are friends with Japan now, so in no way am I being traitorous. When I was shopping, I jokingly asked the car dealer in Conway if I could get one with the requisite fifty-odd liberal bumper stickers pre-applied, but he laughed and said that was a do-it-yourself, aftermarket upgrade. I like this car, Gerald. Her name is Becks, she is twilight blue, and she has fog lights. I think we are going to be best friends.

I wish I could buy my parents' place, but the current owner, a prickly old pine cone named Batty, won't be swayed by any offer, no matter how ridiculously high. She's in tight with the historical society ladies, and owning the historic Browning house must give Miss Batty Holt something to lord over the other biddies. Now, I do look at all the other houses that come on the market, but none of them is quite right.

I think you would have enjoyed the shopping-for-a-house part of life. It feels just like spying. The real estate agent opens the door and someone's inner life is exposed for you to see. No staging around here. Reality is hanging loose. From the unlocked gun safe by the bedside to the Playboy shower curtain in the bathroom to the dirty dishes hidden behind the oven door, the news that people won't buy houses that look lived in hasn't reached Menotomy, Maine. Neither has the news that the book is dead, as shown by the fact that overstuffed bookshelves are the number one decorating choice of the region. Number two is a pair of antique snowshoes or wooden skis mounted over the mantelpiece.

Speaking of books, Booker—that's what I have decided to call the man who walks while reading—was on Fight Brook Road again today. "What are you reading?" I called out. "*The Wendigo*" was his reply, given without a glance in my direction. I guess if I were reading about a demon wendigo while walking beside thousands of acres of empty wilderness, I'd be afraid to look around me too. I don't know what to make of him, Gerald. Since we now pass by one another on a daily basis, I'd like to get to the stop-and-chat stage, but Booker, he's polite, but closed. Then again, that's any Mainer for you.

The river is sparkling today, her ripples splintering sunlight into a dazzling display. Some would be enchanted. I am touched by her efforts, but try as she might, I am not ready to forgive. Of course, she's all a-glitter, she has you.

I love you,
Mimsy

Dear Gerald,

Ate lunch with Aidan at the new roadhouse on River Street. Its walls are bedecked with bawdy pictures of Marilyn Monroe and Betty Boop and vintage pics of Errol Flynn in boxing gear and Elvis gyrating. Aidan, a big, tall guy with ridiculous shoulders, blushed when he realized that we were surrounded by such suggestiveness. Little does he know, poor innocent kid, that I am unshockable. But I won't be the one to burst his bubble about the sweet old granny he's befriended.

It's so nice to have a new companion and so refreshing that he isn't a musician. I tired of their talk long ago. Conversation with a policeman gives you a brand-new, eye-popping perspective on the world. The moment he crossed the threshold the ambient noise level in the restaurant dropped as a whisper passed through the dining room... *here comes the law.* At least nobody knocked over their chair and raced out the back door. I'm not up for police chases anymore, but you may remember me being a bit more game in my youth.

My favorite apple, Black Oxford, you remember, the purplish ones, had just come ripe at Cat Pond Orchard and you took me there to steal some. It was dusk. I was filling my skirts and you had a pailful when we heard the squeal of brakes and saw the sheriff's car stop on the side of the road. We dropped everything and ran. The sheriff caught up with us, yelling, "I told you to stay away from that boy, Margaret!" You pulled me into the river to escape. The water was damn cold that day, but we swam across and hid in the woods, sharing the spoils, a single fruit you'd shoved deep in your pocket. No apple since has been so crisp or tasted so sweet.

Needless to say, I did not confess my crime to Aidan, though it made me feel a little hinky when he ordered a big slice of apple pie at the end of the meal.

Aidan wanted to talk about his partner. Of course, "talk" in these parts equals about two sentences followed by, "Ah, well, it's nothing. I'm fine." His partner was a young lady, and I can tell he is at war within himself as young men are these days between feeling he had failed as her protector and allowing that she was his equal and needed no protecting.

"Drowning is a horrible death," he told me. "After I graduated from the academy up in Vassalboro, I completed public safety dive training and took part in extra practice dives whenever they came up. But Shelly, she didn't have as much dive experience. I should have gone in her place."

I put my hand over his to comfort him. He seemed to be cheered by the gesture so I left it there a few moments. My, oh, my, the contrast was shocking. I guess I don't look at myself so often as I did in my vain, younger years. My hands are wrinkled and bony now; there are age spots all over them. His hands were huge, I could see most of his wide fingers and elastic, young skin, tanned and smooth, beneath my tiny claw. But I won't let myself think about that. I had my days of being new and beautiful once. He has his now.

For my part, I told him all about my house search. That I want something very close to town that feels like it is in the country. Something with apple trees or a small woodlot, preferably with some wildflowers, though I would take gardens. A house with big windows would be nice, especially if it has a view of the mountains. That there has to be a bathroom and a bedroom on the first floor in case I eventually get old and can no longer climb stairs. He liked my list. Lives in an apartment himself and is beginning to have a hankering for his own place, but hasn't amassed the funds quite yet. We tussled over the check. I wanted him to save his dollars to put toward his future home, and he has no idea that I have more than enough money in my bank accounts and investments to cover lunch through the next century. I let his gallantry win this time and told him the next meal was on me.

See, Gerald, I am making connections, friends, here again. They may not be with my contemporaries, the historical society biddies, but then again, I am not a historical society kind of bird. I am going to mix it up a little bit this time around, choose friends that I like rather than choosing them because they are like me.

Time to say goodbye. The river is very calm today. At this spot she is wide and slow. She's sorted out an inviting sandy beach, but it is so full of water that it might as well be quicksand. You think you are stepping on solid ground, but you sink eight inches deep, making it quite a slog to get to the water. But that's not going to stop me from sending your letter. Nothing she can throw at me will.

Your little fugitive,

Mimsy

Dear Gerald,

She's raring for a fight today, Gerald. It rained for three days straight and I have never seen her move so quickly. I know the word slipstream is meant for the air, but that's how she is behaving today, swift, frictionless, slippery. Her water is also darker than usual. Probably picked up a lot of sediment. She's running high, and I know better than to get anywhere near her when she's like this. I'm going to toss the bottle from the rise where the teenagers camp. Maybe I'll collect a few of the empties they leave behind for when I run out of my store of pretty vintage bottles.

You know, I think of you grown up like me when I am writing, but of course you never got to grow up. You were only twenty when you died. I only grew up myself about two decades ago. I think it was the aftermath of my sixtieth birthday party that fast-forwarded the clock. That was a blowout! Lawrence planned it as a surprise. I think everyone I ever knew was there and all of them were staggering drunk by nine. We sang and danced through to the next morning, though we did neither very well. When I woke up on the floor, hand-in-hand with Lawrence, unable to move, that's when I knew our extended childhood was over.

Don't get me wrong, the party was a blast. I was so pleased to spend time with old friends (it was only the bandmates who would cause trouble later) and to be the center of attention for a day. But the chilling realization that neither Lawrence nor I were immortal came upon me suddenly and hard. No matter how I tried, I could not get my legs under me. Lawrence was in no better shape. I cried out and some of the younger guests gave us a hand. They had partied all night, but when I called they jumped up easily from whatever clandestine tangle they'd found themselves in and helped us to our feet. We had partied all night, and we were flat on our backs and immobile on the floor. That helplessness, the realization that we couldn't depend upon each other to get ourselves out of sticky situations anymore, made me think the unthinkable for the first time. We were getting old. And we'd better grow up quickly or we wouldn't get much older.

As it was, Lawrence didn't make it to eighty. But he made it to a very respectable seventy-five and he did not die helpless on the floor. Quite the contrary. He died in an extremely comfortable hospital bed with a steady stream of adoring young nurses (of both sexes!) to entertain him. I was there too, of course. It was the final stages of heart failure, treatment wasn't working, and he lasted only a few days. Not as grueling or as prolonged as some fates, and so I was at my best for him up until the final day. He apologized to me, Gerald, right before he died, for not focusing on our marriage, for all the women he dallied with on the road. I was so stricken with guilt, I felt like all the blood in my body had drained out the bottoms of my feet onto to the floor. It was I who should have apologized. For not being present in our marriage. For sleeping with his best friend. For your memory always coming between us. And yet, despite his unselfish gesture, I couldn't respond generously.

I did climb into bed with him and held him and sang his favorite songs until he passed away in my arms. But I was too immature, too damaged and selfish, to give him the peace he gave me. As I said before, you wouldn't have recognized me when I was with the band. I was so bitter and afraid. My heart was closed. I hope I've matured in the past few years, enough at least that you'd recognize me now.

Of course, the river would never make that mistake, she's always seen right through me.

Mimsy

Dear Gerald,

I've heard the less snow we have in the winter, the more snowmobiles are up for sale come spring, and this year's Ski-Doo crop is bountiful. There are several on the lawn of the outfitter, probably older models they are retiring. And dotting the roadsides, six of the noisy, smelly beasts appear to have run aground, pitifully immobile on the dirt and grass. In the mountains, we are defined by our transportation, the reality of months of deep snow directing our choices: pickup trucks, Subarus, snowmobiles. Once we had trains, though, more powerful than snow.

I thought of them when I crossed the old Mountain Division tracks on my way to the river. The rails run empty now, parallel to a new paved trail where people walk their dogs and ride their bikes. Trains stopped running decades ago. Menotomy took a step backward when it lost its rail lines. We shipped so many of our crops and products via those boxcars. Folks used to take the train to Portland for fine dining, Christmas shopping, and visits with relatives. At a time when not everyone had a car, especially women, the train represented freedom, a ticket to adventure, a way out of the woods.

You and I never had the cash for travel, but remember when we rode for free? Leave it to you to suggest we hop a freight train. I'd say that was the most dangerous thing I'd ever done in my life, but clearly canoeing the river out-dangered it. I can still feel the strain in my shoulder as you pulled me up beside you onto the platform. Some of the cars were filled with lumber, some with potatoes, some with hay. You had the poor judgement to pick an empty flat car, not realizing how hard it would be to stay stable. We clung together in the center as it rocked back and forth, flying through the wilderness. And we clung harder and dug in our heels when the engineer started braking for the next stop. It was amazing we weren't flung off into a tree trunk or a cow pasture at fifty miles per hour.

Transportation was on my mind today for a reason. You remember Jack Bourgeois? He was but a tot himself when you knew him. When I crested the hill by the river, there at the top was Jack's youngest son, the caboose baby, in the middle of the road trying to command—of all the awkward vehicles in the world—a unicycle.

The kid had stacked plastic crates and was using the stack to steady himself as he mounted. It really was an unfortunate spectacle. An unsteady rider. A huge hill. The tarmac lying there, sharpening its claws, just waiting for a victim. I know it was cowardly, but I race-walked by so I wouldn't have to witness the inevitable crash. However, he was still alive and upright when I passed by on my way home. I introduced myself, proclaimed him the bravest soul in Menotomy, and told him I knew his dad when he was baby. He told me his name was Jack just like his dad's, and that he already knew all about me and the band.

The kid's a fan of '60s music, Gerald. There's no escape this time. I've got me a groupie.

Yours,

Mimsy

Dear Gerald,

I have a date!

We're going to a performance at the fancy-pants arts center in Brownfield. Don't be jealous, dear one, my gentleman companion is all of sixteen, and the only thing he is trying to woo me out of are stories of my days on the road. He's a sweet talker though, and he's already finagled free copies of two of the band's albums, a concert t-shirt, and private fiddle lessons. But, I ask you, how can I be expected to resist a boy who rides a unicycle?

I'm hoping to keep a low profile and just be a regular audience member at this concert. Burnt Meadow Music specializes in folk and bluegrass, and the band had periods exploring both of those genres. There is no way the Burnt Meadow Music staff won't have heard of us, though they might not have heard of me. But I will be accompanied by a young herald who, as an over-excited fan, has not been at all discreet about my fame. I suppose I should just steel myself for the inevitable. Kiss any hope of anonymity goodbye. Surrender will make it easier to relax and enjoy a grand time with my young friend. Plus, even if he outs me, I've heard the concert hall is serving my favorite tonight, turkey pot pie. It's Young Jack's favorite too. Despite our age difference, when it comes to what constitutes fine dining we are simpatico.

Now, from successes to failing friendship attempts. I came across Booker when I visited the historical society searching for Batty. I was there to ask her once again to sell me back my parents' house. But there was Booker peering into old tomes. He dresses a bit too nattily to be from the region, more Orvis and Filson than Carhartt and Cabela's. He even tops off his outfits with felt hats, the kind with a decorative feather tucked into the ribbon around the brim. I wonder what his story is. All I could get out of him, despite my considerable efforts and charm, was that he is looking for information on his father.

I couldn't continue my interrogation of Booker because Batty appeared. Gerald, she's a rock on this one. Bedrock. No way she's selling the house. You'd be sickened by the amount of money I offered her, especially since you haven't exactly been keeping up with real estate values. Which she clearly has, as her eyes widened considerably when I whispered the sum, but still no deal. I give up. I am not getting my childhood home back unless she kicks the bucket before me. She's several years younger and those years have been full of clean living. I'm old and have lived like there is no tomorrow. I'd be a fool to bet on this race. Time to set my sights on something new.

Love,
Mimsy

Dear Gerald,

My fame preceded me. The Burnt Meadow Music director made me stand up and take a bow before the crowd. Surprisingly, they applauded. Then I was handed a fiddle and invited up on stage to play. Good thing I'd taken my date with Young Jack seriously and had worn a dress. I would have been embarrassed to appear in my usual outfit, a sweater and jeans.

I don't know if it was Young Jack who ratted me out or if I was recognized, either by my name, which I used to reserve the tickets, or by my face (which has deteriorated a bit since the last press photos that went out but is still obviously me). Whatever the circumstances that got me there, once I was onstage, I was in heaven. I played one song, my favorite from the band's third album, the one with all the fiddle Lawrence layered in especially for me.

I haven't performed in front of a paying audience in years. But I still practice every day, and before Lawrence died, I toured and jammed with the band. But lately, Jack's lessons are the most formal thing I've pursued. Still, the music flowed. In this magical venue carved from trees and starlight and glass, all the weight of old expectations floated away and there was nothing left but the music.

Then the audience stood up and clapped for me. Gerald, I received a standing ovation. Well, me and the pianist. But mostly me. Not the band. Me.

Over the moon,
Mimsy

Dear Gerald,

Still feeling the high of last night's show. I was so keyed up this morning, I had to get out of the inn, so I took a victory stroll down to the river looking for blue flag irises, thinking they'd be in bloom. My steps stirred up some unexpected walking companions. Three tiger beetles, their metallic green backs making them look like wet subtropical sparks against our dark boreal landscape, lifted off and settled, lifted off and settled, lifted off and settled, always keeping just a few paces ahead of me. Their flight was the perfect accompaniment to the rhythm of my steps.

I was so absorbed playing chase with the wildlife, I didn't notice the clouds brewing over Mt. Washington. They say if you can see the mountain, you'll feel her winds. Well, you'll feel her winds all right, her winds, her rain, and her thunderbolts. If the river wanted me to turn back she could have just said so. But yesterday she was all sunny and smiles, so I should have known today she'd have a trick up her sleeve.

She's in legion with the clouds. I mean, where else does her water come from? But a lightning strike right up the road? That is a serious screw-you move. My hair stood up and then my skin prickled. The white light was so brilliant, my retinas are still burning. The concussion shook the ground. The oak it hit split down the middle and started smoldering. I was too slow covering my ears, and the ringing in them continues even now, hours later.

Gerald, I have never in my life seen anything so impressive. Wow. What a great way to die! Instantaneous! Legendary! People pointing out the spot where it happened for years afterward. I definitely would have made town history and earned my place in the ground. That is, if there was anything left of me to bury!

Despite wanting to get a letter to you, I wasn't a complete fool. The sky was still swirling like a milkshake. And since lightning can strike twice, I turned back. Mackey's wife, who had been hanging her washing on a clothesline strung between the ell of the house and the barn when I passed her on the way up, was looking up the hill at the smoking, demolished tree as I made my way back down. She called me over and we went inside to have a pot of tea. The first thing I wondered was if, following up on my tip, Oswald had also dropped by to share a cup of tea this week. Didn't know if there was a polite way to ask straight out, so I held off.

The girl is tiny, Gerald. She's eye to eye with me and I've shrunk a good three inches since you knew me. I should have followed all the alcohol I drank over the years with milk chasers to keep my bones strong. Anyway, her name is Cécile. She is Québécois. I had a bit of trouble understanding her. Her accent is quite strong. She's alone down here in Maine; all her family is in Canada. She's much younger than Mackey. When I asked her how her husband was doing, her tone became pensive and strained.

Once the clouds had passed and the sun came back out and it was safe to do so, Cécile and I went back outside. She showed me to the burial ground I'd asked about. There are eleven headstones. The dates ranged throughout the 1800s, each engraved with the years a beloved member of the Browning or the Wright household passed into, and out of, history.

The Wrights who took over the farm after my relations died were some kind of cousins of my cousins which I believe makes Mackey and me related, something I was not ready to bring up with Cécile, being uncertain the exact nature of their strife and not wanting to appear to be on anyone's side. I sat on the lichen-covered stone wall looking at the patches of columbine, primrose, and lily of the valley that had been planted to pretty up the place. I mentioned that I hoped to be buried beside my ancestors, being that they were the closest family I had in town, as my parents had moved out of state before they passed away.

With that, the girl burst into tears. She told me that she misses her family terribly and worries she won't get much time with her mémé before she's gone, but she hasn't visited in over a year because Mackey needs her here. He's struggling, she said. He doesn't do well when she's gone, even for a short while.

I figured this was a good moment to ask her if she knew Reverend Oswald Martin, and surprise, surprise, she did not. Gerald, I was raging internally at that silent, sanctimonious fraud of a community leader. But what I said aloud to Cécile was that Oswald was a good man, and Mackey had gone to his church when he was a boy, maybe she and Mackey might like to try that again? I stopped at that gentle suggestion, thinking I'd said enough, but she seemed to take it as an opening.

"Mackey's not who he used to be, not the man he was when I first met him. He got hurt doing a construction job. Ever since he's been in constant pain. He can't work. Most days, he just sits in the recliner staring out the window. I have to help him with almost everything. Some days he can't even get dressed."

This time, seeing as I was right beside her and we'd been properly introduced, I did sweep her up in my arms and into a big hug, and I let her cry. She was embarrassed when she pulled away, but I think the kindness did her some good. Clearly, I need to keep an eye on her. She even gave me an opening to visit when I headed out, saying that she sees me walking by almost every day and that I should stop by again soon.

Gerald, life is so delicate and so complicated. One moment you think you have everything and the next moment it's all gone. She misses him so much and he's right there. I miss you, though you are long gone. The river and her thunder and lightning spared me today, so I have some tomorrows to try and make things better. I will start by giving that fool Oswald a piece of my mind. Cécile's trust is not something to neglect.

Lucky Strikes,

Mimsy

Dear Gerald,

Young Jack has it in his head that he should write an article for the local newspaper about me, "Local girl leaves town, becomes famous rock star, returns home a washed-up old lady" or some such foolishness. He ambushed me in town, coming around the corner on that unicycle like a madman. He's learned to dismount rather gracefully, I give him that. He's also relentless. I told him his grandfather was never so cheeky and he'd best learn some manners if he wanted to get his way, so he gave me a long, drawn-out "please" and made his eyes all big for an extra-plaintive look. Sucker that I am, I told him yes.

I put him off for a couple of days on the actual interview. I had business to conduct beneath the spiky steeple of the Congregational Church. And conduct it, I did. Oswald was playing the organ, probably preparing for evening choir practice when I entered like the storm cloud that has filled my nightmares since the lightning strike last week. Lucky for me, I know his full name, Oswald Pingree Martin, and when I deployed it in the tone of an angry aunt, he sat up straight and listened. There are people in this town, I said, who need you. Who need you more than the congregation needs a pretty hymn on Sunday morning. Mackey and Cécile need you.

Then he stood. And he looked at me with the same exact expression he'd had on his face after I kissed him all those years ago. Like I was some kind of test for him to pass in order to earn his angel wings. And though he is as old as I am, there was no tremor in his voice when he spoke:

"Where have you been all these years, Margaret? You come flying back into town and just now are oh so concerned? While you've been away playing rock star, we've been fighting for our young adults, those brave enough to stay in this beautiful town even though there aren't many jobs and not much to do. We open the food bank when they run out of money before payday. We buy their kids good winter coats. We fill up their oil tank when it runs empty and there's still one more month of winter. We'll bury their parents for free in the churchyard. We host AA meetings here every week. We get that crooked-toothed teenager of theirs to the orthodontist.

"A couple weeks ago, you didn't even know the name of Mackey's wife. You might know some of our old folks' names, even my middle name, but you are an outsider. It's too bad, Margaret. If you'd stayed, you'd get it. As it is, you might as well be from another planet. And, by the way, I did ask Mackey to come to see me. He refused."

Well, for the first time ever in our acquaintance, Oswald has given me something to think about. I didn't expect a welcome home party when I came back here, Gerald. I've tried to keep a low profile. But what if I am butting in where I don't belong? Oswald is right about some things. I've missed sixty years of history, I can't rely on my memories to make sense of everything, and I'm nobody's fairy godmother. But, Cécile, I held her in my arms while she cried, and Mackey, well, he's kin, distant kin, but still, he's family. I may not be on the front lines like Oswald, but certainly I can do something useful?

I saw Young Jack on the way out. Told him to postpone the article, at least for a few weeks. When you aren't sure if you are the good guy

or the bad guy in the story, an interview seems like too much exposure.
Where are you when I need you?

Mimsy

***

Dear Gerald,

I am still reeling from my confrontation with Oswald. It isn't going to
be as easy as I thought to weave myself back into the fabric of this town.
I think the fame and money and time away may be insurmountable
barriers. But I hope it is not impossible, as I am staying whether they
remember me as one of their own or not.

However, I am getting on well with the other outsiders. Aidan must
have been listening carefully to my wish list at lunch the other day. The
giant, black, off-road truck that the Menotomy Police Department just
bought screeched to a halt beside me as I was walking this morning
along Fight Brook Road. Aidan jumped out and ran toward me excited
as a child who'd found a puppy. "Mimsy! I found the perfect house for
you!" He opened the passenger door and motioned for me to get in. I
tried to clamber up, but it was like scaling Mt. Washington getting into
the thing. He waited until my third try, lost patience, and lifted me up
into the seat.

We didn't so much drive as roll over the roads until we were back
in town. I felt like a doll in the passenger seat, but the truck did have a
commanding view! A quick turn onto Route 5 and a hairpin left, and
there it was, a tiny farmhouse painted green, completely surrounded
by pine and white birches that had grown up where wide-open fields
were back in our day, Gerald. I fell in love instantly. Best of all, it has
an enormous flower garden! I couldn't go in, but Aidan had been inside
when they got the call that the owner had passed away. He said the
house is sturdy and sweet and the majority of the living space is on the
first floor. I told him he'd make a good, but very macabre, real estate
agent if he ever tired of police work. Like an ambulance chaser, but one
gruesome step beyond that. Then I thanked him with a big hug.

So today is looking up in many ways. There's the house, and when I
sat on the banks of the river, there were at least twenty lovely damselflies

flitting through the shrubbery. They are so unusual they hardly look real. They have ebony black wings and metallic bodies, some are shiny green and some are electric blue. They fly like prehistoric creatures, heavily, awkwardly, and erratically, nothing like the big green darners we used to see down by Cat Pond. I know damselflies start life in the water, and if the river is sharing them with me, maybe I can share something with her, the memory of you chasing me, telling me those green darners flying around us like fighter jets were going to sew my mouth shut. I didn't believe you, but I shrieked and ran anyway, for the game was on and the resulting catch and tumble with you too delicious to resist.

Your soon-to-be homeowner,

Mimsy

Dear Gerald,

I am still shaking as I write this. I knew something was going to happen, Gerald. I knew it, but I didn't do enough to stop it.

I was on my way to the river yesterday when I saw Booker coming down the hill toward me. I had made up my mind to stop him and engage in conversation about the novel he was reading when we both heard screaming from Mackey's. We looked at the house, its faded cedar shakes and mossy roof deceptively quaint, then at each other. In the same instant, we both took off running toward the front door. I didn't give any thought to what we might find.

We ran straight through the flowerbed in the front yard. Through an open window we heard Mackey cry out, "You are better off without me." Booker ordered me to stay and he entered alone. I pulled out my cellphone and dialed Aidan. He picked up the phone immediately but was three miles away. Then I heard Booker through the door, speaking in a calm, level voice, "Everything's going to be all right. Just let me take the young lady outside. Then we can talk."

When I heard Mackey yell "Get out!" I pulled the door open a crack to see what was happening. Cécile was kneeling on the floor beside Mackey who was standing with a gun pointed at his own head. Cécile was begging him to stop. Mackey was right on the edge. I'd seen the expression on his face before; one of our roadies committed suicide publicly after losing a long battle with alcohol and pills.

When Booker took a step toward Cécile, Mackey shouted, "No! No! No!" His plans were going awry, and he was highly agitated. He emphasized each "No!" with a violent, reckless shake of the gun, each movement dropping the barrel down toward Cécile or lifting it up toward Booker.

Booker moved suddenly and fast. I didn't see it coming. He scooped up Cécile in his arms and took the four or five steps out of the house in one giant leap before Mackey could react. The screen door slammed shut. We ran until we heard the shot. It rang out, across the garden, between the apple trees, and across the freshly mowed lawn. Mackey's life completed with a singular and final note.

Booker stopped. Cécile started keening. It was an unholy sound, like demons were tearing the breath from her lungs. Booker set her down in the grass and ran back toward the house. I sat next to her, folding her in my skinny arms, wishing I were more substantial, softer, more of a mom, with a pillowy body better able to absorb her heaving sobs.

Aidan, in his black truck, roared into the driveway followed immediately by two police cruisers. Booker came out of the house, spoke to them briefly, and then the three officers went inside.

Cécile was babbling semi-coherently. We shouldn't have interfered. She could have saved him. He'd tried to kill himself before and she'd talked him down. But this time was different, this time he wasn't high... he was out of everything. "Don't tell the cops," she whispered to me. "I've been buying for him. You have to understand, he's sick. He's so sick. It started with the painkillers, the Oxy for his back, then the damn doctor wouldn't give him any more. He just needed a little bit every day to stay even, and heroin is cheap, so that's what I bought him. But I didn't get any work last week or the one before, so we don't have any money. He tried to go off it. He thought not being able to get any was a sign he should get clean, but he just couldn't. You saw him. I didn't know what else to do. I didn't know what to do."

I just stroked her back and told her she did okay. And I wondered if Booker and I did okay. Because there had been nothing else to do.

Gerald, I failed.

Mimsy

Dear Gerald,

It's been one rough week. I'm still sick about what happened at the Wrights'. If I let it, my mind careens wildly, trying to figure out what I could have done differently, how I could have prevented Mackey's death, but each scenario I entertain ends the same.

When I made my statement at the police station, I could barely keep my composure, my voice cracked and I had a hard time catching my breath. They said I did fine, but I felt like there was something missing from the story, some detail, turn of phrase, or revelation that would make it all make sense. Maybe there is no sense to it. Maybe it's just biology. The drug changes your brain and you can never be free until you are dead. I know how it is; I feel the pull every day. These past few days more than most. Even seeing the horrifying end addiction brought to Cécile and Mackey, I can't deny that every time I heard or said the word heroin over the past few days, something inside my brain perked up, remembering, craving.

Luckily, I had Cécile to care for, a responsibility and distraction. Since she has no one here in Menotomy, I rented her a room in the inn. When she's not sleeping—which is how she spends most of her time, despite having refused the sleeping pills the doctor prescribed—she comes to my room and we talk. Or mostly she talks and I listen, or she cries and I quietly hold her. The first night, she was so distraught I accompanied her back to her room and sang her to sleep. You know I'm not the best singer in the world, but I had some voice lessons on the road, and the band has a whole album of dreamy, calming songs. I went through them all.

Cécile is certainly not ready to go back to the house yet. I suggested she call her family in Canada, and she finally did, but I ended up doing most of the talking. I've also been over to see Jim Holt at the funeral home. Cécile is in no state to make funeral arrangements, so I am doing the routine parts and encouraging her to make the important decisions. I told her not to worry about the cost. She chose a lovely carved casket, as Mackey had been a woodworker. Next, someone is going to have to go select an outfit for him out of his closet. But neither of us is ready for that yet.

You know, Gerald, there were far fewer mortuary choices back when you died, not that I got to make any. I do know that you would have wanted a simple pine box and to wear your old wool hunting jacket into eternity and that your mother would have had you laid out in a heavy oak coffin and in that brand-new suit from Sears, the one you had to wear to church every Sunday after your dad was promoted to deacon. But neither your mother nor I got to make those decisions. You went to your maker barefoot wearing nothing but cutoff jeans, and your casket was the sandy riverbed.

As you probably figured, I didn't have the heart to walk past the house to the river today, though it is generally my favorite route because of all the wildflowers. Instead, I came through town, walked between the post office and the park, up the hill past the summer rentals, down by the horses, and past the farm stand. Then I crossed the bridge to the town beach. There were a number of kids down there with their parents, wading in the shallows or floating on inner tubes spinning lazily in the sun. I made my way to the old bridge. All that remains are the stone footings that once supported the original crossing. She's made some slow progress toward wearing them away, but has years of work ahead before they come tumbling down.

I've run out of bottles, as you can see, so I'll make this letter into a paper boat. The river will snatch it away pretty quickly and probably aim to swamp it before it gets far. Doesn't matter. You'll still get it. You and the river are one.

Love,
Mimsy

Dear Gerald,

Booker's been by the Hobblebush Inn every day checking on us. His real name is Robert Thompson. I still prefer the nickname. He said that with all we've been through, I can call him anything I'd like. He's a long-term visitor to the town, doing genealogical research, and is staying in the log cabin up Fight Brook Road, which explains why I pass him so often. He makes all his forays into town on foot. He's some kind of web developer, whatever that is, so he can work remotely while he does his detective work. We had a long chat about graveyards, him being interested in who is already in them and me in how to get into one myself.

He's been to every plot in the county that might have a gravestone with his mother's surname on it. So far, he's found three family members and dutifully photographed their memorials. He's also been pouring through vital records. As one would suspect from his demeanor, he is a bookish, methodical, and thorough man. He kindly brought me a number of books from the library since he knows I have pretty much sequestered myself in the inn, not wanting to venture far in case Cécile should need me. And knowing Cécile was in no state to read, he brought her a bouquet of flowers and a video about songbirds he said was very soothing.

Aidan has been by on a number of occasions, too. He seems to have taken a special interest in Cécile. At first, she was worried that someone had ratted out her drug buying history, but I don't think that's it. He's witnessed senseless death, as any police officer has, but also experienced it firsthand and has experienced the gut-wrenching guilt that goes with it. I think he's keeping an eye on her mental health. Anyway, once she got over her fear of him, and he started coming after work, out of uniform, he became a calming presence in our little makeshift sitting room, the nook we set up in the bedroom to meet callers who want to offer their condolences.

Of course, the sitting room in the inn is only a temporary refuge. Cécile's sisters are coming on Friday to help finalize the funeral arrangements and to accompany her to the house to get Mackey some clothes. She is adamant she wants to return home. That it's her and Mackey's place and she could never leave it. But she is not sure whether she will stay there overnight on Friday or just pick up some things. She'll know when she gets there, she says. I'll keep her room rented at the inn, just in case.

I read somewhere that your brain holds on to bad memories longer and in more detail than good memories. Being present at the death of a loved one is a transitional moment, so vivid it overwrites your other memories of them, leaving the rest colorless and grey. Eventually you wall yourself off from the thoughts, not wanting to suffer their death over and over again.

I see you drown every time I think of us riding through the woods, picking apples, or kissing behind the school. I see Lawrence's chest rise and fall one last time every time I think of him onstage, with the top down in the Jag, or brewing his special shade-grown coffee. Cécile will hear that shot when she remembers her wedding day, recalls Mackey working at the lathe, and every year when the hundreds of flowers he planted in the garden along the front of the house bloom.

Still…

Your Mimsy

Dear Gerald,

The funeral was on Saturday. I still don't have any closure, even though that's what funerals are designed to do, right? Bring a sense of closure to the living? I know Cécile didn't find any. Her two sisters—neither as tiny as she—flanked her during the entire ceremony, at times holding her upright when her legs gave way.

I heard a bit of the backstory prior to the service. Apparently, Mackey always joked that he'd imported Cécile from Canada. "Where," he would add, "they make the best beer and the finest women." Cécile had worked in hospitality at a large resort near Hudson Bay where they met by chance. Mackey was on a fishing vacation. She was leading a northern lights program for the hotel guests. He'd brag that they met under an electromagnetic sky, their fate written across the heavens. He brought her across the border with him at the end of his stay. Her transition here was seamless; she found work at a resort in the White Mountains. They married two weeks later. People remembered them all lovey-dovey, holding hands around town, their demonstrativeness standing out among the reserve of the general population.

All the funeral tales were upbeat memorials, but later in the parking lot, I learned that when the resort where Cécile worked closed during the recession and the others tightened ship, she found it impossible to get a full-time position and she had to take cleaning work to get by. Around the same time, she and Mackey discovered that they wouldn't be having children the natural way and neither of them wanted technological help or adoption. Mackey's client list dried up as the real estate market tanked. He was a cabinet maker, doing custom woodworking. They'd taken out a loan to fill his workshop with equipment and were having trouble paying it back as all he could get were occasional construction jobs. Then Cécile's car, a 1999 Oldsmobile, breathed its last breath and they piled on a car loan atop their other loans and bills. They would have gone under long ago if the Wright house hadn't been his free and clear. They scrimped on everything, thus the clothesline and the huge vegetable garden, but it was never enough.

Then Mackey fell from a roof while helping his handyman friend with a spur-of-the-moment job. His friend wasn't licensed or insured. Mackey didn't feel right about suing the homeowners for what he considered his own careless mistake. The couple had the cheapest health insurance. It had a huge deductible so it didn't cover any of the bills. And at that time, doctors were handing out opioids like candy and Mackey gratefully took whatever solace he could get. After that there were no more hand-in-hand walks through town, just stress and bitterness and drugs and pain.

The funeral itself was beautiful, Gerald, as was the graveside service. Oswald outdid himself. The man is eloquent, his words a comfort to Cécile. I could see there were tears in his eyes when he spoke. I suppose I have to forgive him. Mackey was too far down the road of addiction. There was nothing Oswald could have done.

The river is extraordinarily beautiful today. Overhanging bushes and trees are reflecting in her slow waters. A heron lifted off from the opposite bank as I sat down and a gorgeous kingfisher streaked by searching for fish. Conciliatory gestures. I'll admit it is soothing today to rest on her shores. I might stay awhile.

Yours in Mourning,

Mimsy

Dear Gerald,

Cécile did stay at the house and did not return to the Hobblebush Inn. Her sisters stayed with her for a week to make sure she'd be all right. When they left, Booker, Aidan, and I took turns visiting. We all agree that

Cécile makes a mean crêpe, especially when it's topped with some of her homemade blackberry preserves. She showed me where the blackberry canes grow behind the barn. A huge patch, replete with vicious thorns, but holding the potential for edible, sugary delights. When they are ripe, we'll pick them and she'll teach me to make jam. I told her she'd be wise to give me my own portion so I won't ruin the whole batch. Keeping her busy and focused on the future seems to help. Booker tells me he's been teaching her to play gin rummy. Aidan helps her weed her garden. And if she takes on teaching me how to cook, that could keep her occupied (and probably frustrated) for years.

I am having dinner with Booker tomorrow to talk about his search for information on his father. He's going to ask me all sorts of questions about our schoolmates. On the phone, he made it sound like the Spanish Inquisition. He said he wants to know everything about everybody. What everybody's home life was like. Who dated whom. Which kids were best friends. Which ones were enemies. Who moved away and who moved into town. Were there any scandals. Luckily, I was so busy hiding the stuff you and I were up to that I didn't have time for anybody else's secrets. Booker's a tenacious researcher though. If there is any juicy information hidden in my memory banks, he'll pry it right out of me.

I made a less than graceful approach to the river today. I stumbled and slid down the riverbank on my ass. My balance is worsening, I'm afraid, and it frightens me not to be able to trust my body. Anyway, I was a mess. My hands were caked with mud and I had to wash them off before I started your letter. Her water is warm this time of year, at least in the shallows. A crayfish scuttled under a rock and tiny fish scattered when my fingers touched the surface. Reminders that she may not be my favorite resident of this town, but she does have a purpose.

Your Muddy Mimsy

Gerald,

I met with Booker today to talk about his father.
Did you know? How could you not know?
Or did you know and choose not to tell me?
You had a son.

M

~~~

Gerald,

When Booker showed me the puzzle pieces he'd gathered—the track medal you'd given his mother, the back engraved with the initials "J. F." and the team yearbook photo with the caption below, labeling you with the nickname, "Jerry," in quotes—they fitted together into a different picture than I'd expected. A portrait of some guy, Jerry, I never knew.

Someone who slept with a girl, got her pregnant, and never took any responsibility. Someone who did not object when Anne Thompson's parents sent her away. Someone who acted as if the teenage mother of his child never existed. Never once mentioned her or the baby.

You must have known. Even if she didn't tell you, everyone knew what it meant back then when a girl got shipped off to live with an aunt. Did you offer to marry her? Offer to help support the child? I can't imagine you did, because I know for a fact you were silent when the school hallways filled with hateful gossip.

You prided yourself on how we told each other everything. Except, apparently, this one enormous thing. Now I feel like I never knew you at all.

Mrs. Bell

P.S. Booker said his mother never spoke of you except once, right before she died.

Gerald,

Since I moved to town, whenever people ask me how I spend my time, I tell them, "I write letters to a dead man." They laugh, think me eccentric or heartbroken, and wonder how that works, exactly. They are wrong in their assumptions. I am not eccentric, and I am no longer heartbroken. And as for how it works? Not well. The problem is that you cannot expect a reply from a dead man, even when you desperately need answers.

I am not sorry it has taken me over a month to write. I don't even know why I am writing now. I have heard the saying "the ground fell out from under me" hundreds of times in my eighty years, but never once had I experienced it. Not until Booker found his answers and in doing so filled my world with questions. When I have hope that by some strange twist of fate you didn't know Anne was pregnant, I want those answers. In the moments when I am certain that you did know about the baby, I don't. They wouldn't be answers; they'd be the excuses of a coward and a liar.

The river can have you, Gerald.

M

Gerald,

It is ninety-five degrees and I walked all the way down to the damn river after picking blackberries. My hands are stained purple and my arms are covered with scratches. The extra-bonus mosquito hatch is going full bore, and I just picked two deer ticks off my shorts. So why am I down here? Because I just can't cool the rage I feel when I think about the fact that I moved back here to Menotomy for you. Sixty years of my life was spent following Lawrence around and then I up and decide to spend my last days following you! When I think of all the hours I wasted daydreaming about our days together. The unfair comparisons I made between you and all other men. The pedestal I erected for you. What a fool I was.

I will tell you, though I am loath to give you anything, that your son is a solid, upstanding man. You would be very proud of him. Heck, I am very proud of him and he is none of my making. He doesn't look much like you; he takes after his mother's family who, as I remember, were of Scandinavian stock and much taller, thinner, and blonder than your people. Booker is smart and brave and loves to read. His mother told him about you on her deathbed, but over the years he forgot the details, remembering only that you had once given her your track medal. She died when he was only ten years old, and Booker was raised by his great aunt and uncle. He was married once, to his high school sweetheart, Ginger, but he lost her ten years ago to breast cancer. They had no children.

He really wants to get to know you, through me. Every time he brings the subject up, I feel panic rising in my chest and I can't breathe. He says he understands, but I am going to have to get a hold of myself and tell him the stories he desperately needs to hear, because he is my friend, and I don't want him to think that I think less of him because you shamed his mother, abandoned him, and lied to me.

Then again, maybe that last one is all on me. My mother, my father, the sheriff, the headmaster, and the minister all warned me against you. As an adult I see that they were right, but, of course, back then I didn't listen.

M

~~~~~

Dear Mr. Booker Thompson Fessenden,

As you know, I am struggling to give you what you need. Not from a lack of concern for you, but from fear that the underlying narrative that I've used to make sense of my whole life was, from the very beginning, a lie. That being the case, I do realize it is selfish of me to put what amounted to only a few years of my life above the decades of loss you've felt not having a father. Since I cannot seem to get my emotions under control, I am writing instead of speaking with you about Gerald. I think this is for the best as my thoughts are clearest when I write them down, and with this letter in hand you will not have to remember every word I say. You will have a written record of a portion of your father's life.

Gerald was born at home to Joseph Fessenden and Doris Sullivan. Their family was of Irish descent. He had two older brothers, Billy and Donald, but they went off to war in Korea and one was killed and the other went missing in action. His parents' grief at the loss of their elder sons colored everything they did. I remember the melancholy that hung over the house. The few meals I ate there included prayers referencing them, and their photos, draped in black cloth, were prominently displayed upon the piano that his mother stopped playing the day she was notified of her eldest son's death.

To be fair, despite their incredible pain, his mom and dad tried to put on a good face for Gerald. They were busy running the grocery, but made sure he did his homework, made extra special meals for him every Sunday, and they showed up for his baseball games and track meets. His mother died quite suddenly and mysteriously when he was fifteen years old. Now that I look back, it is possible she committed suicide. But such things were not talked about back then. His father did what he could, but from that point on Gerald, having witnessed the fragility of life, was determined to live every minute as if it were his last—unrestrained and free.

I met him when we were both five years old. He tripped over me when I was lying in the sand on the town beach, pretending to be a whale. He'd been backing up trying to catch a ball. He apologized profusely and went on playing and tripping over people for the rest of the afternoon. Baseball was pretty much all he did until his mother died. He was a good player. People didn't go so crazy about kids' sports like they do today, so I doubt he had any trophies to show for it, but the pleasure for him was in perfect pitches and numerous strikeouts.

Though we grew up alongside each other, always part of each other's background, Gerald and I didn't start making eyes at each other until the seventh grade. But despite our families being somewhat equal in stature in town, my father being an accountant for the bank, his owning the only grocery, our budding romance was discouraged. That, of course, made him all the more interested in me, and I in him. We were flirtatious, but we didn't get together romantically until we were sixteen. Your mom left school the year before Gerald and I began to go steady. We probably would have gotten married, had the accident on the river not taken him.

Booker, you should know that your father was unlike any other person I have ever known. He lived entirely in the present moment. He was fearless. On Halloween, he broke into a haunted house so he could spend the night with ghosts. He tracked bears, not to hunt, but for the high he got when he neared them, all his senses ramped up, even his hair on high alert. He played pranks. He drank too much. He aggravated all his teachers with his accurate, but arrogant, diatribes against convention and tradition. He and I stole apples, canoes, horses, and beer. But all his wildness was for the purpose of adventure. Not badness, but freethinking. Not disrespect, but adrenaline. Not foolhardiness, but bravery.

I think the story that most illustrates who your father was and why I loved him is this one: In those days there were many active mines in the mountains, their owners digging for granite, feldspar, mica, pegmatite, and gemstones. Gerald had a collector's heart and he would spend his spare time sifting through the waste dumps, searching for overlooked gems. Mostly he found common stones, smoky quartz, garnets, and beryl. He had a shelf at the store where all his specimens were arranged, labelled, and displayed as if in a museum. He loved minerals as much as I loved the wildflowers, and we encouraged each other's collecting forays.

One day, he was working at the grocery when he overheard some older gentlemen talking about a huge tourmaline find in the mountains several towns over. He was young then, thirteen, still looking like a kid and a ragged, motherless kid at that. He had never seen tourmaline, but as soon as he heard it described, he had to have it. So, he charmed the men. He showed them his "geology museum." He spoke eloquently about his dreams of owning a mine one day. He casually dropped the "almost an orphan" card, and found himself the youngest hire of the most famous mineralogists who ever passed our way. From thirteen until he died, he worked at the mine. He earned some money but he was also paid in gems. And by the end of his tenure, he had a collection worthy of a small museum. I always thought, if he hadn't been truant so often, sabotaging his grades, his father might have noticed his passion and sent him up to the University of Maine for formal study of geology.

Your father had tourmalines of many colors, but the pieces in his collection he most cherished were called "watermelon," stones banded green and pink, some with a little yellow or white in between just like a cross section of a watermelon. One specimen was small, but perfect, and he took it to a jeweler and had it threaded on a gold chain. I thought he might give it to me. But he'd noticed that his mother's best friend, Iva, was still as heartbroken about his mother's death as he was. So, Gerald presented the necklace to her, saying that the colors reminded him of the big southern watermelon his mother always ordered in summer, the ritual she had for slicing it to show it off beautifully on the plate, and how she always invited Iva to join them for the first picnic of the season. Later, he confessed that the smile on Iva's face took his breath away. And that is how he always treated me, listening until he knew my heart's desire, fulfilling it, and then basking in the afterglow.

Your father was an original. Like you are, Booker. Different in his interests, but wholly devoted to them and to living life fully. You should be proud to be his son.

Love,
Mimsy

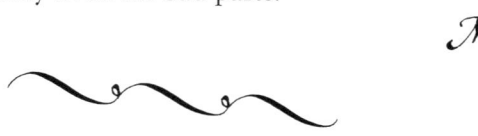

Gerald,

Don't think I'm not still glowing with rage. I know what I wrote to Booker might as well have been an ode to a saint. But don't think for one second that I have forgiven you. I told him the truth. The good parts of his father's story. He's already lived the bad parts.

M

Dear Mr. Gerald Fessenden,

I don't think she'd like that I am writing to you, but do I think you have a right to know that Mimsy has been in the hospital for a couple of days. She had a TIA, a mini-stroke. Probably brought on by the stress caused by the unsettling events of the past couple of weeks. She'll be fine, but the doctors want her to do a little outpatient rehab. She took a nasty *fall during the event. I am picking her up at the hospital this afternoon and will look after her.*

Sincerely,
Officer Aidan Ward
Menotomy P.D.

Dear Mr. Gerald Fessenden,

You know, if you were alive today, acting like Mimsy has been telling me you did back in the '50s, it would be my pleasure to be your arresting officer. I know you did wrong by Booker's mom, but I think it is the horse thievery that gets me the most. My mom raised quarter horses. I am surprised one of those innocent animals you "borrowed" didn't end up with a broken leg. I know bad boys get all the glory with the girls, but Mimsy really picked some winners in her life. Still, I see that she is feeling really down lately without her routine of visiting the river and writing to you, so if you found some way to apologize for being such a dick, maybe we could convince her to start back up again.

Sincerely,
Officer Aidan Ward,
Menotomy P.D.

Gerald,

I know that you know I was in the river today. It might have seemed like forgiveness, but nothing could be further from the truth. It was what they call "aquatic therapy," water-supported exercises to help me regain my strength. I tried it at the pool for a week. But I have always hated the stench of chlorine; the high probability some kid let loose and pissed in the water; the noxious, pallid blue tones; the slippery deck; other people's infected toes spreading athlete's foot across the bathroom floor. It is just not my scene.

It was actually Young Jack who came up with the solution. This time of year, he and his friends swim in the river every day. They keep a close eye on me and I can finish my water exercises without my hair smelling like it just came out of the bleach load. Though I had sworn never to set foot in the traitorous river again, I am content with the compromise. The moving water is invigorating. The sand under my feet is soothing. The young people's laughter is contagious. And I get the exercises done. Know I am here on doctor's orders. I need to regain my strength. I am not going on a downward spiral toward death because of a tiny blip in my brain or one little fall. If preventing that means I work out in your river, so be it.

M

Dad,

Your son, Robert, here. I have wondered about you for such a long time.

Mom never talked about you when I was a kid. That made me worry that maybe I was the product of a rape or that you hit her or you were her teacher or a hundred other bad things that could have led to your name being banned from our house. But when she was dying she told me, "Your dad wasn't a bad guy." I chose to believe her and went on with my life. I got married and had a good career. It was a standard, happy existence until my wife died of cancer. By choice, Ginger and I had no kids, and so I suddenly found myself without any family at all.

One of my co-workers had been going on for years about the genealogy websites available to the family historian. I humored him when he'd launch into long, boring recitations of his ancestors' names, when they were born, what they did, who they married, etc. But one particularly lonely day, I asked him to show me his research. Of course, the platform he used was useless to me as I didn't have your name. But my co-worker said before the Internet people did boots-on-the-ground research. Going to county seats to see vital records. Looking in the family pages of passed-down bibles. Traveling to graveyards. Reading old newspaper articles on microfiche. Finding copies of high school yearbooks.

Yearbooks! I remember feeling a bit of hope when I heard him mention yearbooks. Instead of researching forward from a name, I could research backward from a place and time. I knew where Mom had grown up, as she spoke of it on occasion, mentioning how beautiful the landscape was compared to where we ended up. I just had to go there and search for you.

I did all the graveyard and vital records research I could do. Which got me nowhere with you, but I found a lot of data on my mom's family. Then I pored over the yearbook photos wondering which guy was my father. I started asking around town to find people who had been in the school when my mother had attended. I talked with a historical society lady, Batty Holt, but she was too young to remember my mother. She suggested I speak to Mimsy. Which was ironic, because Mimsy had been trying to speak to me for weeks.

I blame myself for Mimsy's stroke, though I know Mackey's death was probably a factor. Mimsy was certainly distraught over it. But the stroke didn't happen until after the meeting when we put two and two together and realized that her high school boyfriend was my father. She is tough, but she's eighty. I knew from my own great aunt and uncle that as they got older they couldn't handle things as well. Any bad news about friends or negative family gossip knocked them right off their feet. The emotional fragility only came on in their later years. But Mimsy is in her later years. She's just so vibrant I forgot to be careful. My excitement overtook my good sense. I should have done things differently, and I am really sorry.

Of course, now Mimsy is furious with you on my behalf. I am going to talk her down. You died when I was a toddler. I wouldn't have remembered you if I had known you. I am happy to have the stories about what you were like. I am happy to have two sides of a family tree. I am happy to have Mimsy as a friend. All these things come from you. I understand that times were different. My mom grew up in a strict religious home. I know she didn't tell her aunt and uncle who the father was. I am sure she didn't share your identity with her parents. She may have been too ashamed to talk to you. You were both so young and times were so different then. I don't blame you. I know if it had happened today, you and my mom would have made different choices.

I know Mimsy gave up using bottles for your letters. She says she no longer has anything to hide from the river. But mine's in a bottle, a formal introduction from your son.

Love,
Robert (Booker) Thompson

Gerald,

Booker gave me a good talking to. I am not sure if he is just worried about my health (both he and Aidan have been all over me about starting up my walks again) or if he is really just all peachy keen and la-di-dah with what happened in the past. He does have a steadfast and calm demeanor. Maybe it's more than skin deep; maybe that's his true nature. Maybe for him it's all good that he was fatherless for sixty-four years. If it were me, I would be furious. But then fury has been my default state for decades.

What I did not mention—because if he is in a good place about it, who am I to bring him down—was the error in thinking that since you died when he was little, he wouldn't have remembered you. But if you had taken responsibility for Anne and for him, you never would have been on the river with me. You wouldn't have died. He would have had a father for a long, long time, probably even longer than he had a mother.

When Lawrence and I fought, which was often, we had a hard time making up. The resolution usually required the redefinition of some relationship, his and mine, his and his mom's, mine and his best friend's, his and the girl from the last city who was still on our tour bus four days later. It is time we redefine our relationship, Gerald. We can't go on being teenage lovers forever.

Too much of my identity is wrapped up in hopping trains, stealing horses, and hanging out by the river with you to just end it. But I can't continue to erase myself by mooning and swooning over you until the day I die. We'll have to hash out the terms of a new relationship. I'll write again when I am ready.

Your river is tranquil tonight. There's a veery singing somewhere down the river corridor, his notes spiraling down the scale. Nothing is blooming. The trees and shrubs have on their dark summer greens. For the first time in weeks, I feel calm. Her stillness is a sedative.

Your old friend,
Mimsy

P.S. When Booker spoke to me today, I noticed, for the first time, that he tips his head and lifts a single eyebrow when he is expecting a "yes" answer and only a "yes" answer, just like you used to do.

Dear Gerald,

I have thought about it long and hard. Let me tell you where I'm coming from.

The experience of being in the band only because Lawrence wanted me in it made me feel like an impostor most of my life. So, at first, when I found out that you'd been intimate enough with someone else to make a child, I felt the same white-hot jealousy any betrayed teenage girl would. But when I got over that, I realized it was not having been told you had a child that hurt the most. It made our relationship, the trust in which I cherished above all things, feel counterfeit. As if all my successes and feelings had been fabricated by the actions and lies of men.

Now, let me tell you what I want.

I want to go to the river without watching you die in the film reels of my memory and I want to go to the river without imagining that all your adventures with me were just a way of running away from the fact that you were a teenage father. To do that, I have to write about today. What is happening now. What I am doing. Like I would to a pen pal overseas. I am angry with you. But I know that I can't ride that feeling any further and still be healthy. I stood up and played fiddle onstage at Burnt Meadow Music and that was all me. I took care of Cécile and that was all me. Brace yourself, because you're going to be hearing a lot less about us and a lot more about me and my life from now on.

Your friend,

Mimsy

Dear Gerald,

First letter of our new friendship. I'll start with the latest happenings in town and see where that gets us.

It's Bike Week. Harleys farting down the road. Sport bikes buzzing like bees. The accompanying roar of revved engines and pooting tailpipes has made for a less serene soundscape, but my vision has been full of some wonderful scenes. I even found the perfect image with which to inaugurate the camera on my new phone. There was a biker idling at a red light, an older man in a leather jacket with sparse white hair gathered in a ponytail. In the mirrors: twin images of his face, snow-white beard, and blue-tinted wraparound sunglasses. In that moment, I caught him both coming and going.

I stood there waiting to cross, watching the endless river of bikes, thinking I'd like to ride a motorcycle one day, knowing I no longer have the balance to. You'd think with the company I've kept, I'd have done this already, but the opportunity never came up. I did once pose reclining atop a custom chopper for an album cover, but I never thought of it as more than a prop. The folks driving through this week certainly don't think of them as props, more like engines of freedom.

Anyway, I was standing beside the road, suppressing my desire to stick out my thumb and hitch a ride on a hog when I saw someone I knew. A very unlikely someone: Oswald. He spotted me. I stuck out my thumb. The next thing I knew he was buckling his helmet under my chin, and we were on the road on his Harley. Of course, he had to show off. Once we were out of town, on the sinuous roads that wind through the national forest, I had to wrap my arms around him tightly just to stay on. The old fool still has his balance though, I'll give him that.

Biker chick for a day. With a long white braid, no less. Well, no one can say this old girl is becoming mild-mannered or cautious with age.

Where the rubber meets the road,

Mimsy

Dear Gerald,

This getting old thing is crap. Since the stroke, I have more doctors hovering around me than I saw in all the younger years of my life combined. And let me tell you, at some of my lowest lows, I could have used a whole herd of doctors! Today, my orthopedist insisted that I attend balance classes for seniors at the hospital. It is pretty sad when you to have to attend classes to stand on your own two feet. And to add insult to injury, I had to pick up four prescription bottles at the drug store. The pharmacist, an angular divorcée with fierce eyes, commis-erated with me. She's in her fifties and she says she knows it is only a matter of time before she has to start handing over half her paycheck to Big Pharma. I paid up and took my pharmacy bags home. My stash now contains only legal drugs, a lot less fun than the illegal ones.

Later, Batty came to see me at the inn. The dead lady's house is still going through probate, so I haven't officially bought it yet, but everyone in town knows that the offer is in and has been accepted by the heirs. Now that Batty no longer thinks I want to steal her home out from under her, we were able to have a civil conversation. She was angling for details about the Anne/Gerald/Booker scandal, for "historical" purposes, of course. And, you know... I just blurted out everything. The whole thing happened sixty-four years ago. Booker appears completely unfazed by the scandalous circumstances of his birth. And I have been wrestling my anger into a tangled knot, getting nowhere. Then a sympathetic listener sits down across from me and pats my hand gently and the whole story unwinds in a tearful rush. She was great about it. She held my old wrinkled hand in her old wrinkled hand like we'd been best friends forever, and said something I can't get out of my mind, "Mimsy, dear, history is never pretty. It is always complicated. One thing we cannot do is get hung up on the details. We have to look for progress within the big picture."

In a few minutes I have to go to physical therapy, but I wanted to tell you that I have discovered some trees on the riverbank that glow like molten gold in the sun. Their bark is smooth but the edges flake and curl. These particular ones, possibly siblings, gently touch all the way up their length. The river has spared their bank. Their home juts out a bit and the water eddies gently around it. It won't be that way forever, of course. She'll take them out in a flood or slowly undermine their roots. That's progress I guess. But in this moment, they are a pretty picture.

Mimsy

Dear Gerald,

Since I look to be reliant on friends for the rest of my days, I guess I should try harder to accumulate some. My newest candidate, Batty, called to ask if I wanted to join the silver sneakers group. They walk in the high school gym. But as long as I have the strength for it, I am keeping my sneakers firmly upon the country roads and woodland paths. I couldn't hear myself think in that group with all the tittering and gossip, and I need quiet to compose my letters. They don't spring complete out of my mind the moment I sit down on the riverbank, you know.

Seeing that my participation in the silver sneaker parade was a no-go, Batty then asked if I wanted to come to the "History Slideshow Sundays" that she holds in the basement of the historical society every weekend. I think the look on my face was enough of an "I'd rather saw off my own arm" response to make her pause. Finally, she tried to overcome my resistance with an offer to volunteer with her at the food pantry. I was slightly tempted. But one thing I know about myself is that volunteering doesn't make me happy, and that following in an ex-boyfriend's footsteps is no longer my thing. Oswald would be so proud to hear I'd jumped into community service, I had to say no out of spite. I did, however, write her a big fat check for the pantry, which shocked her enough to stop her relentless friend-making attempts. I wonder what happened to make me so desirable all of the sudden? She did nothing but evade me before.

Mimsy

Gerald,

Now I know why my popularity is on the rise. I enclose the copy of a column from The Jockey Cap Tattler that went to press this week. I have a rogue publicist; you can probably guess his name. Cub reporter Jack Bourgeois Junior's mini unauthorized biography was ninety percent rock history and ten percent sensationalism, including a paragraph about my "heroism" at Mackey Wright's house. And worse, he mentioned your death and my letters, which are very personal things. He meant well, but he's young. Since the cat's out of the bag, a stern talking to would be pointless, so I won't subject the boy to one this time. But next time, I won't be so lenient.

Speaking of the Wrights, I walked by the house today. Cécile's sundresses were flapping on the line. I felt like stopping by, but since the robins are already singing vespers, I better send this letter first. I will visit on my way back from the river. I'll tell you how she's doing tomorrow.

Hopefully the fans of the band who read The Jockey Cap Tattler article won't be waiting downstream to fish this letter out of the river to sell to collectors before you receive it.

Good night,

Mimsy

Gerald,

It was dark by the time I left Cécile's last night. Her location is spectacular. We watched the full moon hanging low over the ridge, spilling an apricot glow across the pond, the exact same creamy orange as the sunset. Green frogs were chorusing. A few gray tree frogs chimed in. The wind was still, the air full of lilac.

Cécile's hanging in there. Her sisters take turns calling. Oswald has been by on a number of occasions. Aidan has taken over lawn mowing and the daily maintenance of her vegetable garden. I'm to come by bright and early tomorrow as we have preserves to preserve. Booker has plans to come over later with scones after all the work is done and the jam is ready for tasting.

One of Cécile's friends from her hotel days goes with her to the cemetery several times a week. Cécile says that she thought the reminders in the house would be the hardest thing, but even worse is the churchyard grave. She can only stay a few minutes before morbid thoughts start to intrude, and she imagines, vividly, the grisly scene underground. I told Cécile that there was no duty to visit the grave so often if it was causing her this much distress. No one was keeping count. No one would judge her. And I mentioned that she should talk to her doctor and Oswald about her dark thoughts.

I don't know if she'll heed my words, but I did get to thinking again about the whole burial thing. How I can't possibly ask her to bury me on her farm in the graveyard under the pines. I can see she'd be compelled to sit there with me every day even though she's prone to gruesome ruminations. That is not how I want anyone to live their life, tending to the dead, especially not someone as sensitive as Cécile. So, the search is still on, Gerald. Maybe I can find a more private place to lay my bones.

Sincerely,

Mimsy

Gerald,

The weather is wild today. High humidity, bright and sunny one moment, dark clouds flying across the sky the next, a sprinkle, some hail, then clear and sunny again. Definitely afternoon thunderstorms in the works over the mountains. Exactly like the day of your accident, Gerald.

So, you'll understand that I freaked out a little in the IGA when I saw the young couple with the shopping cart full of beer. It's high summer, so jeep-loads of twenty-year-olds keep arriving for weekend river parties. I'm afraid I just couldn't keep my mouth shut. "You kids watch the sky and get off the river immediately if you hear thunder." What a downer I've become. A total buzz-kill. An anxious, meddling old lady. They kindly told me that they would, but you and I both know after they knock back a few of those beers and get naked, they aren't leaving that river come hell or literal high water.

I wish we'd been smarter. You and I both heard thunder in the distance for at least a half hour before the storm hit. Those first heavy drops pummeling the water's surface, painfully striking our skin, didn't dissuade us from our course. It had been raining all day upriver, and the runoff plus the rainstorm turned the river into a churning, hateful maelstrom. At any point we could have landed and taken cover. But we were testing our bodies against the elements, as young people are wont to do.

And we lost.

Mimsy

Gerald,

I forgot that when you buy a house in Maine, you have to accept that it won't really be yours until you leave it. From the day you move in, despite all the papers you signed, titles you insured, and the check you wrote, the house will forever be referred to by the name of the former occupants. And any infamy associated with the former owners will be brought up every time you share your address. Furthermore, it is likely that some degree of guilt by association will have been transferred along with the deed.

"You Mrs. Bell? You're the one who moved into Jimmy Hensworth's house! You know what he did, right?" That's what I heard when I took Becks the Subaru in for an oil change. Men don't shy away from gossip in Maine; my new friend was practically vibrating with excitement at being the first to break the big story. I sat precariously on a highly unstable stool at the counter listening to the dark-haired mechanic unwind a tale of intrigue as devious as any my bandmates could have executed. As he spoke, I gradually became cognizant of the fact I'd moved into the one of the most notorious homes in town.

The former owner, Jimmy Hensworth, was married to the church music director, Helen, a gem of a woman, the one who recently passed away and whose house I now own. Her husband was less than a gem. He was, in fact, a deeply flawed man. Sean, my new mechanic friend, described him: "Jimmy was a stout fellow, handsome despite his size, but he had wormy lips, smiles coming out one side of his mouth, lies from the other." He was also a gadabout. Flirting his way out of bar tabs. Flirting for extra muffins at the bakery. And that wasn't the only muffin he was enjoying.

Jimmy seduced Oswald's wife with sweet nothings and an endless rain of compliments. Now, knowing Oswald, I can see how his wife might get her head turned by the slightest hint of romance, and apparently Jimmy was laying it on thick. And as he was stealing Mary's affections away from Oswald, he accused his own wife, Helen, of doing exactly the same. He started making comments at church about how much time she was spending with Oswald in the practice room. He staged an argument in which he publicly accused her of adultery. It was all gaslighting, an artful show, to divert attention from his own misdeeds, cast doubt on Oswald's fidelity, and clinch his hold on Mary.

The two of them ran away under the cover of night. He literally stole her out from under the covers of her marital bed. Sneaking in an open window, taking her hand, and leading her down the ladder out to his running car.

Oswald was devastated. Helen was devastated. The torrent of gossip this unleashed was unbelievable. Neither Oswald nor Helen could leave their houses without being bathed in it. Sunday services were filled with whispers. Helen quit the church. Jimmy's believable lies had made it easy for the townspeople to misplace blame.

I never in a million years would have guessed Oswald had been married. I'd assumed he'd forsaken the sins of the flesh forever after our ill-fated kiss. But he did forsake love, after it left him. Never remarried. Never dated. Buried himself in his work. No wonder he's shouldered so many charity projects.

So, I guess I am going to have to get used to living in Jimmy Hensworth's house, even though he hasn't lived in Menotomy for forty-five years. I guess the next occupant can live in Mimsy Bell's house and hear all about my dead boyfriend and my drinking and drugging, my rock 'n' roll years, my false "heroism," and whatever gossip-worthy stories I get myself involved in next.

Sincerely,

Mimsy

Gerald,

The last thing I thought I'd be doing this week is hanging out with someone from the band. But if I could choose from all of them, it would be the one who called me yesterday all excited about spending time with me during his vacation in the White Mountains. A week with Aran Sky. I don't know whether to be flattered that he's kept up with my whereabouts or freaked out because I had thought I'd closed the door permanently on that part of my life.

Aran was Lawrence's backup singer. He also played some sweet guitar, but his real talent was getting naked on stage, especially in the rain. There was just something about Aran Sky unbuttoning his wet shirt and peeling it off so very slowly that drove the fans to communal orgasm. And I'll admit it, there was something about Aran just being Aran that brought me to his bed, over and over again, more times than I'd like to admit.

The last time I saw him was at my sixtieth birthday party. I spent almost no time with him; by that point his continued attentions toward me drove Lawrence over the edge and I did not want a scene. I only slept with Aran Sky when Lawrence and I were fighting, but, as you remember, I was a scrapper, so that was often. You'd think free love would be nirvana for men: I've my woman and all the other women too! And it was all good when they woke up in a papasan chair curled up with three beatnik chicks. But surprise! The sight of their own girlfriend in their best friend's bed awoke not a feeling of joy at her free experimentation, but raw animal jealousy. The Pill might have ignited the free love movement, but drugs and drink were required to keep it burning. You can't get that angry about things you're too trashed to remember.

Though I do remember a handful of those hot, wet, rainy nights with Aran.

Scandalously,

Mimsy

~~~

Gerald,

I asked the pharmacist if she could slip a couple Valium into the bottle with my Warfarin, but no go. Instead, she asked me why I'm so anxious. I told her I was going to see an old boyfriend tomorrow. She commiserated, but said since she'd dumped her old boyfriend and sworn off men, she no longer felt the need for Valium. She also said that word around town was that my old boyfriend was dead.

I told her this particular old boyfriend is still alive, at least he was as of his last text an hour ago. Aran is five years older than I am, a member of the 85-and-up club. In fact, I might not even need the Valium; each day is a crap shoot at his age. We'll see if he makes it to lunch tomorrow. He could keel over at breakfast, and then all I'd see of him would be his obituary.

I am feeling a keen sense of excitement along with my dread. Nostalgia is nudging me to satisfy my curiosity. Memory is waving a red flag in my face. Vanity is pushing me to decide what to wear. Aran Sky, the barefoot wet dream of every female flower child of the sixties, wants to see me, and I'd like to be worth seeing. That means staying out of my trunk full of old stage costumes and my closet full of walking shoes and taking a trip down to the boutique in Bridgton. Something new. Something memorable. Something red.

I don't feel you, Gerald, down here today. Maybe you're jealous, sulking. All I feel is the rush of thousands of gallons of river water, unstoppable power. All I see are people in boats. But Aidan tells me there weren't any accidents during the big storms last weekend, so either my anxious warnings to the young couple in the grocery store saved their lives or the river chose to spare them. Zero drownings and we are more than halfway through the year. Keep your watery mitts off all those happy young people, river!

Even curses have expiration dates,

Mimsy

Gerald,

I hoped my eighty-first birthday would slip by without mention this year. I liked the idea of playing fiddle with Young Jack and writing your letter and having a burger at the roadhouse with Aidan without anyone knowing I had completed another trip around the sun. But little did I know, far beyond the borders of Menotomy, there was a man who had my birthday written on his calendar.

Aran spent the past year traveling across India visiting world heritage sites, the Mahabs, Hampi, Ajanta. In an homage to what's left of the Hippie Trail, he smoked weed on the beaches of Goa and on Freak Street in Kathmandu. But when his adventuring led to an extended stay in the hospital in Mysore, he decided to come home early. And what was on his calendar? Considering that he'd planned to be away for two years, the band was on break, and his wife had divorced him a couple of decades ago, very, very little. Except a notation that on a certain day very soon, Mimsy Bell would be turning eighty-one.

He told me he took that singular entry in his datebook as an invitation. He asked around and discovered I'd moved back to my childhood home. Then he searched out the one and only spiritual destination within a fifty-mile radius of Menotomy, the highest mountain in the northeast, Agiocochook, a.k.a. Mount Washington. Aran Sky has definitely not lost touch with his roots. He's as tuned in as they get when it comes to sacred places. A once-in-a-lifetime event for my birthday was his goal, as if he were still in competition with Lawrence, who had celebrated my birthdays as if I were my own country and each year was the bicentennial.

Aran decided that summiting the mountain on my birthday would be an auspicious way to begin the next year. I couldn't have climbed that impressive mountain even when I was a teenager, and even the thought was laughable in our eighties, but luckily there was a cog railway in place to take us to the top. I think Becks was a little disappointed she wouldn't get the "This car climbed Mt. Washington" bumper sticker, but being piloted up a narrow, cliffside road by an octogenarian put her at high risk of experiencing her last trip ever, so she parked at the bottom of the mountain without complaint. Since I felt guilty about leaving her behind and I have been lax about helping her fit in with the other Subarus, I bought her an oval "WASH" decal and a "I brake for moose" bumper sticker from the gift shop to slap on her pristine backside.

On the biggest mountain grow the smallest flowers. There is a whole new world of plants up here I never knew existed. Low to the ground to withstand the brutal winds and dryness, alpine plants cover the grey rock, balancing its somber hue with the green of growth. The living carpet was sprinkled with pink and white blossoms, flowering even though it was only forty-five degrees.

Aran didn't worry much about the flowers. He spent his time cross-legged on a smooth expanse of stone, looking across the Presidential Range and feeling the strength of the mountain seep into his bones.

It was a good birthday, Gerald. If it were to be my last, I'd be satisfied.

Mimsy

Gerald,

I completely forgot about Young Jack, my biggest fan, the only other person who knew about my birthday. While I was wandering atop Mt. Washington with Aran yesterday, he bought party food and decorated his house. Guests were assembled. But Young Jack's call begging for an "emergency" fiddle lesson went straight to voicemail. He was used to me always being available, and hadn't factored in that I might be whisked away by an out-of-town guest.

I noticed the message this morning when I was having coffee on the porch of my new house with Aran. He'd been complimenting me on the choice of a home right next to such a powerful goddess. He was talking about the river. I'd just begun explaining the details of my strained relationship with the "goddess" when I heard Jack's voicemails. I felt terrible. My friends had prepared a nice party for me, and I was off gallivanting with an old boyfriend! Connections in my new life derailed by connections from my old.

Aran, witnessing my distress, declared there was only one thing to be done for it. We had to call the boy back, apologize, and ask him if we could make up for it with a special jam session today. Aran had seen the article Jack had written, taped to my fridge, and had a feeling the kid would appreciate the chance to play with a second rock legend. I was quietly flattered that I was the first rock legend in this scenario.

So, I called Jack back, begged forgiveness for being a day late, told him I was bringing a friend, and to get his fiddle ready. Jack exploded in a fit of fanboy happiness when he saw Aran Sky. The three of us set up and we had a private concert for his dad in their living room. And you know, I played really, really well. Guilt has always been my muse.

Your friend,
Mimsy

Gerald,

I picked Aran up at his hotel and we took a trip up the Kancamagus Highway today. I drove. He gossiped. Unlike me, Aran wasn't estranged from our bandmates. He'd kept up with every tiny detail of their lives. Unfortunately, many of the details were similar to the woes you might hear in the halls of an upscale nursing home.

Aran mentioned that Peter Sketcher had recently been diagnosed with lung cancer. He was our token Brit, our nod to the Fab Four, Lawrence's first recruit, our pianist, and my worst nightmare. He truly thought I was a country bumpkin, a naïve rube Lawrence found in a dairy barn somewhere in the woods. He was the one who kept thrusting his leftovers on Lawrence, girls he thought would be much better matches for him than me. I'll admit to being awful and holding a grudge; I didn't even react to the news he was sick.

But Peter, annoying as he was, wasn't the one that finally drove me from the tribe. That distinction was reserved for the one who had started out the journey as my best friend, Glimmer Linkletter. Of course, her first name wasn't really Glimmer, any more than my companion's original name was Aran Sky. Offstage, she was a Barbara, and a really, friendly, fun Barbara, too. For decades we were as close as twins. She was a singer and tambourine player, the youngest of us, the only one with the good sense never to sleep with any of the other band members. In the later years, she was the one who rustled up gigs and booked tours. But after Lawrence's death, she became very critical of my work and went so far as to hire another fiddle player to back me up. Then I was out for a month with pneumonia, and when I returned I'd been replaced. Despite the animosity between us, when Aran told me that she'd had attacks of gout and had toes amputated because of her diabetes, I instinctively wished to reach out to her. Then I remembered that she didn't think enough of me to want my sympathy, and I mourned our friendship all over again.

Aran didn't have sad news about Ron Hodges, our sitar player and percussionist. He was doing well. He hadn't suffered any big health scares, but he did complain about going bald. Ironically, he'd had the longest, thickest hair among us. His hearing loss is severe, but he can still feel the music, especially the drums, so he keeps right on playing with the band.

Our bass player, Charlie Walsh, is in a nursing home now. Dementia. He was inducted into the Rock and Roll Hall of Fame recently, but could no longer comprehend the honor, though Aran says he enjoys showing off the statue to staff, visitors, and the other residents.

Amongst all this nonstop talk, Aran and I did see the sights of the national forest we were driving through. We waded in the pool below Sabbaday Falls and crossed the Albany Covered Bridge. We encountered a young porcupine. Aran was enthralled. It was making a mewling, plaintive cry, normal for a porcupine, but Aran was so concerned about its welfare, it was all I could do to stop him from gathering it up in his arms and bringing it home with us!

We drove into the parking lot of Aran's hotel at dusk. And I felt that with my night vision shot and having exhausted myself driving on winding roads all day, I shouldn't drive home in the dark. I headed toward the counter to see if a room was available, but Aran held me back. He said he hadn't wanted to be presumptuous, but he'd chosen a two-bedroom suite when he made his booking, and he hoped I'd share it with him tonight.

Turns out, we didn't need the second bedroom. I decided that here was an opportunity to lie close to someone, to make love, an opportunity that might not come around again in this lifetime. Aran is as safe a place as I can think of, and he is leaving at the end of the week, so there are no strings to entangle me, only a warm body and arms still strong enough to hold me tight.

Mimsy

Dear Gerald,

In retrospect, lunch with Aran Sky and Booker Thompson—not a good idea. Booker and I have a standing date at Bay's Luncheonette every Tuesday, where I tell him stories about you and your family and what it was like to grow up in Menotomy in the 1940s and 1950s and he asks perceptive questions and writes down everything I say exactly as I say it. Since the conversation is always about you and me, I probably shouldn't have sprung Aran on him like I did. From the moment Booker and Aran met, the two were instant rivals.

Aran is, and always has been, a gentle soul at peace with the universe, friend to all living things, so I was surprised when he started to bristle at Booker's rather standard questions. My first thought was maybe he'd gotten some bad stuff. He'd definitely downed some edibles and was tripping. High Aran was generally groovy, but this Aran had an edge I'd never seen before. Booker was, as usual, his uptight, methodical self. Polite to a fault, but when I entered with the lanky, salwar-kameez-wearing octogenarian with a flower in his hair, he was startled. An off-balance Booker was also something new, something I was pretty sure I didn't like.

For the duration of the meal, an undercurrent of jealousy threatened to pull them both down to new lows. Booker's: "Exactly *how* do you know Mimsy?" "What *kind* of name is Aran Sky, anyway?" "Are you *high*?" and Aran's: "Was your father... *anybody*?" "It's not like Mimsy is *your* mother." "Now that you've found what you were looking for, *when are you going home*?" were driving me crazy. Honestly, if I hadn't been so starved—I'd been served a huge plate of bacon, sausage, and toast—I would have put a halt to the meal immediately.

As it was, I got to witness the two rams locking horns. Aran, loyal to Lawrence and perhaps uncertain about his own place in my life, seemed offended to learn I'd had a big love before the band. Booker, knowing about my late husband but firmly in camp Gerald, was standing up for his dad and obviously put out that there was another major character, an in-the-flesh, living, present-day man, complicating the fairytale.

It was appalling really, that two men were quarreling about who should or should not be in my story. Like my real life didn't align properly with the versions that played in their heads. I scolded both of them. Sent Aran back to the hotel, alone, to get over himself. Told Booker that I would author my own life, and if he didn't approve, we'd no longer have lunch on Tuesdays. They both appeared appropriately chastised as they got in their cars. You would have been proud of me, Gerald. I remember how you looked at me on occasions when I stood up for myself, when I was brave. Like I was the most powerful, amazing person on the planet. Thank you for always reflecting my strength back to me. When I saw it in your eyes, I could never doubt it was there.

Your friend,

Mimsy

Dear Gerald,

We made up from our spat yesterday. Aran apologized for being rude to Booker. I forgave him for acting territorial. I reminded myself that neither Aran's nor my own tomorrows are guaranteed. If he gets a bit possessive of the few we have together, what does it matter in the larger scheme of things? If being a fallible human complicates only one day out of our week together, that's a pretty good track record. And, honestly, I don't want to give up any more time in his bed. I missed him last night. It's been years since I had the luxury of a man's touch. Someone to stroke my hair, to kiss, to feel the weight of on top of me. Sure, it wasn't the gymnastics of our youth, and some might not call it actual sex; I don't keep progesterone cream on my nightstand anymore, and Aran didn't think to pack the Viagra. But the slow caresses, the kissing all over, the rediscovery of pleasure filled my spirit to overflowing, and if I can have four more nights like this, I want them all.

We'd intended to spend the day in bed, but kept getting interrupted. Cécile knocked on the door. "We're naked!" I yelled. She left the basket she was carrying on the porch and excused herself in a hurry. But she wasn't quite quick enough to spare herself the view of a hungry, nude hippie bursting through the door and diving into her homemade crois-sants. To my eyes, Aran Sky is beautiful, but the poor young lady was forced to cover hers. There are some things a girl just can't unsee.

Soon after we'd had our fill and snuggled under the covers, the phone rang. It was Burnt Meadow Music. Their Friday act had cancelled at the last minute and they were rounding up local talent to fill in. The director wondered if I might be available. I told her she could have me and Aran Sky, too, which made her doubly excited. We were to practice with the others today and tomorrow morning. The performance is tomorrow night.

After I hung up, I instantly went into a panic. It took Aran two hours to calm me down, even though calming me down has been his specialty for decades. A full show might be too much for us! No way could we do it on such short notice! We'd just embarrass ourselves!

I was hysterical. But Aran did his thing, murmuring and stroking and radiating peace and inner tranquility, and soon I could breathe again, then my heart slowed to a normal pace, and I was able to carry my fiddle to the car. The actual meet-up with the band went fantastically. I actually had fun.

As we left the session, a wind came up from nowhere. Thousands of ripe maple seeds blew from the trees along the edge of the parking lot. Maple keys, because they are unevenly weighted, swirl like helicopter blades in a tornado, spinning deliriously until they hit the ground, burying themselves headfirst in the soil. I appreciated the surprise and dazzle, but Aran was inspired to action, grabbing my hand, running right into the shower, and spinning with the seeds. At that moment, he was one hundred percent pure Aran Sky, blissing out on the beauty of life. How could I not join him? We twirled as the maple seeds rained down upon us, then we fell into a heap on the ground, dizzy and laughing. The Burnt Meadow Music staff member who'd been lured outside by the commotion held up his camera triumphantly in one hand and yelled, "Well, here's your next album cover!"

What a day!

Mimsy

Dear Gerald,

They aren't kidding when they say that the cure for a bad breakup is a new man. And while Aran isn't a *new* man or even *my* man, Gerald, I think I am ready to call our falling out over Anne Thompson done with. I have been sorely lacking in perspective. A sixty-four-year-old secret is nothing but a whisper from a parallel universe. It tempts you with what might have been. But what is, is enough. Without the secret, you and I would have never spent those four years together. Without you and Anne, Booker would never have come into my life. And though he has an irrational fear of prayer beads, patchouli, bare feet, and everything Aran, I love him because he is part of you.

Yes, even during the weeks I was full of spit and venom, I still loved you.

Mimsy

Dear Gerald,

Aran says he legally changed him name on the advice of a sky spirit he met during a vision quest. But I have always secretly believed he changed it because his last name was Garfinkel and that wasn't going to go over so well at Woodstock. Luckily the competition, Simon and Garfunkel, skipped that gig, and before his near-namesake ever knew he existed, Daniel Garfinkel stood before a judge and became, forever, Aran Sky.

Our youngest fan, Jack, is well aware of our aliases and various name changes over the years. When we picked him up to take him with us to Burnt Meadow Music, he greeted us as Aunt Margaret and Uncle Daniel. Great-great-aunt Margaret and great-great-uncle Daniel might have been more chronologically accurate considering the decades upon decades between us, but I am not complaining. He thinks of us as part of his family!

Rehearsal went well. Afterward we were served crab bisque at lunch with the staff. I was asked to sign autographs for the first time in years; I'm afraid the hallmark swirls and loops of my once practiced calligraphy are a bit shaky these days. I remember the hours I spent as a young girl on the tour bus, filling notebook after notebook to perfect it. I still have some snap to my wrist and can saw and reef the bow without pain, but wrapping my fingers around the narrow barrel of a fountain pen and producing artistic signatures may be a skill of the past.

Impressively, despite the cancellation of the originally scheduled act, three quarters of the seats in the auditorium were full. There were some newcomers who came just to see us. Aidan and Cécile had their own table. Jack's school friends and his father were at another. Jack, whom we'd invited onstage to play with us, was beaming. I'm afraid to tell his father, but I'm pretty sure we've ruined him for anything besides life on the road.

Right before we took the stage, Aran caught my eyes with that starry, interplanetary gaze of his, and I knew the night was going to be magical. And it was, Gerald! Somehow our new band wove together an evening of sound that held the audience spellbound. The consensus in the first rehearsal was to play traditional music that we were all familiar with. Our rendition of "The Two Sisters," though a shadow of Jerry Garcia's, galvanized the crowd to join in on the last stanza. Toward the end of a verse, the electricity went out. The audience continued to sing together, their faces lit by moonlight streaming through the newly darkened glass.

When we left the stage and collapsed in the waiting room, the staff member we'd seen yesterday, the one with the camera, came over to congratulate us. And, Gerald, this is the best part! He handed us each a CD he'd burned, *The Maple Keys Live at Burnt Meadow*. On the cover was a photo of Aran and me, arms outstretched, twirling under the maple trees. We put out so many, many albums over the years, but this raw, in-the-moment creation was the most beautiful I have ever held in my hands.

Deliriously happy,

Mimsy

Dear Gerald,

I don't usually sketch people, mainly because I am bad at it and they turn out looking a lot like plants, all viney and barkish, with either the tall posture of a pine or the sprawl of a juniper. But Aran insisted. He found my sketchbook under a pile of field guides and apparently was so taken by my very minor talent that he proposed a sitting right then and there. So, I say it is not my fault that his finished product combined the lean length of a string bean with the delicate venation of an oak leaf. He loved it though, carefully put it in the trunk of his beloved Kharmann-Ghia, and took it with him when he left.

I stood by the mailbox and waved goodbye as Aran Sky drove out of the driveway and onto Route Five, his convertible a low, red flash amongst the greenery. As soon as he was out of sight, I returned to the house, which now felt unfurnished, as if movers had come and emptied it while I had my back turned.

Aran has always been a balm to my soul. His visit has mended things I didn't even know were broken. He's headed west to commune with the universe under the dark skies of the Sonoran Desert for a while, but we made a plan. He's coming back for our local county fair in September to see the stage where it all began for Lawrence and Mimsy Bell.

The river runs slow and easy today like it has all week. She's been recognized as a goddess, appeased by Aran's devotion and soothed by his tending.

Gerald, he's been gone an hour and I already miss him.

Mimsy

Dear Gerald,

Cécile noticed me moping around town and invited me to see a movie at the Zoetrope, a special screening of *The Wizard of Oz*. I am not a huge fan of modern movies because they move too fast. I can't even process the images on the screen in an action film anymore. But nostalgia rules at The Z. They play one classic film for every four modern ones. Cécile was right to think I needed some cheering up. I have been pale and dispirited ever since Aran left.

The theater could give any big city art cinema a run for its money. The lobby is decked out in antique film nostalgia, you can operate real zoetropes in the foyer, the popcorn is to die for, and the theaters have balconies and red velvet seats and curtains and stages. I was in heaven. Lawrence and I used to go to the movies every Friday night in Boston. The advertisements before the picture are a little bit different here in Menotomy: docks, gun shop, redemption center, and whoopie pie bakery, but the movie trailers are the same. Sometimes they reveal so much and I get so deep into the story, I forget that I was here to see another movie! But the *Wizard of Oz* starts out in sepia, and only later gets to color, keeping the feature film distinct from all the elaborate teasers.

So, with soda in one hand and popcorn in the other, I let myself be Dorothy for two hours. She has her troop of true friends. I have one by my side, and just like Dorothy, more back at home.

Cécile cried at the end; she says she always does at happy endings. I held her hand and we sat quietly watching the credits until she was ready to leave.

Love,

Mimsy

Dear Gerald,

I took a walk down by the bog, and I saw a for sale sign on the side of the road. Remember the glade that had all the wildflowers in the spring: huge patches of bird-on-the-wing, painted trillium, lady slipper, clintonia, trout lily, and Dutchman's breeches? Today, the viburnums are in flower, covered with tiny bees, beetles, and butterflies. I identified witch hazel, spicebush, and alder in there too. There's an old mountain birch grown tall in the middle of the trail with delicate white bark so thin in places it looks like it has pink stretch marks. I think I've found a new place to love.

I called my real estate agent. She says there's been interest from a local developer. The lovely spring ephemerals will have all gone to seed by the time this place sells. The developer won't even know what he's destroyed. I am sure he won't see beauty in delicately shaded bark or know the difference between the ten different ferns I can see from the road. The native shrubs, he'd call trash trees. The idea of the exquisite bark of this elder birch torn and ripped by the saw! It's wrong, just wrong, Gerald.

I can't stand it. In my mind's eye, I see a tiny community obliterated. Tromped over by bulldozers and ripped to shreds by saws. Dragged off to rot. The ground compacted, houses built, and glade and forest replaced forever by the hateful green of lawns.

The very idea makes me sick to my stomach. I am here to find community, and I have found it in many places, including these woods. I know that in our youthful protest days the band and I would have climbed the trees and refused to leave until the bulldozers backed off. In my old age, I have a different way to fight. I am calling my real estate agent back, and I am paying full price.

Your wildflower warrior,

Mimsy Bell

Dear Gerald,

I stopped by the hardware store; the gossip mill is running full tilt. Aidan Ward is its grist. It seems that our friend's vehicle was observed parked *all night* outside Cécile Wright's house. I find it astonishing that Aidan has lived here well over a year and he still doesn't know better than to employ a little stealth in matters of romance. He could have tucked his truck in the bushes down by the beaver dam or left it at the end of the road up by the river. Folks would have thought he'd set a speed trap or was using the vehicle as a decoy to scare away teenagers. But no, he's invited the whole town to speculate on whether one of our town role models, a police officer no less, ought to be dating a woman widowed so recently!

I have a half a mind to ask him the same question myself,

Your Mimsy

Dear Gerald,

Well, before I had the chance to interrogate Aidan, the river made her second attempt on my life. This time she took advantage of the weakness of my old age rather than the foolhardiness of my youth and used my lack of balance against me. One minute I was crossing my arms and lifting my knees, doing my water aerobics as directed, the next I was underwater. The weight and strength of her held me down. The current pushed my body along the river bed. I remember reaching, weakly, for the light at the surface, then nothing more.

I awoke to see Aidan's worried, angry face inches above mine. I could hear the sirens of the ambulance and feel the presence of the paramedics, working on and around me. But Aidan's voice soon drown out everything else, "You, of all people, should know better! What were you thinking? Mimsy Bell, if you so much as set foot in that river again, I will lock you up for your own protection!" Later I learned he'd also threatened to arrest Young Jack and his friends for endangering an elder, which I don't think is an actual crime, and that he'd screamed at the ambulance driver to go faster or he'd ticket him for underperforming in an emergency, which is absolutely a made-up infraction.

I was in no shape to reply to his scolding, having inhaled so much river water, but had I been able to, I would have agreed with him. What was I thinking, Gerald? My aim was to make peace with the river, not to hand myself over to her on a silver platter. I caused Aidan and Jack great anguish. They say I wasn't breathing when the kids pulled me out of the water. They experienced hours of fear and guilt because an old lady was too stubborn to know her limits. I had no right to place that kind of burden on them. I have to be more careful. Especially when I am around her.

I didn't realize the river still has her eye on me, Gerald. Maybe I was meant to be the third victim. Sixty years ago, she took only two.

Solemnly,

Mimsy

Dear Gerald,

Oswald came to visit me in the hospital today. He brought flowers and an old album for me to sign. Probably thinks he better get my autograph quick; it will be worth more in the church auction once I'm dead. And I say he is right to do it now. This is the closest to death I have ever come. I coughed up blood this morning. Pneumonia and a possible pulmonary embolism. No number of blankets can keep me warm, I am chilled straight through.

Oswald looked very concerned when he saw me, and I assume he sees a lot of folks on death's door so I must really be in bad shape. But he didn't feel compelled to give me last rites so there's some hope.

We talked mostly about the river, me about how much I hate it, and him about how it inspired his career. He remembers hearing his grandfather talk about the baptisms performed there, congregants gathered along the beach, the minister holding the babies up to God then immersing them in the flowing water. When Oswald was a kid he used to take his cousin's dolls down to the river to baptize them. Later, when he came back from divinity school, river baptisms had long been abandoned, a stone baptismal font substituting for the river bed.

Nowadays, though he thinks his insurance company would frown upon it, he has it on his bucket list to perform one.

Lest he be inspired by my experience, I told him my near-drowning doesn't count as a baptism. That I came up just as irreligious as I went down. And that this river doesn't have the power to wash anyone clean of sin. She's not in the business of salvation. She's a goddess in her own right with her own voracious appetites.

And then we talked for a while of curses. Oswald wondered whether believing in them is what keeps them alive. My only concern is evading their inevitability.

Booker will be delivering this letter. They are keeping me here for a few days.

Love,

Mimsy

Dear Gerald,

They sprung me! Eleven days in the hospital. Good thing Lawrence pushed me to get that Medicare supplement. All our riches combined wouldn't have covered that bill. I am still very weak. No short, medium, or long walks allowed so I am sending this from my backyard. Good thing I didn't see the river hiding on the other side of the lovely birch forest when I first looked at the place or I never would have bought it. But waterfront has its benefits. With the river a hundred yards from my back door and the mailbox a hundred yards from my front door, it's just as easy to send letters to the dead as it is to the living.

For a few days there, I was really afraid I wasn't going to make it, Gerald. I've had pneumonia before, but never so bad as this. Batty said I was blue around the gills. The nurse mentioned being worried about pulmonary edema. But I don't think my young friends knew how bad it was; they were so busy trying to outdo each other entertaining me. Well, all except Aidan, who refused to enter the hospital. He waited for Cécile in the parking lot, arms crossed, glaring up at my window. He knows how close I came to letting the river take me.

I am going to call my lawyer tomorrow, amend my will. There are a lot of new people in my life that I need to make provisions for, just in case this reprieve from death is short lived.

The river is showing off her fecundity tonight, displaying a healthy crop of fish and frogs, her fertile waters alive with abundance.

I love you,
Mimsy

~~~

Dear Gerald,

I figured Cécile finally intended to spill the beans about her and Aidan when she invited me to go with her to pick up baby chicks for the farm at the post office, but she didn't. She must know that everyone in the whole town knows they are sleeping together, so why not broach the topic? All I could think was that she was having a hard time telling me that she's moved on from Mackey.

When we returned from the post office with our precious cargo cheeping from inside their perforated box, Aidan was waiting for us in the kitchen with a pot of coffee and some breakfast. The ceremonial box opening was a welcome distraction from my musings. Had all the chicks survived? The relief in the room when we counted twenty-five noisy little beaks was palpable. Though Wright Farm had hosted many generations of barnyard chickens in years past, this was the first run for Cécile. She and Aidan took to their duties like new parents, cooing over each baby as if it were the cutest thing in the world, and then carefully setting each tiny bit of fluff into the warm brood box.

I ate while they mooned over their babies. New life on a two-hundred-year-old farm. New beginnings for two young people. And despite the fact I hacked and coughed out remnants of the river all morning, Aidan apparently had decided that my near drowning was another topic that should pass into history without further discussion.

The river is particularly charming tonight. She's aglow, stealing the light of the pink sunset, blushing at all the new life bursting forth around her.

Love,
Mimsy

Dear Gerald,

Cécile and I drove by the potato fields today. There are rows upon rows upon rows of lush, dark green plants topped by thousands of clusters of white flowers, stretching all the way to the hills in the distance. You'd think people would grow them in their flower gardens, potato blossoms are that beautiful. I guess having to pick off hundreds of Colorado potato beetles every day makes them a lot less appealing.

Cécile and I were practically salivating discussing all the dishes she will make with the local potatoes when they are available by the ten-pound bag at the farm stand. This illness has left me as thin as a reed. Maybe some scalloped potatoes, potato soup, poutine, and potato pancakes will put some weight back on me. I've noticed Aidan's waistline has responded to Cécile's bountiful table.

The cough, the weakness, the weight loss, Gerald, I am not kicking this thing. Supposedly, it is no longer life-threatening, but I still can't take in a full lungful of air and I am tired all the time. I haven't been cleared to start walking again and feel cooped up. That's why we took the scenic drive to the hospital where my doctor works. I needed to take in some beauty, see some mountains.

Love,
Mimsy

Dear Gerald,

Earlier today, Batty and I played a game of turnabout-is-fair-play. Last time it was me pestering her incessantly about buying my house back. This time she was stalking me. When Nancy at the bank handed me an envelope of twenties, she announced that Batty was asking around for me, then Carolyn, who had my take-out order ready at Bay's, mentioned I should catch up to Batty soon, and finally, Rolf at the hardware store asked if I had crossed her, because Batty was lit up like a live wire, frantic to find me.

Turns out I wasn't the problem; I was the solution. Batty's sweet old friend Lilac Peary, who had just turned eighty-six on Friday, was overwrought with worry about one of her relatives. Her great nephew had found himself in a mess of legal trouble and Lilac wanted to help him out of it, financially. Batty, sensing her friend was about to hand the keys to the kingdom over to a deadbeat, had heard I'd bought property on the same road where Lilac owned sixty acres of untouched woodland, and wondered if I'd like to expand my empire. I asked if the great nephew was worth it. Batty said, "sort of… maybe… no." I asked if it was correct to assume Lilac would sell or mortgage her house to help him if she couldn't sell the land. Batty nodded, resignedly. I asked the price. Upon hearing it, I smiled and told her it was a deal.

I'd passed by the parcel numerous times on my walk, but we drove over anyway to take a look. It was rich habitat that hadn't been logged in a century. I loved it. Batty asked me what I was planning to do with the properties. I told her I have always felt the need to look after the plants, the most defenseless members of our community. Trees and shrubs and wildflowers can't escape or even voice a protest before being bulldozed by developers or crushed by skidders, so I was making a preserve.

Batty smiled at this. "I think I know what you mean. You feel the same way about the wildflowers and developers as I do about Lilac and her no-good nephew."

And so, as fellow avenging angels, Batty and I finally bonded.

Love,
Mimsy

Dear Gerald,

I was weak this morning, but I wanted to be outdoors, so I asked Bert the mailman to help me drag a lounge chair down to the river. Bert has a white knight complex. I hear it originated twenty years ago, the day he found the barber's wife tipsy and hopelessly tangled in her clothes-line after an unfortunate tumble off a ladder. He spun her around six times, unwound the line, freed the helpless damsel, and earned himself a midday slice of blueberry pie and a shot of whiskey as a reward. Ever since that day he's been on the lookout for opportunities to repeat the performance.

After Bert passed on some gossip, a couple of music industry magazines, and another bill from the hospital, he carried the chair to my backyard. Once it was perfectly placed with a sweeping view of the river, the intervale, and the mountains beyond, I lay for a long while staring at clouds, not thinking much of anything. Then I noticed one turkey vulture flying, wings in a V-shape, in the thermals above me. Then two, then three turkey vultures gathered, circling directly overhead. Occasionally, one would turn a beady eye towards me, and I'd feel compelled to shout up to it, "I'm not dead yet!"

Unnerved, I returned to the house so the scavengers wouldn't mistake my afternoon nap for my final rest. Inside, I found I carried half the riverbed back home with me in my shoes. There's sand everywhere in my house, in my driveway, along the road, in town, even miles from the riverbanks, evidence of her reach. She's cut a serpentine path through the landscape over thousands of years. That's the way of rivers—they twist and bend and cut themselves off at the pass; cast wide loops and claim more ground, then retreat, straighten out the crooks, and race downhill. At one time or another any given patch of ground in this town could have been hers. I wonder how much more she's taken since the dreadful day she took you. I can't imagine she's been content within her banks.

Thinking of you,

Mimsy

$$\sim\!\!\!\!\sim\!\!\!\!\circ\!\!\!\sim\!\!\!\circ\!\!\!\!\sim$$

Dear Gerald,

"The grayest state in the nation," that's what a columnist in the Sunday paper called Maine, as if retirees who stay in Maine—rather than shuffling off to Florida to be properly warehoused, adjacent to a putting green, until they die—are a burden. We like it here. That's why we stay. That's why we come back after long exiles. Plus, Maine doesn't put its old folks out to pasture. Most of the gray hairs I've met are still working. For God's sake our minister is eighty-one and our selectman is ninety-five! As Aran Sky says, we are full of elder power—a ripened version of flower power—the power of peace through wisdom. We should be celebrated, not dismissed.

Speaking of age and staying in Maine forever, Booker discovered another cemetery and invited me to explore it with him. He had a lead on his great-grandparents. The drive to Denmark was lovely, even if the trip's soundtrack was a recitation of Booker's entire family history, his pedigree from first begat to last begat, all the way back to the 1600s. I told him he was now officially as boring as the coworker that introduced him to genealogy a year ago. He laughed, and said he knew.

A lot of the old gravestones were covered by gray lichen. Those that were not stood ghostly white. Several lay cracked in half, the thin stones victims of a fallen tree branch. It only took Booker a few minutes to find Sarah and Micah, his great-grandparents. Your grandparents, Gerald. I remember you talking about them. If I had known he was looking for people on your side of the family, I would have brought flowers. Aran once told me about the Jewish tradition of putting a pebble on the gravestone in memory of the deceased. Since Maine has more rocks than flowers, all I had to do was look down. I set one on top of Sarah's headstone and one on top of Micah's headstone. I told them they were from you.

All this cemetery visiting has me worried. I really need to find a place for my earthly remains. The vultures know it. I know it. Time is running out.

Thoughtfully,

Mimsy

Dear Gerald,

Last night on the way down to the river, I rolled my ankle on a pine cone, and this morning my left foot was swollen up like a balloon. That prompted a trip to the hospital and an X-ray. The technician discovered that I have a fractured first metatarsal, and now I find myself clunking around in a very uncomfortable, rigid surgical shoe. This is the first I've heard of my metatarsals, they are particularly fine bones, and it is unfortunate we've been introduced under such painful circumstances.

Lately, I feel like all my letters have been written by a very boring old lady. My lungs! My heart! My foot! There's a reason old people talk about their ailments, there's no time left in between all the doctor's appointments, rehab work, balance exercises, pill counting, and keeping up with insurance coverage to do anything else worth talking about.

The drive home was interesting as always. The state line looks much the same as it did in your day, Gerald, but instead of tractors and hay wagons on the lawns, we've got many new adornments. On the back road to Conway, I passed by a plastic deer full of arrows in the front yard, a Chevy up on blocks in a side yard, and a bass boat covered in a blue tarpaulin, the pride of someone's driveway.

My old neighbors, "Massholes" as we so delightfully call them here, would die a thousand deaths if their neighbors proudly displayed chainsaw art or a decommissioned plow blade on their lawns. But here they are conversation pieces. It's this taste for eccentricity, the public delight in oddity, and the exposed, naked display of manual labor and her machines that makes me think my neighbors have an independent streak that runs pretty deep. Whereas, in the Massachusetts town where Lawrence and I lived, sameness was a virtue.

I was so tired from the doctor visit, I fell asleep on the couch as soon as I got home. It was almost dark as I made my way down to the river. She is sleepy, too. There are no ripples or curls in her surface. Your letter will be on a slow boat tonight.

I love you,

Mimsy

Gerald,

Today I got a postcard from Aran Sky. It was postmarked Gila Bend, AZ. There were only a few words written on it, but they were good ones. "Life's short. Marry me!"

Help!

Mimsy

Dear Gerald,

Well, tending baby chicks must have made Cécile broody, either that or Aidan proved himself good daddy material with those little practice babies, because she's pregnant!

I guess life is too short to wait around!

This blessed event has me leaning slightly toward saying yes. Aran and I get along great. We love each other. Not like you and I loved, more of a loving friendship, but still, we are certainly not indifferent partners. But more than those things, my question is why the hell not? We are so old that if there is a chance for companionship why not take it?

But the devil is in the details. Where would we live? I doubt he would be happy in Menotomy. He'll probably want to keep on touring. I can't walk more than a hundred yards without being out of breath. Will I hold him back? He's also still using mushrooms, pot, peyote, who knows what else? How can I be around him and stay clean? And what about the money? I've made a will. The money is deliberately allocated for the wildflower preserve, my new friends, and Burnt Meadow Music. If he outlived me, would he inherit? We'd have to have our lawyers draw up a prenup, which seems ridiculous at our age. Also, I can't forget that I made a promise to myself to stop following love and start blazing my own trail. Aran Sky is larger than life. Marriage to him would not be a trail blazing experience. I'd be perilously close to becoming a groupie instead a member of the band.

I need more time. I will write back that we will talk about it seriously when he comes to see me in September.

I love you,

Mimsy

P.S. It's a cliché, isn't it, for the deceased's best friend to marry the widow?

Dear Gerald,

Ugh, more carnage. Jack and I drove by a new logging cut yesterday. If
it was man-against-tree in a one-on-one fight, the men using crosscut
saws and the power of their own arms, like it was done in my grandparents' day, then maybe it would be fair. But these vicious circular
saws operated on long robotic arms, that's just a massacre. I suppose
they are following the letter of the law. They leave trees standing here
and there. Of course—as they know full well—without the support of
their neighbors, the trees they spare will end up blowdowns in the first
big winter storm and the sunlit gaps they leave will soon be filled with
invasive plants. Gerald, I know that people do need wood and jobs,
but when I see a sign promoting "Forest Fixers," the mark of a logging
outfit that clearly has no problem with irony, I can't help but get angry.

But for me, anger precedes action. I have two properties of my own.
I can't stop people from doing what they want with their own land, but
I can match them parcel for parcel.

It might be time to make a visit to town hall and peruse the tax maps.

In league with the trees!

Mimsy

Dear Gerald,

Town hall has been moved from the stately Victorian in the center of
town, where it originated, to a nondescript rectangle on a side road. The
clerks are as efficient as ever, handing out dog licenses, car tags, burn
permits, and receiving fines, back taxes, and dealing with complaints of
all types from everyday to whackadoo. I had the misfortune of standing
in line behind a whackadoo who wanted a permit to burn down her
barn because there were bats in the hayloft, so it was a good twenty
minutes before I could approach the counter. The clerk wiped her hands
along her sleeves brusquely, as if her last customer had been shedding
cat hair like crazy, before leading me to a table where I could spread out
the tax maps and see just who owned the land I want to buy.

I am thinking six hundred acres might do it. Large enough to contain different habitats and small enough to be contiguous. There are some hundred-acre parcels as well as a number of smaller sized lots surrounding my property. I checked with the planning board to see if anyone had submitted plans to develop them. None on file. Now is the time to strike.

Land Baron,

Mimsy Bell

Dear Gerald,

You know, this whole grave search would be a whole lot easier if I came from a normal family. I could just be buried beside my parents in Boxboro, MA, and be done with it. But after your death, I pushed my mother and father away. They said all the right words, but I could see in their hearts they were relieved. Mom and Dad's reaction to your death was more "good riddance" than "goodbye." And though I visited and cared for them in their old age, I never forgave them.

To be perfectly honest, there is a burial plot with my name on it in Massachusetts beside Lawrence. It is in an old cemetery that looks more like a garden than a graveyard. The Bells have their own section, surrounded by mountain laurel and rhododendron, with brick paths and granite benches. He waits under the earth with certainty that I will join him. But I was widowed before I was married, and you are waiting, too, at the bottom of the river, certain I will come.

Lawrence and I had our storybook, all the way from "once upon a time" to "the end." You and I are an unfinished novel. The original story, *The Story of Gerald and Mimsy*, never made it past the first few chapters. Being buried here, near you, is the only way I can think of to give us our happily ever after.

Love,

Mimsy

P.S. Funny, I completely forgot about Aran in this calculation. What certainties does he expect from an exchange of wedding rings?

Dear Gerald,

I have been taking a lot of scenic drives in the mountains lately trying to decide what to do about Aran's proposal. I turn the music up loud, put the windows down, and drive faster than is probably safe at my age. The combination of wind, sound, and the hair whipping my face distracts me from the decision I must make, right away, like tomorrow.

When I crossed the border into New Hampshire, I noticed that their state motto, emblazoned on every license plate, is "Live Free or Die." That's a strong statement, a commitment to non-commitment. Perhaps I should take their advice. It's not entirely at odds with the philosophy I adhered to in the 1960s. Why should Aran and I bind ourselves with laws and sacraments? We've embodied free love for almost six decades. Why cut a good run short?

The river is swirling beside me. She's hungry for your letter and laughing at my hypocrisy. Thinking about marrying another man when I am so wedded to you. But what she doesn't know is that when one is very old, loneliness and nostalgia are powerful aphrodisiacs.

Love,
Mimsy

Dear Gerald,

Aran and I made a date without knowing if either of us would be able to keep it. Fortunately, old age hasn't done us in yet; we both lived to see September and attend the county fair as promised. The two of us found our way to the band-shell where a rockabilly band was playing. I directed Aran to the center of the bleachers, four rows up, precisely where twenty-year-old Lawrence sat decades before.

I noticed Lawrence that day because he was on the very edge of his seat, his eyes fixed, not on my face, but on the motion of my hands. As soon as I finished playing, he disappeared. I remember looking wildly about, in all directions, frantic to find the handsome young man who seemed so appreciative of my music. I walked off stage and toward the exit, intending to search the crowd for him, but there he was, coming in the doorway with a handful of wildflowers.

Lawrence was absurdly cocky. His introduction came with a deep bow and a line I'd never fall for today, "Baby, I'm the one who's going to make you famous." I took the flowers and I took his hand, and in that moment, history changed. My future, diverted once before by the river, took yet another turn. Changing course, slowly and broadly this time, toward a life on the road. And then inevitably circling right back to the place where it started.

After the rockabilly band in the band-shell played their last set, Aran and I rode on the same carousel horses—then new, now vintage—that Lawrence and I were astride when we first kissed. Aran was all over the experience, from the calliope music to the brass ring. A big kid, playing oversized knight on his wooden charger. I watched him like I'd watch a movie star. Aran has the power to fascinate. You fall under a spell just watching the way he moves. You are bewitched by his pure joy in living.

Hungry after our ride and uninspired by cotton candy or fried pickles, Aran and I went looking for something heartier. Lawrence had loved the fire department's chicken barbeque. We made a meal of that at least five times over the course of the week we courted. The closest Aran and I could rustle up from today's vendors was hot wings. So, we ordered an extra-large portion and carried it behind the crafter's building, where we leaned against the clapboard and shared from the same container.

Lawrence always loved to feed me by hand. I don't know if he found it erotic or if it was a nurturing gesture, like a papa bird to its nestling. But there was always something on his plate that ended up dangling in front of my lips. Most often it was something I otherwise would have passed on. Twenty formative years eating boiled dinner and brown bread had dulled my palate. Lawrence never ordered for me or critiqued my choices. He just shared his, opening me up, patiently, to the world.

By nine p.m., Aran and I were exhausted, and we decided to go home, but then he spotted the fireworks. If I thought his inner child was on display before, now it was fully incarnate. He started running circles around me, herding me like the sheep dog we'd watched work earlier that day. Aran did not want to miss a moment of the show, but we had to get past the Ferris wheel and the tilt-a-whirl to find an unobstructed view. I limped painfully along with him nipping at my heels.

When we arrived, it was about ten minutes into the show. The brilliant shimmers and slivers of light blotted out the stars. We stood side by side—my sides heaving—and allowed the split-second bursts and spirals and rockets of color to bathe us. Their beauty was so fragmentary and ephemeral, it made me think of love. I looked up at Aran and his face was washed with green and then red, blue and then gold. He felt the touch of my gaze. And, as if it had been planned all along, he got down on one knee and proposed.

Behind him, my favorite fireworks, the ones that send down spirals of fuzzy whistling curls, exploded in front of the distant mountain backdrop. Aran was silhouetted in the classic pose of earnest men throughout time, supplicant and awaiting grace. And though I'd practiced saying no, I said yes.

I am sorry,

Mimsy

Gerald,

There is a new ring around my finger, recycled platinum decorated with conflict-free diamonds. It weighs much more heavily on my hand than the delicate gold band with the diamond solitaire that Lawrence gave me when he proposed onstage one year after we met. That first engagement ring sits in its original box in a drawer in my bedside table. Up until last night I wore my wedding band every day. I tried taking it off a few months after Lawrence died, but the indentation it had made over fifty-four years of wear was ugly to my eye. This time, because I am practically skin and bones, it slipped right off without leaving a trace.

I wonder what you would have offered as an engagement ring? With boxes and shelves full of semi-precious stones, I think you would have come up with something special, maybe a deep red garnet or a clear blue topaz, maybe a startling combination of gems in a whole range of colors. Stone mined from the earth under our feet set in river-panned gold, it would have been a commitment between you and me and the land, commemorating our deep connection to this place.

Don't forget that I love you,

Mimsy

Dear Gerald,

Aran and I dropped by Cécile's to show off the ring and announce our engagement. We brought a baby gift, a basket full of books on pregnancy that I'd picked up at the bookstore in Bridgton. She was cooking omelets and set aside her spatula to wash up and take a peek through the titles. She said they looked very reassuring, far different than the websites and online forums she'd ventured onto which were already giving her anxiety attacks with their conflicting advice and fear-mongering.

There was an injured hen in a box in the corner of Cécile's kitchen. I eyed it warily as it was missing a lot of feathers, covered with gashes, and looked as if it had lost a game of paintball, its scattered wounds painted blue with antiseptic. I was told it refused to go back in the coop last night and must have tangled with some of the local wildlife. Cécile sighed when she mentioned that keeping chickens wasn't exactly the great fun she thought it would be. Good practice for parenting, I thought, but did not say aloud.

Aidan offered to take Aran down to the target range with him, and to my great shock Aran agreed. I think this was some sort of fatherly gesture on Aidan's part. He's very protective of me. And as the new fiancé, Aran probably wanted to get in good with the closest person I have to a dad, even if that dad is five decades younger than I am. I watched them head out. Aidan walking straight and tall, carrying a tan pistol case in each hand and Aran, empty handed, galumphing beside him like a puppy. He's going to need therapy tonight, I thought. I am certain this will be the first time Aran's ever held a weapon. Crazy that he was doing it for me. To be part of my family.

Love,
Mimsy

Dear Gerald,

Aran slept in, so I drove a load of garbage over to the dump. Becks the Subaru is wonderful in many ways, but when I have stinking bags of trash in the hatchback, I'm tempted to trade her in for a sedan.

I got in line, which was not moving at all because Archie Cyr is up for reelection in November and he thought today was a good day to stump at the dump. He was pontificating and promising, passing out campaign literature, kissing babies and shaking hands. I really don't think he thought through this campaign location. There's not enough hand sanitizer in the world to banish the germy handshakes of one hundred people on trash day.

Guess who else I ran into at the dump? Oswald. When he asked how I was, I told him I had accepted a marriage proposal. Upon hearing the news, instead of congratulating me, he said—very rudely, I might add—"It's not that hippie is it? Tell me it's not him."

Saw Aidan at the dump too. He reported that yesterday's outing to the target range went okay. Aidan had managed to convince Aran to get off a single shot, but only after he removed the paper with the "bad guy" silhouette from the target and after he promised, repeatedly, that firing a revolver at an inanimate object was not going to result in Aran's eternal damnation or his reincarnation as a beef steer. Luckily for me, and probably because he has to deal calmly with people from all walks of life and in all states of inebriation, Aidan found Aran's reluctance amusing. It also didn't hurt that Aran wasn't half bad for a beginner, his one shot hitting the cardboard target just a few inches off center.

Love you,

Mimsy

Dear Gerald,

I've been a little distracted, but I finally pulled out my tax map research and called my real estate agent. We're going to approach a number of landowners with offers. Who knows, if I am tenacious, maybe I can cobble together vast holdings!

I also finally took time to read the genealogy that Booker gave me weeks ago. You have a colorful history, my dear. There's quite a rogues' gallery in your lineage: arrests, family feuds, cheating wives, bastard kids, runaways. I guess you come by your wild nature honestly. And I can see now why my family tried to keep me away from yours!

Considering it is essentially just a long list of ancestors, it's a pretty exciting read. Booker did a fantastic job.

I made up for some of Jack's missed fiddle lessons with a double session. I wish you could hear him play. He's devoted to practice and it shows. He has a whimsical touch. He can surprise you. Right when you think he's going one way, he flips and twists and goes another. I think he's got the potential to be great. But, of course, I am biased. He is my first and only student. I'll get him to come down by the river to play sometime, then you can judge for yourself.

I am able to get things done today because Aran left for a series of gigs along the East Coast. He'll be gone for two months. When he gets back, we'll have just under a month to organize the wedding. We've set the date, December 21st, winter solstice.

I know this is sudden. I hope you are doing okay with all of it, Gerald. I can't imagine that you'd begrudge me companionship at my advanced age, but still, I've dropped some promises into this river over the past year and I wouldn't blame you if you felt that I have been fickle or dishonest.

Forgive me,
Mimsy

Dear Gerald,

Booker called me. He's going to the bean-hole bean supper at the grange tonight and wanted to see if I would come along. He's trying to pry me out of the house. After an initial burst of excitement, I holed up for a week after Aran left, filled with doubt and worry that this whole marriage idea is going to be one big disaster and that I should call it off.

I suppose I could use an outing, but pork and beans, potato salad, and yeast rolls are not foods for someone with cold feet. They are picnic foods for the lighthearted, someone deserving of lemonade and pie. Not for someone who makes decisions in the spur of the moment and has to take them back, someone who breaks hearts and kicks puppies. That person should be forced to subsist on frozen dinners and stale beer. I told Booker I was going to wallow in my self-loathing a little longer, but he ignored me and told me he'd pick me up at five.

On the way over he told me I was being an idiot. That he has no idea what I see in Aran, but what he sees in me when I am with Aran is something worth keeping. That I would be a fool to screw it up. He advised that whenever he and his late wife, Ginger, had stopped being open with each other, worries festered and turned ugly, slipping out sideways, wounding the relationship. He said I shouldn't make that mistake; I had to talk to Aran. I was tempted to argue with him, but he wasn't entertaining any back talk and we finished the ride in silence.

We arrived at the grange just as the cooks lifted the cast iron pot out of the bean hole. The coals that had surrounded it were gray embers, extinguished by eight hours cooking underground, but the scent of molasses and maple and pork wafted warmly, tantalizingly, from under the lid. I knew Booker was approaching this meal as a historical reenactment, but I'd had bean-hole beans at the grange every year from infancy until I left town at twenty. It was plain old everyday comfort food for me.

As you know, there's not much to do in Menotomy, so everyone was at the supper, including Oswald. As soon as I spotted him, I shackled myself to Batty and her biddies so that I would be engaged in conversation every moment and not available for small talk with the disapproving minister.

Batty told me she is leading Halloween cemetery tours every weekend in October. "Walking on My Grave" is what she's calling them. She insisted that I come to at least one. I pointed to my foot, not long out of its post-op shoe, and shook my head. She said, "Nonsense! We'll just sign you up for the Snow Burial Ground. It's no more than twenty yards long and twenty yards wide. We'll plant you in a chair in the middle, put you in costume holding a scythe, and you can be Emma Snow, beloved matriarch and hardworking agriculturalist." When I shook my head a second time, she cajoled, "You can hand out candy."

I've never handed out candy. Parents rarely encourage their children to knock on the doors of tour buses for trick or treats. And Lawrence and I lived in a gated home for security. No trick-or-treaters getting past the guards there. My new house in Menotomy is set right where the speed limit jumps up to forty-five and I doubt I'll have any little costumed visitors wandering up the highway to knock on my door. Gerald, I have not given so much as a single lollypop to a child in all my eighty-one years, but the idea suddenly seemed delightful. And so, the answer was an enthusiastic yes.

Love,
Mimsy

~~~

Dear Gerald,

Aran called me from Atlanta. He wanted me to drop everything and fly down to Raleigh for their next show. He must have forgotten that my band, The Maple Keys, has a gig later this week. So, I reminded him I am not putting aside my music for his. If he wants to be married to me, we're sticking to a "free to be you and me" philosophy. I am not always going to be available to hop on a plane, because, finally, at eighty-one I am exactly where I want to be, doing exactly what I want to do.

He seemed kind of shocked to receive such heavy stuff in response to a simple invitation, but after a couple of beats, he rose to the occasion. It was easier than I thought to speak directly and honestly like Booker suggested. I guess after all those years with Lawrence, I equated communication with conflict. But Aran is so easy to get along with, there was no blowback for expressing my feelings, just patient understanding. I can't even begin to explain what a relief that is.

Love,
Mimsy

~~~

Dear Gerald,

Aidan delivered the news that there has been a drowning. It was well south of here in Cornish. A sixty-year-old widow, out fly fishing. Campers found the woman's body caught in a snag in the middle of the river early this morning. And so, with that, the river's six-month fast has ended.

I imagine the scene. A woman accidentally hooks a sunken log and is reluctant to cut the line. The fly she is using is one of a kind, tied by her husband. So, she wades out into one of the river's deepest channels to retrieve it. Every step toward her goal is slippery and treacherous, the water fast and deep. Just a little farther, a little farther. Reach for it. You're almost there. Now, just duck under the water and retrieve it. The river whispers directions, luring her in, using what she loves most as bait. She can't backtrack even when she knows she's in too deep. Her waders fill with water. She can't leave that fly. I know this about the woman, because my heart, too, has been trapped in that river for more than sixty years. Impossible to extricate.

Stop it, I tell myself. You are being morbid. But I can't stop the flow of images in my head. My thoughts might be fiction, but the power of the river is real. She can even reach through time. Upon hearing the news, I was right back in the river myself, trying and failing to hang on to the slippery sides of the capsized canoe. Bludgeoned by the furious waters, moments from being swept away. Then she decided instead of taking me, to let me watch you die.

I am sitting on the riverbank. There's a corn crib on the farm in the intervale way across the river. The old wood is glowing, reddish gold, ignited by the western sun. The hayfield in front of it is burnished copper. But the river is dull pewter, her surface a shroud.

Sorrowful,

Mimsy

Dear Gerald,

Cécile called me this morning in hysterics, unable to form complete sentences, and I rushed right over. Aidan's truck, throwing up a cloud of dust, sirens on, lights flashing, was right in front of me when I turned onto Fight Brook Road.

I was transported right back to the day Mackey died. The level of emergency, blood coursing through my veins, sweat like rivers running down my body, my heart clenched in a tight fist. Was Cécile hurt? Was the baby okay?

I was relieved when I saw her standing in the driveway. Doubly relieved when I got closer and saw she was unharmed and holding a tiny kitten. But then I saw her face, tears streaming down and dripping off her nose and chin. The shuddering intake of breath in the middle of each word she was trying to say as she spoke to Aidan.

By the time I parked, Aidan was running off to the barn. I wrapped Cécile up in my arms, again wishing I was a motherly sort, and she told me what she found in the barn this morning. Five of the barn cat's kittens had been killed in the night. All of them except for the runt of the litter, the one in her hands, a little money cat that had the presence of mind to hide under a bucket.

Aidan returned after he'd cleaned up the mess in the barn and viewed the recordings from the night vision cameras they'd set up after the earlier attack on the chicken. He identified the culprit as a fisher.

We took the kitten into the house and made up another box for it beside the hen. Cécile was not sure what to do, because the kitten needed to nurse, and its mother was nowhere to be found. Even if the mother cat returned, she was feral and wouldn't come in the house, and there was no way Cécile was putting this baby back outside. I called the vet. He asked us to bring the kitten in. An hour later we came back with a clean bill of health and twelve cans of kitten formula. Mama Cécile and Papa Aidan are going to get some practice with midnight feedings.

Gerald, I can tell already that I'm going to have nightmares after this. Not about fishers. But the memories of Mackey's face and the sound of the gunshot and the police officers and of Cécile's keening are already knocking. This will trigger bad memories for Cécile too. Though, I suppose they are always there, every time she closes her eyes.

I miss your strength,

Mimsy

Dear Gerald,

The barbershop is a vile den of lies. I thought the hardware store was bad. I knew the salon was infamous. But unlike the flag, the red, white, and blue of the barber's pole in front of Sam's Shave and a Haircut clearly does not symbolize honor. Booker was getting his daily shave from Sam this morning when he overheard Oswald, who was having his ear hair trimmed, share a story about how he once rejected the advances of a rock star. Me!

Booker could barely contain his laughter as we breakfasted together. Your son, not a man prone to mirth, was so amused by the image of Oswald and me together that he almost choked on his eggs. And he should choke. He swallowed Oswald's tall tale whole! I couldn't even get in a word of correction without him bursting into another round of laughter. I certainly hope he's amused by this story, because it's the last one he's ever going to hear about my past.

And what the hell is Oswald bragging about? Who is he trying to impress? You'd think he'd be afraid to mention our little tryst on the log bridge considering the embarrassment he experienced there. It would not make him look like the big man around town if it was revealed that he was so frightened by my kiss that he fell in the river! Perhaps he's in the beginning stages of dementia. That's the only excuse I'm going to accept.

And believe me, I'd better hear some excuses out that slandering mouth of his, heaps of them.

Love,
Mimsy

P.S. Aidan got his buddy, the animal control officer, to set some traps around the property. Cécile insisted on live traps. Even though she has a fierce hatred going for that fisher, she doesn't want it dead. Which pretty much parallels my current (most charitable) thoughts about Oswald.

Dear Gerald,

Town meeting tonight. Archie Cyr is ninety-five and has one good tooth, but despite his age and his pronounced lisp, he still smacks a mean gavel. On the town's agenda tonight is the bottling plant, so it should be contentious. I hope to corner Oswald when the volume rises. The battle will drown out our own personal disagreement.

It has been difficult to maintain the fury I had yesterday, because early this morning at my doctor's appointment I got the all-clear on my lungs. The cough has been tapering off for weeks and I am now officially on the mend. And to my great relief—with the doctor's okay—I was able to take a very short walk with Cécile from her dooryard down to the pond and back again. We saw a muskrat and you'd think it was a unicorn from how excited I was. I don't think it is time to start hiking over hill and dale on my own again, but at least I no longer feel like an invalid.

The ravens were having a bit of a to-do behind Cécile's farm when we got back from our stroll. I also heard the chuck, chuck, chuck of chipmunks, the mournful creak of the autumn field cricket, and the wild shrieking racket of the blue jays. I've never been much of a composer, but I thought it would be interesting to incorporate those sounds into some music. So, when I got home I pulled out my fiddle and tried to do them justice. I think I have a fair replica of the cricket, him being a fellow fiddler, but I am not sure if I am capturing the others. I am going to have to take the fiddle out into the woods so they can teach me.

River's got some clarity today. Wish me luck trying to rein in Oswald tonight.

Inspired,
Mimsy

~~~~~~

Dear Gerald,

Of all the stubborn old men, Oswald Pingree Martin is the worst. The most sanctimonious. The most prideful. Despite these massive character flaws, once I lined his pockets, he agreed to a cease fire.

It helped that I mentioned that every story has two sides and in my version of the breakup story he does not come out looking quite so good. Remember freaking out over sins of the flesh, Oswald? Being unable to reconcile the mind-body dichotomy? Taking a plunge into the cold river to cool your jets? That last one gave him pause, but then he brought up some foolishness about freedom of speech and history being a shared experience owned by all.

In the end, it came down to blackmail. Another big check for the food pantry. We agreed that he can tell whatever tales he wants after I'm dead and buried. Until then, no more tabloid "my brush with a rock star" brags.

Blowups with Oswald might not be as volatile as those I had with Lawrence, but despite this fight's milder nature and quick resolution, I find myself in need of comfort. I wish Aran was home. His embrace makes bad feelings evaporate, just float away, replaced by this Aran Sky dreamy peace.

Mostly, Lawrence and I fought because I was high as a kite and spinning out of control, but sometimes our fights revealed deep divisions. Lawrence defined himself by that which he rejected. Blasé, contemptuous, he was the darling of the media. They loved putting him in front of a camera. No one—not even I—could predict what he would say when they handed him the mic. But Lawrence was a rebel for rebellion's sake, and even he had a hard time keeping track of what he dismissed. Were the Trotskyites in or out? Had he condemned this capitalist tradition before? Or was it that patriarchal one? Where was he on the issue of leather?

It was never clear if Lawrence was an icon or an iconoclast. His music certainly was worthy of veneration. But he was reckless in his declarations. At the height of his career his words held so much power it frightened me. His fans could be turned toward or against an idea with the briefest mention from stage. I begged him to leave the political stuff alone, abandon the movement, and focus on the art. I was ever so thankful when, finally, age and maturity slowed him down.

But never as slow as this river tonight. She's dead in the water—if you can say that about a river. Satiated and full.

I miss you,

Mimsy

Dear Gerald,

Well, clearly Batty chose me to be in her graveyard program because I was the only one who could fit in the dress. It's an original, found in a chest in the attic of the Snow homestead. It has the tiniest waist of any of the period dresses in the collection. I had my doubts during the fitting that they could get it buttoned up, but they manhandled me into a girdle and it slipped right on over that. I looked so much like a ghost with my pale skin and white hair and old-fashioned, off-white gown that some of the kids were reluctant to approach me, but once they saw the full-size candy bars in my basket, they got over their fear.

The fact I fit into that dress at all has made me hyper-conscious of my weight, or lack thereof. You know I was never one to pay much attention to my figure, but honestly, I barely exist. I need to get over to Cécile's for supper, and breakfast, and lunch more often. Batty, however, was thrilled by my miniaturization. Apparently gaunt old ladies are all the rage on the Halloween circuit. She wants me to attend all the tours now. She thinks I'll be a big draw.

As we waited for more visitors, Batty prattled on about the six grave-yards in the series, including Fight Brook Burial Ground. I mentioned that I wanted to be buried there, that I had relatives in it, and it looked like there was room. She dismissed the idea and explained that there were several graves without stones, so whether or not it looked like it, it was full. I told her I was still graveyard shopping, then I asked her what her plans were. She explained that her plans did not include death. But if that strategy fails, the Congregational churchyard will do. For me though, she understood why I might not want to be buried there, because of Oswald—wink, wink, nudge, nudge.

In a desperate attempt to change the topic, I asked the old gossip where she recommended I be buried. She looked at me and repeated her list of closed graveyards. Then she asked me what they all had in common. It took me a couple of guesses, but I landed on the fact they were all old family burial grounds. Batty said that the historical society ladies were, of course, primarily interested in the old ones. But there are new ones. And that in Maine you can legally bury anyone you want on your own land as long as you fence it in and register it with the town clerk.

That's it! I've searched in vain long enough. I'm going to build my own damn graveyard!

Your not yet dearly departed,

Mimsy

Dear Gerald,

This morning, I caught the scent of wood smoke, the volatile flavors of oak and ash drifting through the air. Seasons here turn subtly at first: a single red leaf on the swamp maple, a change in the night-singing insects, and then the goldenrod blooms. Before you know it, you can see your breath as you take your coffee on the front porch, the migratory geese line up southward in the sky, and you feel a sudden urgency to install snow tires on your car.

Cécile swung by with lunch. Oddly, she didn't eat what she brought me. She had her meal all measured out into tiny glass containers. Got to get exactly the right nutrients in, I guess. I've heard of pregnant ladies having food cravings, but acai berries? That's a far cry from pickles and ice cream, but what do I know, other than it was nice to not have to share my pulled-pork poutine.

Otherwise, it was a quiet day. I wandered around the yard looking for the most suitable portion to fence in. There's a nice grove of birches near the back porch, but they aren't long-lived. The pines are too dark and gloomy. The front yard would be inappropriate in so many ways. I made a trip over to my properties to see if I liked it better over there. I lay down in the center of a witch hazel thicket; it was quiet but also lonely. So, it looks like this is it, the wide bank by the river, the place where I come to rest at the end of each day and where I write to you.

Having found the perfect place, I raced over to the town office to fill out the application for a family burial ground permit. They checked my paperwork and told me that once I have a fence installed, my burial ground is legal! I was so excited I went a bit nuts, enamored with the idea of digging my own grave, I grabbed a spade and started chopping at the sod. Within minutes, the ground became too hard and the spade became impossibly heavy. I collapsed on my back in the hole, struggling to breathe, contemplating how much easier it would be not to have to breathe at all, fully aware that that day is right around the corner.

I wish you could see the sky tonight. To the west, there is a long line of clouds that look like waves breaking across the sky. A cross-section of the ocean in the air.

Ready to rest in peace,

Mimsy

Dear Gerald,

Looks like our neighbor across the road, Ronnie Gagnon, got his deer. His hunting season over and done on day one. The buck is hanging in the dooryard, field dressed and gutted, aging. For the rest of the month, pickups will litter the roadsides around here. Fellows wearing blaze orange, shouldering rifles, disembark before dawn, singly or occasionally by twos. They hike across the fields and disappear into the firs. The percussion begins at first light, singles and volleys; the retorts continue until sunset. Each bullet a spin on the roulette wheel for the prize of a full freezer come winter.

We used to have venison once a year when I was a child. Always the day before Thanksgiving. My dad must have gotten it from a friend, because he was no hunter. He cooked it exquisitely and served it with a honey cranberry sauce. I remember back then the wild taste was a delicacy, a rare treat. Mom liked it too because that was the one day all year she had off from cooking. Of course, preparing the feast the next day cancelled out any rest she'd gotten on her day off, but I remember how she'd take her time cutting slowly, savoring every tiny bite, partly enjoying the flavor, partly enjoying every moment of someone taking care of her for a change. I think I'd like to renew that pre-Thanksgiving tradition.

It is cold and the mist is rising from the water's surface. A whitetail doe in the field across the river stands, head high, ears forward, poised on the edge of flight, her accusatory stare speaking as loudly as words. You can't eat what you can't catch. She has a point. I'll never get one the traditional way, but like my dad, I'll barter with the neighbor for a roast.

Love,
Mimsy

Dear Gerald,

Cécile and I drove down to South Portland today to go maternity shopping. She's getting big now and her jeans won't button. There wasn't an elastic waistband to be found in the trendy shops in North

Conway. A surgical strike was what she was after. Get in, get clothes that fit, and get out.

Gerald, I've never been an expectant mother, but Cécile doesn't seem particularly excited about this turn of events. I understand that her fashion choices have now diminished to stretch-panel leggings and long flowing shirts, and that is upsetting, but it's more than that. I can't pin down exactly why I'm worried.

I've noticed little things here and there. She never touches her belly. Most moms I've observed hold the baby before it is even born. They rub their baby bump, cradle it with two hands, or rest a single hand upon the top. Cécile didn't want any of the extraneous baby things I picked up around the store either. Tiny booties, cute bibs, little lambie doll. Didn't even look at them. I bought them anyway when her back was turned, but I feel like that should have gone differently. There should have been oohs and aahs and "That's so cute!" exclamations. Something doesn't feel right.

However, this river doesn't care about my worries. A strong wind has kicked up small waves across her surface perpendicular to her current, ruffling her hair, antagonizing her. She wants to regain control, at least on the surface.

Love,
Mimsy

Dear Gerald,

I'm so relieved that winter is not far away. All the people who willingly enter her waters will migrate uphill to the ski slopes. They will escape the river's curse for another year, and she will grow hungry and lean waiting. This year, she only took the one woman down in Cornish. There is only a small window left for her to act, to collect two more. The leaf peepers are gone. The skiers and snowmobilers not here yet. Maybe she is satisfied. Maybe she'll rest.

You know, back in the city, the eternal struggle was man vs. man. You could win, maybe, if you were lucky, but the deck was stacked against you. There are just so many men and only one you. Ultimately, they wear you down. Defeat will be empty and graceless. Rejected by a mid-level health insurance bureaucrat and you die without insulin. Your building permit is delayed on a technicality and your brownstone's floor caves in beneath you. Some asshole blocking the box so he can turn left on red accelerates and flattens you in the crosswalk.

But here in Maine, it's man vs. nature. You are going to lose and lose spectacularly. Swept off the picture-postcard rocky shore by a rogue wave. Obliterated by a magnificent, heavy-antlered moose smashing through your windshield. Frozen to death when you wander away from your out-of-gas car, lost in a glittering ice storm, as treacherous as fairyland.

Sometimes I wonder what is preferable. A mundane end or a spectacular one? Maybe the difference comes down to what or whom your loved ones get to blame.

Sorry to be such a downer, but you know how she gets to me.

Love,
Mimsy

Dear Gerald,

Today, I picked up my fiddle and drove out to the property I bought from Lilac Peary. First, I sat on the stone wall and listened. Then I played, quickly scaring off all the wildlife I was trying to imitate. But I improvised by trying to capture the wind in the leaves and the creak of tree boles. Eventually the birds and crickets became curious and returned.

I think I have the beginning of something. As I said before, I've never tried to compose music. I left that to Lawrence and Aran. Left a lot of things to them. Things that would have made me a better musician. Just kept to my role, pretty barefoot girl with flowers in her hair who walks in from stage left, fiddle on her shoulder, and dances across the stage playing her part in Lawrence's masterpiece, only to exit stage right a few bars later. It never occurred to me to step outside those parameters when I was young. I slept with composers, for God's sake. You'd think I might have paid attention and learned something. But song making was their time together, the sacred space, the bounds of which were never crossed, even by lovers.

And I can see how hard it is, now on my first try. Hard to make my fiddle tell a new story. Must have been impossibly hard to combine and fit and weave so many instruments and voices together in the band. I am finding there are infinite choices, not all work together, not all sound fresh and new. Even with chipmunks and crickets, blue jays and ravens, I find myself repeating old melodies, relying on old patterns. And when I hit just that right combination, I risk losing it in the folds of my mind, for age is not a friend of memory.

As difficult as it seems now at eighty-one, and despite how frustrating it is to realize that it would have been so much easier at twenty-one, composing music is exhilarating. Certainly, I am creative when I play, and as a teacher I've passed that playfulness on to Jack, but this is another whole order of creation. This is art. This is playing God. Direct communication from my mind to my instrument. No following directions. No interpretation of others' work. My work. My slow, painful, excruciating, maddening, new, beautiful work.

Growing wings,
Mimsy

Dear Gerald,

After I told Aran about my song, he overnighted me a package of staff paper and a box of vintage E. F. Blackwing pencils. He also offered to help me when he gets home, but I am not going to let him. He's composed plenty of songs in his life. This one is all mine.

I dropped by Cécile's today. She was being very weird about the kitten, keeping it in sight at all times. Even though she had bacon sizzling away on the stove, she followed the little calico cat from room to room as it flung itself all over the place like a crazed pinball, jumping off couches, bouncing off walls, and swinging from the drapes. She and Aidan still haven't caught the fisher that killed the rest of its litter. It is obvious this kitten will not be going back out in the barn, nor will it ever set foot outside if Cécile has any say over it. She's named it Copper, I think because it's a money cat, with patches the color of a copper penny, and not because her boyfriend is a police officer.

I had a late lunch scheduled with Booker, but he made a mysterious disappearance, calling at the last minute to say he had to fly out to the West Coast. I was so disappointed. With all my Halloween hauntings and other carousing, I haven't seen him in a couple of weeks and I miss him. We've been talking about how he's finished documenting the genealogy of his mom's side of the family and is compiling it into a book. He offered to do mine next. I can't imagine why. It is generous of him, sweet even. I will probably say no. At this late point in my life, I don't need a family tree to tell me who I am. I know who I am. I am the girl who raced his father up Mt. Tom, on a weekly basis for four summers in a row, and won each and every and time.

Sweet dreams, slowpoke,

Mimsy

Dear Gerald,

I couldn't sleep so I bundled up and went outside. The humidity is low and the sky is sparkling. How is it that I forgot that night is supposed to be filled with stars? There's Orion; I remember him, his belt, three stars in a row. There's the lazy W of Cassiopeia, paler, lopsided. Cepheus, a geometric dullard of a constellation if I've ever seen one. Ursa Major, somehow both leggy and boxy. Ursa Minor, petit mimic of major. Draco, clearly more intimidating in the imagination than in the constellation. And, of course, the most spectacular sight—absent from every city I ever toured or lived in—the Milky Way, a trail of silver glitter cast from horizon to horizon across the sky. How did I live without this view for so many years?

I've been spending every spare moment writing music. These Blackwing pencils Aran sent me seem loaded with a magic of their own. They fly across the page, jotting down notes as soon as I think of them, and I have made more progress on the piece today than all the rest of the days this week put together. Aran included a note that many famous composers, including Sondheim and Bernstein, used this brand. I think my fame is behind me, but heck, just being able to mark the page with the notes that come to mind, solidifying them before they drift away, has been a blessing. I had Young Jack come over for a first listen. He approved wholeheartedly of where I was going with it. He even gave the guitar part a try. We ended the session by making a pact to play it for you first, once it is finished.

It is past midnight. Barred owls are calling in the distance, their voices spectral and seemingly in communion with the universe above. The cold has seeped through the sweaters and jackets and tights I layered on in order to come out here so late at night and I am shivering. I am going to go back to my bed, eyes full of starlight. Hopefully sleep will come soft and easy.

Dreamily,

Mimsy

Dear Gerald,

Well, yesterday was awful. It started out with a storm, a real gully-washer, and ended up in the emergency room. I lost power and headed over to Cécile's where they have a generator. Aidan wasn't there. Cécile said he'd been out for hours following up on emergency calls and looking after the road crews and line workers. She looked like she hadn't slept a wink. There were huge dark circles under her eyes. I could tell she hadn't had a thing to eat, either. I started some scrambled eggs, but while I was whisking, I heard very quiet keening noises. At first, I thought the kitten might be trapped somewhere, but the sounds came from where Cécile sat, curled up under an afghan on the couch. I set the mixing bowl aside and went to her.

Her full, round belly was emphasized by the blanket's soft, clingy drape. When I sat down beside her, she stopped making the sounds I'd heard and looked up at me without expression. "It's Mackey's birthday," she said. I kicked myself; I should have been on the lookout for just this sort of thing. Your birthday, Gerald, still throws me for a loop. I used to take it off when I was with the band, disappearing for the whole day, wandering around whatever city we were in and ending up crying by the water. So, it was with great sympathy, understanding, and more than a little guilt that I scooted closer and put my arm around her shoulders.

But she shrugged me off and spat, "It's your fault!" at me. I was shocked, so shocked I didn't respond right away and she continued on without pause. It was an accusatory rant much like the one on the day Mackey died. Her tone of voice was not tragic, though. It was high and disjointed, her words fast and manic. And her words, as they tumbled, became far uglier than they were on that terrible day.

"It's the wrong baby," she said over and over as she pressed her hands frantically into the sides of her belly as if wishing to expel it. I pulled out my phone to call Aidan, but as soon as his photo came up on the screen she slapped it out of my hand.

"We tried for years to have our baby." She was referring to Mackey again. I was desperately trying to reach the phone with my foot and having no success. But then Cécile started keening again, and then began scraping at her belly with her nails instead of pressing with her palms. She didn't seem to hear me at all when I begged her to stop. It was terrifying, almost as if she was asleep and acting out a nightmare.

I thought of a ruse to distract her, to break her out of her delirium. I yelled, "Oh my God, Cécile! Copper looks sick. We have to take him to the vet." Then I picked the kitten up from the floor where he was sleeping. Luckily, he'd been in a deep sleep and stayed limp in that floppy way kittens have. The exclamation and his limp body startled Cécile. Then I started asking frantically about his carrier. To my great relief she got up and went to get the carrier. I slipped the phone in my pocket when she stepped away, and I popped Copper into the cage immediately upon her return. I put the handle in Cécile's hand so she would feel some agency, and said, "Hurry, I'll drive. We've got to save him." This got her in the car. I pulled the seatbelt around her and she stared through the cage door at her nonhuman baby, who thankfully had gone back to sleep.

I know I am supposed to take it easy in my old age with slow reaction time and imperfect eyesight, but I made it to the hospital in under twenty minutes. Once I got Cécile and the kitten inside, she suddenly realized where she was. When the nurse approached, she started saying, "It's the wrong baby. Get rid of it. Please, get rid of it." The nurse guided her to a seat in triage, and I quietly explained to a second nurse Cécile's sudden and dramatic change in mental state. They took her to a room to wait for a doctor and said they were paging the psychiatrist. I immediately set down the carrier and called Aidan.

I didn't even know what to say to him when he arrived ten minutes later. How could I tell him she didn't want their baby? But he didn't even look at me when he crashed through the emergency room doors. I sat down in the waiting room. Feeling helpless, I scrolled through my contacts looking for Aran Sky, but my thumb stopped at Oswald Pingree Martin and I called his number.

Oswald was there in what seemed like hours but was only thirty minutes. By the time he'd come in, the doctor had come out to question me about exactly what I'd seen and heard. But she wouldn't tell me any more about Cécile's condition. Oswald waited for the doctor to finish, then sat down and held my hands, which in an incredible show of restraint had waited until this point to start shaking.

Cécile had been given a sedative and was resting comfortably when I left. Aidan said they'd done a number of tests which all came back normal and afterward she'd been transferred to the psychiatric ward. His face was stricken with grief, so I knew she'd been ranting about the baby while he was in earshot. Aidan gave me a hug and told us both to go home and get some rest. Oswald stood up and gave him a kindly pat on the shoulder and handed him his card with his phone number if he wanted to talk. It took me forty minutes to drive the thirty minutes home.

There's still no power,

Mimsy

Dear Gerald,

Aran is coming home today. Boy, do I need him here. After the events of this week, I feel like I was hit by a truck. I spent the whole night tossing and turning; sleep did not come at all. I'm so worried about Cécile and Aidan.

When Aidan finally called this morning, he briefed me on her condition in the tone he'd use for updating one of his officers. The doctors have diagnosed Cécile with prenatal psychosis and post-traumatic stress disorder. Cécile and the baby's physical health are fine, but she will be in the hospital for a while until her mental health improves. When I asked him how he was doing, Aidan changed the subject, thanking me for taking the kitten home with me, and then he hung up. Well, he should thank me for taking the kitten; the little clawed devil has already scattered my sheet music across the floor twice. But wrangling this beast is the least I can do for Aidan. He's the very first friend I made here, and no matter how much he doesn't want to talk about it, he must be devastated. I'll have to find a moment to talk to him, when he's calmer, maybe tomorrow when the doctors have a clearer picture of what's going on.

Well, it's time to drive to the airport in Portland to pick up Aran. Because the power's not back on yet, we decided to have a nice dinner at a fancy restaurant, go to the symphony, and nestle in at a downtown hotel for the night.

Love,

Mimsy

Dear Gerald,

We're back and so are the lights!

Aidan showed up on my doorstep today, unshaven and bleary-eyed. He dropped by to pick up the kitten, who has been terrorizing my furniture. We chased it all over the house. It was all a wild game to that crazy baby. He led us through the equivalent of a full obstacle course before we cornered him in the bathroom. Aidan scooped him up, looked at his tiny, ferocious face, and his eyes began welling up with tears. I wasn't quite sure what to do. Aidan is the most stoic person I have ever known. I was better prepared to watch a pillar of granite suddenly dissolve in front of me than to watch this particular man fall apart. But I didn't get a chance to do anything because Aidan turned and walked right out the door without saying goodbye.

Oh! With all the horrible things going on, I forgot to tell you. I finished the song! I think it's good, though you'll have to judge for yourself. I did my best to capture the sounds of the woodland animals that inspired me to take this leap, and I fashioned the whole thing to sound like the music was adrift on a raft in the river, moving farther and farther from the listener until it disappears. Young Jack, Aran, and I are going to perform my composition for you at three p.m. today. Be there or be square, as my old beatnik friends would say.

Menotomy's newest oldest composer,

Mimsy Bell

Dear Gerald,

For goodness sake, it is freezing outside, and yet Aran decided it would be a good idea to take a polar bear plunge. I caught sight of him emerging like the god Neptune from the river, naked, water streaming over his broad shoulders, lips blue, shivering with cold. I ran outside and gave him a piece of my mind, asking how many more boyfriends I should sacrifice to this river. He waved away my concern and said I should join him next time. Next time! I am sure he'll be back in for another quick dunk tomorrow and probably every day after that.

I hung out at the auto shop for an hour having the snow tires put on my car and gossiping with my dark-haired mechanic, Sean. He had much to say about recent goings on in town. A volunteer firefighter, he'd responded to a chimney fire down Lake Vista Road. "You'd think with a fancy vacation house like that, they could afford to have their chimney cleaned once in a while," he said, intending every ounce of judgment loaded into the statement. I took Sean's comment as a compliment, because if people are sharing their true thoughts about flatlanders with me, I must finally be considered one of the locals!

After that errand was done, I dropped by my real estate agent's office. She's been working hard to obtain the land for the preserve. Of everyone we've asked, most were more than happy to sell, especially for what I was offering, but there is one major holdout, and it is Oswald. It turns out the southern parcel is an old family property. That plot contains botanical rarities that must be protected, including rattlesnake fern, blue cohosh, and baneberry. How a man of the cloth can refuse to ensure the preservation of such vulnerable and exquisite forms of life, I do not know.

Booker replied to my text invitation asking if he would be back in Maine for a party I am planning to honor my father's Thanksgiving Eve tradition. He said yes, he would, and he is bringing a plus one! No information on the guest. But I'll set another place. I also got acceptances from Aidan and Cécile, Batty, Oswald, and Young Jack and his father. I am getting excited. Our first party!

No longer a flatlander,

Mimsy

Dear Gerald,

Aran's headed out on a pilgrimage up to Starks at first light. Starks is the town best known for Hempstock, the Green Love Renaissance, and the Harvest Ball, all legendary pot festivals. None of them are going on now in the cold depths of November and one of them has moved further north to Harmony, but once Aran gets an idea in his head, there is no stopping him.

He was reminiscing about his trip to India a couple of days ago and was expressing that he felt the need to honor the goddess Cannabis in all seasons. I told him what I knew about Starks and he looked up the history of the farm and the festivals online. The very next day he borrowed Becks the Subaru—better than the Karmann-Ghia in the winter—and motored two and a half hours northeast to smoke a joint on the storied streets of Starks. I should have gone with him. It is a long drive in unfamiliar country for an eighty-five-year-old man, but the idea of a five-hour round trip in order to stand out in the open watching Aran Sky respectfully inhale was not appealing. I can see him perform that ceremony right here at home any day of the week.

I took the opportunity to drive Aran's car over to North Conway. It is kind of like riding on the ground compared to the high seat in the Subaru. The pickup trucks certainly look more menacing. I did get some appreciative glances at the stoplights, which made me happy and reminded me of the fun I had driving the Jag. I stopped at the grocery store for a small bouquet of flowers and then tried, once again, to call on Cécile at the hospital. I've been trying my best to inquire but not be disappointed when my visits are rejected. Which they have been every time.

The river is melancholy tonight. Her surface is the color of quicksilver. She babbles a bit, complaints, mostly. Sometimes, even she doesn't get her way.

Love,
Mimsy

Dear Gerald,

We ran into Aidan at the dump, a few cars ahead of us in line. As soon as I saw him, I shoved my trash bags into Aran's hands and leapt into action before Aidan could get away. I pounded on the passenger door, yelling "Open up!" until he unlocked the door. Once in, I ordered him to drive, as if amateur carjacking were my hobby. He raised his eyebrows, sighed loudly, put the truck in gear, and pulled out onto the main road. I've heard that men talk more when they are in cars, when they don't have to make eye contact. It took several miles, but the floodgates opened. And a few miles after that, we had to pull over because he was sobbing.

As best I can understand it, though he has asked to see her every day, Cécile has not agreed to see Aidan once since she was admitted. He's been sick with worry about her and the baby. Worried that she'll never get better. Terrified that she'll terminate the pregnancy. He couldn't get over the hateful tone in which she spoke about their baby. She'd seemed so happy when they did the pregnancy test and saw that plus sign. I considered telling him I'd noticed things that seemed a little out of the ordinary in the past couple of months, but wasn't sure if that would be helpful so kept my mouth shut and listened.

Since they are not married, Aidan is not Cécile's next of kin. Her sisters are. Both of them came down from Canada when I first called, but her younger sister, Helene, has since returned home to care for her small children. Her older sister, Geneviève, is very protective. She told Aidan that Cécile had asked her not to speak to him about her condition, but not to worry, she was going to make sure her sister got the best care and that the baby was safe. Unfortunately, the definition of best care is under debate. With no improvement and mounting hospital bills—Cécile is not on Aidan's insurance either—Geneviève decided to have her care transferred to a hospital in Québec. She's being transported tomorrow. Aidan is despondent about this new development. He's afraid the baby will be born in Canada and that there will be some kind of international custody fight that he has no idea how to win.

I reassured him that I'd call my lawyer later today to find out who would be the absolute best attorney for a situation like his and I'd put that person on retainer. At least the fear and uncertainty of not understanding the law and what he might be up against would be put to rest. I also suggested he write Cécile a letter. She won't see him, but maybe she'd read the letter, or maybe Geneviève could be convinced to read it to her. We found some paper in his bag and he struggled with the words for over an hour. I sat quietly by, trying to radiate encouragement. When he was done, we drove to the hospital. We encountered Geneviève, her coat on and her bag over her shoulder, in the hallway. We approached her very calmly considering that both of us were freaking out so much that we could have been admitted to the hospital for tachycardia.

Geneviève read the letter. By the end she looked up at Aidan with appreciation, and agreed to go back in and read the letter to her sister, but didn't promise anything more, remarking that Cécile's mental state was unchanged from when we dropped her off, though she was calm now that she was medicated.

Aidan and I sat side-by-side in uncomfortable chairs, waiting. I sat upright, anxious, while he leaned forward, face buried in his hands. Geneviève appeared about ten minutes later. She told us Cécile listened the whole way through and then asked to keep the letter. Geneviève said she would call us tomorrow morning with an update. I took this as a good sign, but I still called my lawyer as soon as I got home.

Trying to remain hopeful,

Mimsy

Dear Gerald,

I am going to put a sign on my front door that says, "I don't like surprises." My parents knew that. Lawrence knew too, though he surprised the heck out of me every birthday and anniversary anyway. But these young folks I hang out with now don't know, and they also have surprises.

This was the kind of surprise that could kill an old woman. I opened the door when Booker knocked, and beside him I saw you, standing in the doorway. Your walnut eyes, your square jaw, your jaunty grin. I actually stepped backwards in shock, and stood there stunned and mute. Luckily Aran is an enthusiastic greeter. He wrapped the newcomer up in a warm hug, giving me a few moments to try to collect my heart off the floor.

Maybe all this time you'd been lost and living a life far away from here, I thought, my mind filling with hope. But the dark hair and tiny crow's feet were not the marks of a twenty-year-old man gone missing sixty years. They were the signs of a much younger man entering middle age. But I was slow to recognize this and must have been standing there longer than I should have, staring and silent to the point of rudeness. Booker spoke to me sharply to shake me from my trance, "Mimsy, say hi to my second cousin, Theodore. You'll be interested to know that he's Gerald's first cousin."

My mind's eye slipped back sixty years to your Uncle Roger, whom you favored, standing in his white shirt and pressed pants, pumping gas at the town's only gas station. When I left Menotomy, Uncle Roger still wasn't married, though he was already twenty-two. Turns out, years later, he left for Seattle, bought a small house, and started a family. The youngest of his children was the man who stood before me. The age difference between you and your cousin is thirty years, but your shared gene pool, written all over Theodore's face, transcends time.

Aidan was the only one who noticed I was in distress. Probably because he was too. Everyone else was quite excited about the apparition and they were all talking at once. And so, nobody noticed when Aidan took me by the arm and led me to the quietest corner of the house, the sunporch overlooking the birch forest. He sat me down in the glider and used his long legs to start it gently rocking because my short ones don't quite reach the floor. I whispered that he looked exactly like you. Aidan wrapped his arm around my shoulders and pulled me close, "Booker should have known better than to have sprung him on you without warning like that."

Eventually I recovered enough to tend to the meal, if not to my unexpected guest. When I emerged from my sanctuary, Aran had everything under control. He'd checked the venison, was mulling apple cider, and had the veggie sides transferred into our best serving dishes and was looking around for spoons. I got to work, and the meal itself went off without a hitch.

I could tell that Booker was thrilled to have found his cousin. It wasn't long ago he thought he had no family left. Theodore seemed pretty happy with him too. During his trip west to see his newfound cousin, Booker met a whole heap of new relatives. Theodore was the only one with enough time off to be able to visit the family's ancestral home in Maine. I got to hear all about your other cousins and their children, Gerald, but none of it sunk in. I just couldn't rip my eyes from your—from Theodore's face. And I couldn't stop the memories that flooded my mind when I looked at him.

Why couldn't it have been you? Was I so silly a fool to hope for those brief moments that you'd not died, just been washed away and found somewhere beside the river, forgetful from a blow to the head, and helped by kind strangers to start a new life? That you'd finally made your way back to me?

Crushed,

Mimsy

Dear Gerald,

It is Thanksgiving Day. Aran and I decided after all the stress and surprises this week, we'd nest safely at home and celebrate being thankful for one another.

We started with a wedding planning session over breakfast, but only got as far as the choice of best man before the conversation made a dramatic left turn. What brought us to the subject of death was Aran's choice, his childhood friend, Alexander. The two had played ball and roamed the neighborhood with a gang of kids back in the '40s. But Alexander is ninety years old, and since he has emphysema and cancer, it's possible he might not live to see next month's ceremony.

We played a few rounds of "Well, if he's dead, maybe you can choose…" with each suggested replacement being another gentleman of iffy longevity, before we were completely off course and found ourselves deep into Grim Reaper territory. Speculating no longer about wedding dresses and boutonnieres but about our own deaths and burials, what would and would not make the best perpetual resting place.

Aran voiced his skepticism about my family burial ground. "Let's be buried together in my family plot. We could buy an extra-large coffin so we can keep on knocking bones into eternity," he said with a wink as he grabbed me by the waist and pulled me to him. I'll admit to being grim, but all I could think of was him going first, then when I passed away, my fresh body dumped in beside his mummified skeleton in the coffin equivalent of a double-wide trailer. It was not a romantic image. But Aran thought the idea was great fun. I blame the Grateful Dead for putting images of happy, dancing skeletons in his mind. The reality of death is not rainbow-hued, Aran Sky!

I knew he wouldn't want to be buried here in Menotomy, and I don't expect him to be. There is an "until death do we part" clause in the marriage vows and I intend to use it. It's my loophole, you might say, if I go first. He wasn't pleased to hear that my being buried at home was non-negotiable, and the squabble that followed definitely tabled wedding planning for the day. We'd recovered a bit by afternoon. I'd had a nap and he'd had another foolish dip in the river. Then we ate the prepared feast we'd picked up from the farm stand and made eyes at each other across the candlelit table.

Happy Thanksgiving,

Mimsy

P.S. Oh, I forgot to tell you: despite the slight success with the letter, Cécile was transported back to Canada as planned yesterday. Booker is going to drop by the farm to keep Aidan's spirits up today. I am still shaken from seeing your doppelgänger last night, so Aran and I will wait to see him until tomorrow.

Dear Gerald,

All right, I am going to admit it. I need a hearing aid. At first, I was sure Aran was spouting hippie nonsense all the time, but then I realized that half of what he says does make sense. The other half, I'm not hearing right. "There's some tabbouleh in the fridge" turns into "There's a new shibboleth on the ridge," which is amusing but not at all accurate.

I've probably needed a hearing aid for years, but living alone, I haven't had to try to discern meaning from words spoken from the next room or over the sound of running water. The quiet life of a single woman is uncomplicated. I communicate with myself within my own mind quite well, thank you. It's transmitting information through the air that is getting in the way of my new relationship. Everything is garbled in translation and there are only so many times I can holler "What? What? What?" in a day before even the ever-patient Aran Sky starts to get irritable. In fact, he was the one who called the audiologist and made an appointment for me. He said, "I don't want you to lose the music, Mimsy."

Aidan was getting ready for work when we stopped by early in the morning. The frozen bagel with cream cheese in his hand when he opened the door was a far cry from the restaurant-quality morning meals he'd been getting from Cécile, and the contrast was not lost on any of us.

We accompanied him out to the new chicken coop, a virtual fortress protected by razor wire and the latest surveillance technology. He let Aran, who was bouncingly eager to commune with the hens, scatter the scratch feed. While my fiancé delightedly tossed grain to his newest fans, I checked in with Aidan.

It seems in addition to worrying about the love of his life and his baby, he's also worked himself up into a full-blown panic about whether or not he is trespassing. His reasoning is that if Cécile doesn't want to talk to him and doesn't want his child, she's certainly not going to want him living on her farm. I argued that someone has to feed the chickens, take care of the kitten, and keep the pipes from freezing and certainly he has some rights as a kind of roommate or tenant. "I love this place," he said, with the defeated look he'd been wearing for days. I told him I'd call Geneviève, and worst-case scenario, I knew a very nice inn that would give him an extraordinary deal.

On the way out of the barn, Aran asked about the fisher. Apparently, the devil was caught on camera several times but had so far evaded the traps. Aidan was hopeful it would get desperate during the winter and they'd be able to relocate it before spring when the hens would be eager to forage outside again.

Aran left him with a sympathetic, "Peace, brother," and gave him a hearty pat on the back. That comfort Aran radiated must have connected, because for a just a moment, Aidan's face relaxed.

Love,
Mimsy

Dear Gerald,

Aran and I were able to engage in peaceful wedding negotiations over breakfast this morning. He really wants to get married in a sacred natural space and I agree. Since the site of our first date, the summit of Mt. Washington, is arctic this time of year, he offered two more suitable possibilities, Joshua Tree or Red Rocks. I fell immediately in love with the thought of Red Rocks. I mean, the natural beauty of the park and the site of one of U2's most dramatic concerts ever, *Under the Blood Red Sky*, what more could I ask? Venue? Check!

As for an officiant, Aran just happens to know a shaman who is free on the solstice. I was mostly fine with that, but a rogue part of me wanted to speak up and suggest Oswald. However, the irony of my first boyfriend marrying me off to (what will certainly be) my last boyfriend kept me quiet. Aran's shaman—with whom I have never shared anything, much less a kiss—is a far more appropriate choice. With a place to get married and a person to do the marrying, we called it quits for the day. No need to tempt fate.

It is getting colder every day. I am in the direct sun sending your letter at midday and still my teeth are chattering. The river, she's covered in fallen leaves, the last of the year, from an overhanging oak. Silver beeches, green spruce, black and white paper birch, and yellow birches, intermingle. The diversity makes for a varied winter palette, one that is easy on the eyes, something I used to say about handsome fans, but now seems more resonant when applied to the forest in winter.

I miss you,

Mimsy

~~~

Dear Gerald,

I spent the morning with the Maple Keys going over my new composition. Hopefully they weren't just being polite when they complimented me on its originality. Of course, after several run-throughs, a few of them couldn't help but add their own signature notes here and there, but they only made it better. A few more practices and we should be able to perform it. Then I'd like to get it recorded.

But, don't worry, Gerald, I'm not resting on my laurels. I've already begun composing a second piece. It was inspired by the frost ferns that appeared inside the single-pane windows of my house this morning. The temperature outside got very low last night, and the moisture in the air inside condensed and froze on the cold glass. I remember these surreal icy patterns, the curly ferns, the sharp lines, and the feathery crystals, from when I was a kid, but I haven't lived in an old house in a long time, and modern double-paned thermal windows pretty much eliminate the magic. To translate the icy beauty to music, I am going to need a percussionist who can play antique cymbals and tubular bells. And I am going to have to shell out some serious cash to buy those instruments. Oddly, we don't happen to have any of those lying around the house, although, looking around, we do seem to have an obscene number of guitars.

Aran suggested hitting up his buddy, Ron, the drummer and percussionist in the band, to see if he had any, but I cut that plan off at the pass, explaining that I understood he was still in the band and close with the musicians, but they and I had irreconcilable differences, and I did not want him telling them anything about me or what I was up to. He looked at me a bit pityingly, I thought, then realized from my stern glance it would be in his best interest to agree. "Mum's the word, darling."

On my way back from practice, I stopped by the Congregational

Church to remind Oswald there was still an offer on the table for his land. He was out, so I left a message on his desk. While I was there, I noticed he had a small, framed photograph of Mary, his ex-wife, on the bookshelf. I picked it up. Her broad, guileless smile made me suddenly, terribly sad. I am sure she had no idea when this picture was taken what complexities life would throw at her. How when she was older, she'd end up hurting the one she loved, wounding him so deeply that he'd never love again.

   Does she think of him? I wonder. And if she does, does she smile? Or has she pushed him out of her mind? Or is it something in between, still racked with guilt but blaming him, remaining unwilling to shoulder the burden of her own choices? I pushed the photo back on the shelf, horizontally as if it had accidentally fallen face down, but I have no doubt Oswald will put it right when he returns.

Love,
Mimsy

Dear Gerald,

Your son has returned from gallivanting all over the Pacific Northwest with his cousins and his cousins' cousins and possibly his cousins' cousins' cousins. Your relatives are certainly prolific. He's added so many new names to his genealogy, I can no longer keep track of the entire cast of characters. But you'll be thrilled to know that Booker dove into his new extended family with gusto and came back full of life. I have never seen him so spirited. He says they are a wild bunch, full of adventure, and there's no choice but to join in and enjoy the ride.

   I caught him up on the wedding plans. I did detect a slight eye-roll at the beginning of my recitation of what Aran thought about the when and where and how of it, but he refocused when I pointedly reminded him of his duties as my best man. Aran's got a handfasting planned. I am pretty sure Booker has no idea what a handfasting is, but he can tell it's not straight-laced, everyday, or conservative. I guess the wild cousins haven't completely changed his nature.

   Booker wrote down all the details and then looked at me rather solemnly and asked if I was sure this is what I wanted. I said yes, but you know that's not a complete answer. It's what I want now in this period of my life when other options are behind me. To bastardize the Rolling Stones: at my age, you can't always get what you want; you may get what you need; but most often you choose from the things you can still have. I am lucky. I want, need, and can still have companionship and intimacy with Aran, and I can give him extras—like handfasting rituals and a shaman for an officiant—things he wants, needs, and can still have. There's no sacrifice in that.

The river is freezing up, Gerald. She's got no power over the cold. The deepest channel is open, but soon she'll be still, at least at the surface.

Love,
Mimsy

Dear Gerald,

This morning, I came across the shopping bag with the booties and bibs and little stuffed lamb I bought for Aidan and Cécile's baby and was suddenly, totally deflated.

Gerald, Cécile is like a daughter to me. I miss pretty much everything about her. How she slips into French when she's excited. How she can bake things that are exquisitely beautiful on the outside and so sweet on the inside. How she listens patiently to an old woman. How deeply she loves. I know she means the world to her sisters and that they are taking good care of her, but I want her to come back home. To Aidan, of course, but also to me and to her farm, and if she can find her way to them, back to the good memories of Mackey.

The road to healing is not straight. I should know. There were years when I thought I'd moved past the accident, then I'd see something or hear something that reminded me of you, and my heart would be ripped right out through my ribcage again.

Bereft,
Mimsy

Dear Gerald,

I met up with Aidan at the roadhouse. Before we even sat down at a table, he launched into a tale of criminal stupidity to beat any he's ever shared with me before. Last night's exploit began with a lady's handbag, a fishing pole, and two cases of beer. From there it devolved into a chase through the woods, a couple of stolen sleds, and the perp captured via lasso.

I didn't want to bring him down so soon after his law enforcement high, but I'd gotten through to Geneviève last night, probably while he was on the flexible flyer snaring the perp with a pull-rope. Geneviève said she hadn't thought about it, but when we discussed Aidan's worry about staying in the house, she agreed he should stay, at least for now. She added that she was slightly optimistic about Cécile's progress. Though her sister was still speaking in negative terms about the baby, Cécile had agreed to attend group therapy at the hospital. The doctors said this was a good sign. Geneviève said the letters were really helping. Unfortunately, she had to get off the phone before I could ask what letters.

When I mentioned Cécile and Geneviève, Aidan's face went from animated to vaguely ill in a matter of seconds. I immediately corrected course by saying I had some good news. He could stay in the house and Cécile had agreed to attend group therapy. He picked up the sandwich he'd put down the first time I mentioned her name, so I figured that he'd taken the news positively. I continued by saying that Geneviève had mentioned letters. Letters that had been helpful to Cécile. I asked him if he knew what she was talking about. He set the sandwich back down again and looked at me sheepishly. "I took a page from your playbook," he said. "After the first letter you had me bring to the hospital, I just kept it up. I write her a letter every day. I buy a lot of international stamps. The postmaster is rooting for us."

I put down my salad fork. I was so proud of Aidan. He's not an emotive guy, and he's certainly not from a generation of letter writers. But he knows I love you and you are out of reach, so I write to you. And he loves her and she is out of reach, so he keeps writing to her. And the letters might just be working.

There were two bald eagles flying along the river when we left the restaurant. Both of us stood still, watching them until they were out of sight.

Hopeful,

Mimsy

~~~

Dear Gerald,

Since you are dead and will remain dead forever, I expect time has less meaning for you than for the rest of us living folks, so you won't mind if I just stack these letters up and wait for ice-out to send them. The river is frozen solid. And unlike the postal service, ice is definitely keeping her from her appointed rounds.

I've got a good portion of the second song composed. Notation for the bells and chimes is completely different than anything I've seen before and I've had to learn it from scratch. Let's just say that the saying "can't teach an old dog new tricks" has some truth behind it. I am sure I would have picked this up much quicker when I was in high school. Aran bought me the instruments for Christmas but presented them to me early so waiting wouldn't slow down my work. Yesterday, the Maple Keys and I recorded the first song I wrote. If I keep up this pace I can have seven or eight songs done by late spring. The very idea is exciting. My first album!

Aidan brought us a Christmas tree he cut in the woods behind the farm. It looks a bit scraggly, as wild trees do, but on the plus side we can see the ornaments on both the front and back of the tree at the same time. Aran invited Aidan to stay for drinks, an invitation he heartily accepted. I am relieved that these two get along so well. Especially since I have to deal with Aran and Booker's continuing antagonism.

I don't know if Aran is keeping his invites down to keep the bride's side and groom's side even or because he feels sorry for me, but he wanted only his best man and a friend from college. He must have been listening to what I said earlier, because he didn't even broach the subject of inviting anyone from the band, and I am grateful not to have had that discussion again. I half suspect he purposely doesn't "understand" what happened between them and me so that he can continue to tour with them without guilt. But I don't want to stop him from performing. I know he does his best work with the people he's been playing with for decades. As long as they aren't at my wedding, I'm okay with it.

Have a good winter's rest, Gerald. It's almost solstice, and Aran and I are leaving for Red Rocks. We'll be there through the holidays. I'll write again when I get home.

Until next year,

Mimsy

Dear Gerald,

Well, we're officially hitched! I must say Aran's melding of many traditions yielded a magical wedding. We stood on a stage that has hosted some of the most important bands in history and felt the power of their music in the air. Aidan was the ringbearer. Aran's best man, Alexander, who had moved from Boston to Kentucky and had become a Pentecostal, brought his snake and spoke in tongues. The shaman sang and smudged and prayed. We asked Booker to wrap the cord for the handfasting. Whether or not he thought the union was a good idea, he knotted that rope around our joined hands like he truly wished it would last forever. After the ceremonies, we had a fine dinner at the resort. Then, once Aidan got a cab to the airport and the others retired for the night, Aran Sky and I danced outdoors, alone, under the stars. In case you had your doubts, Gerald, having done it, I can truly say it was right and I am happy.

Red Rocks, Colorado, is beautiful. You would have loved the otherworldliness of it. All the rocks—as advertised—are red. More specifically for geology buffs like you, they were formed from the gently eroded layers of fine and coarse iron-rich red sandstone, the remnants of ancient mountains. There are huge uplifted masses on either side of the amphitheater that are named Creation Rock and Ship Rock. A mushroom-shaped dais, the Seat of Pluto, was the site of many of our best wedding photos.

We returned home to a house with no power. A nor'easter tore through town right before we got back, knocking down trees and dumping two feet of snow in a single blast. The postman came to the door to deliver all our held mail. The latest edition of The Jockey Cap Tattler with our wedding as front-page news was on top of the pile. Bert had clearly read the whole article and shook our hands in congratulations. He then took a good long look at the ring, probably so he could describe it later to the other gossips along his route. After he left, I took a moment to look at it myself. It is finely crafted and perfectly at home on my finger.

Aran and I read the paper together over a cold cereal and ice tea breakfast. The detail in the article was so specific, I think Young Jack must have had a reporter or two embedded at the scene. Two suspects immediately spring to mind, one with research chops and the other with undercover experience.

Because of the power outage, Aran tried to get the wood stove going, but as it was complex and new technology to him, all he managed to do was fill the living room with smoke. We put out the embryonic blaze in the firebox and evacuated to the Hobblebush Inn to celebrate our honeymoon in a more hospitable environment. Though it will be a short one. Aran is going on tour again next week.

There was also in the paper an embarrassing photo of the near-brawl that went down during the Christmas Eve concert at Oswald's church. Despite the solemnity of the evening's event, a verbal altercation between two singers and two musicians resulted in tossed drumsticks, sharp words, and the musicians walking out in the middle of a hymn. This certainly explained the panic I heard in Oswald's voice on my answering machine. Twelve messages, each more frantic than the last. Over a period of days, the members of the church music program splintered into warring factions and as of the last call were on the verge of disbanding. With Epiphany just two days away, Oswald didn't know what to do.

I am clearly far too susceptible to Oswald's pleas, for I agreed to help him. Now, don't worry, I'm not leaping with both feet into a volunteer mission. I am not taking over direction of the sacred music of Menotomy. This is a one-time event. I am assisting in a strictly advisory capacity.

So, despite the fact I have no idea what Epiphany is, and had to look it up to spell it, clearly it is a headline gig of some sort for Oswald. Luckily, I have a lot of experience with taming fractious band members, placating divas, and harmonizing vastly mismatched talents. Years of trying to keep up with the rest of the band honed my practice skills, my raw determination, and my fake-it-until-you-make-it game to a razor's edge. This mixture of catch-up and deception is a strategy I've practiced for decades, something I can teach others how to do. I told Oswald to call an emergency meeting tonight. We're going to straighten out these rascals and get this Epiphany jam on.

I still can't bring this letter to the river, Gerald. The snow is above my knees and who can tell where the land ends and frozen water begins under its thick blanket. I will set it on the mantel with the others. Right now, in the gentle aftermath of the storm, big, slow, fluffy flakes are falling. Remember how we used to stagger around like fools, trying to catch snowflakes on our tongues? We were very unsuccessful, as I recall. But boy did we have fun.

Love you,
Mimsy

Dear Gerald,

I dug a bit deeper into the incident on Christmas Eve. I talked to the pianist and she identified the four instigators: two sopranos, a brand-new drummer, and a brand-new bassist. Honestly the new guys were no worse than the old guys who retired, she said, but being new they were firmly in the sights of the queen bees. "Not good enough." "Not up to our standards." "Too slow." "Too fast." "Ended a bit too soon."

You'd think they were being judged on their performance in bed, she laughed. No wonder they felt threatened. Anyway, the blow-up, when it happened, was epic. Sheet music was flying in the air. Oswald was running around in a panic waving his arms ineffectually, screeching "Stop it, you fools!" at the top of his lungs. It was like an episode of Saturday Night Live. The audience was in stitches.

Later, when the members had been reassembled, mostly against their will, I took Oswald's place as choir director. I knew I would have to be stern but consoling. Oswald had asked me not to bring up the brawl for fear the evening would disintegrate into a blame-fest, and then there would be zero chance of a recovery performance. But I knew better.

Tensions in a band had to be fully discharged or they'd build up again. I'd seen it a hundred times on the road. Hell, I'd instigated half of the blow ups. And I knew exactly what both the instigators and the victims required to quell their rage and hurt feelings.

So, I huddled them up for some Gestalt therapy straight off the tour bus. While Oswald cringed and wrung his hands, I had them reenact the ill-fated evening. There was a lot of "When she said that, how did you feel?" and "Why was this so important to you?" and "How can we let go of unrealistic expectations?" It became clear that the sopranos were highly invested in the beauty of the music as a backdrop for their talent. They envisioned a choir of angels backed by harps. What they were getting was a middle school band. The musicians, on the other hand, just wanted a break from their constant criticism. It took time to jell with a new band. They'd joined just weeks before the Christmas concert.

I was fairly confident things were going to be okay after I got some apologies and promises out of them, but in order to ensure there would be no repeat performances of their bullying, I called the two sopranos over for a private conference. First, I set forth my expectations. Then I bribed them, "If you two leave the conducting of the band to Oswald, I will let you stay here when Aran Sky comes by in a few minutes to help me coach the new band members. If not, you can leave now with the rest of the choir."

I could tell that the two ladies were just old enough to remember the concert poster, the one with Aran Sky, his peace-sign belt buckle resting right above the bulge in his jeans, naked from the waist up, hair, shoulders, and chest streaming with water from Eagle Falls. Probably forgetting how long ago that poster was printed, the ladies became suddenly submissive and agreeable. Of course, they were so sorry they had overstepped their bounds. Of course, it would never happen again. Of course, they'd love the opportunity to meet Aran Sky. Did they have time to fix their makeup?

Peace restored through my old standby trick: bribery. And what better currency to barter with than my husband, the hottest peacenik in town.

Oswald owes me,

Mimsy

Dear Gerald,

The Karmann-Ghia has been sitting outside in the snow since solstice and when we tried to drive it into town, we soon had a flat. We had it towed and it only took my mechanic a glance to diagnose the problem. He pointed out the numerous, parallel divots all over the surface of the tire. Tooth marks!

Sean was very happy to explain that porcupines were not afraid to use their industrial-strength teeth on unprotected car tires in wintertime. They are attracted by the road salt residue. Two of the tires on the Karmann-Ghia would have to be replaced at full cost. Their warrantee covers road damage, not rodent damage. And there is nothing stopping the porcupine from returning tonight to begin chomping on the new tires. At first, Sean had no solutions that didn't involve lethal force, but when pressed he recommended hosing down the tires after every drive, a fun chore when the temperatures have been hovering around twenty degrees.

Last night, Aran and I decided to stake out the driveway. It wasn't long before a black shadow waddled up, plush, pigeon-toed, and protected by quills. It was so comical that it was impossible to hate it, even as we watched it sniff each tire, eager to choose tonight's salty snack. Aran was paralyzed, caught between his love for his classic car and his love of these ridiculous-looking creatures. To protect both, we burst out of the house yelling and waving our arms, hoping to scare the noshing pincushion away.

Have you ever seen a porcupine run? It is a roly-poly affair, its backside a tornado of quills. Aran collapsed in laughter watching it. "I love it!" he gasped. "We have to give it what it wants. It's so cute!" While his enthusiasm is endearing, we are not sacrificing the car to the porcupine. It is too deep into winter to build a garage, but by next year we'll have a solid one in place. In the meantime, I think maybe we'll try to lure it away with salt blocks from the feed store.

The porcupine shed a quill as it hightailed it out of town, apparently as a gift for Aran, who honored the giver by clipping off the sharp ends and sewing the brown and cream tube onto his jacket like a long, decorative bead. Aran picks up everything and everything is a gift. Every horizontal surface in my tiny house is covered with acorns, old coins, and bottle caps. Reminds me a little of you and your shelves full of gemstones.

Time for bed,

Mimsy

～～～

Dear Gerald,

Little black-capped chickadees, their winter voices anachronistically bright in the presence of a below-zero wind chill and three feet of snow, peppered my walk to the river with hopeful optimism. Practicing for the mating season, their "fee-bee" call splits the frigid air, the only sound louder than the crunch of snow under my boots. It has warmed up, albeit fractionally, and I thought I'd check the river. I can see the ice over her main channel is thinner, a translucent window surrounded by a sheet of opaque white. Beneath this frozen helm, she is moving, but she'll be carrying no letters today. Even if the center channel was open, I'd no more trust a path across her ice than I'd trust a tightrope over a knife-filled chasm. Just know there will be quite a lot of reading once I get this stack of letters sent. I haven't forgotten you.

Aran's so softhearted, he was up first thing and off on a mission to protect the porcupine, finding someone who can build a temporary carport for the cars. He's always been softhearted toward me too, even when I was prickly. He surprised me during the wedding vows by telling me something I'd never suspected. He admitted he'd loved me from the first moment he saw me. That he sensed early on that my heart did not belong to Lawrence. He'd always hoped that divide between us would become an opening for him. I came to his bed so many times; each time he fell for me a little more. Each time, he hoped I'd never leave. But I always did. This time, though, he'd caught me. When he recited his vows, he smiled and said, "Now we are together, as joined in life as we always were in bed."

Later, when I thought back to those early days sleeping with Aran, when I was seeking comfort and nothing more, I recalled something. It's a hazy and disjointed image; I must certainly have been stoned when it happened. But I see Aran, down on one knee, presenting me with a bouquet of one hundred daisies, miming a proposal. I'd thought at the time he was being silly, playacting. How I must have hurt him, dismissing his romantic gesture, treating his proposal like performance art.

I would have never disrupted the band, left Lawrence, or complicated my memories of you back then, despite the comfort Aran brought me and the seamless way we got along. In the end, even with the fighting and infidelity, I did love Lawrence. He was brilliant and awe-inspiring and believed in my talent in a way no one else did. Eventually, Aran gave up the fantasy of us together. He opened himself up to the possibility of another relationship and met Shelly, his first wife. But Shelly was constitutionally unable to have fun, and eventually became openly contemptuous of Aran's childlike nature. The divorce was so bitter that he swore he would never marry again.

But during this final act of life, I am thankful that Aran reversed that oath, and I am grateful for the perseverance of his love. The comfort and companionship we had remains and fits much better into this quiet life than it ever did on the road. And so, this time around, when he proposed with fireworks instead of flowers, I am glad I didn't let him down.

No regrets,

Mimsy

Dear Gerald,

I got caught up in watching Aran this morning. He's just always so busy, busy, busy. Right now, he is multitasking, singing John Prine's song "Paradise" about the Green River, trying to convince me I should practice it with the Maple Keys, and hand-writing responses to fan mail. Before that he did the dishes, met with the handyman who is setting up our carport, took a carload of trash to the dump, practiced guitar for an hour, and did his sunrise morning yoga routine. In contrast, my accomplishments included eating a bowl of oatmeal and reading The Jockey Cap Tattler before getting ready to go into town.

I was on a fact-finding mission. I met with Lillian, the director of the Pequawket Land Trust, to ask how the land trust operates and how it cares for its preserves. I learned that if I bequeath the wildflower sanctuary to a land trust, the land will be protected in perpetuity. This sounds a lot easier than setting up a nonprofit to manage it. But there is so much to learn about the process. I need to talk with my lawyer before I decide.

When I returned home, Aran proudly announced that he had conquered fire. He got the wood stove started and the smoke to go up the chimney instead of into the living room. The wood heat was intense, toasty for snuggling on the couch on one of the coldest nights of the year. He's going to teach me how to make a fire tomorrow, so I'll be all set when he goes on tour. I am starting to feel a bit melancholy about his leaving. Newlyweds are newlyweds even in their eighties. At all ages it aches to be apart.

Sweet Dreams,

Mimsy

Dear Gerald,

It was negative nineteen degrees this morning. Warmed up the car before driving into town. I don't care if they say warming it up isn't good for the engine; it is good for my old bones. On the way in, I drove by a long line of snowmobiles waiting to fuel up at the gas station. When I met Aidan for lunch at the roadhouse, the place was filled with sledders, snowmobile suits unzipped to the waist, tops with empty arms dangling comically behind them, boots clunking heavy on the hardwood.

Aidan looked excited for a change. He announced that he'd finally trapped the fisher. "A big, snarly buster," he called it. It was in his truck, so he made me bundle up and go back outside to see it in the flesh. The beast didn't look too imposing reclined against the back of the trap, until Aidan banged on the cage, and it rose up on all fours and bared its teeth.

"I am going to kill it with my bare hands," Aidan said in a dangerous tone I'd never heard from him before. The desperate ferocity of it drew the image of Cécile—her face, horrified, ill; the tiny surviving kitten clutched against her breast—from the recesses of my mind. Her newfound safety net had been ripped out from under her by this blood-thirsty creature. She must have felt so powerless, so vulnerable. I understood Aidan's hatred. If this fisher hadn't brought blood and violence back to her farm so soon after Mackey's death, would Cécile have slid so deeply into darkness?

Aidan was on duty, taking his lunch break, his firearm strapped to his side. He rested his hand on the grip. "It would be easy to shoot it," he said unsnapping the holster with his thumb. I responded, as neutrally as possible, "That's what most people around here would do." Then I placed my hand on Aidan's forearm, halting his movement, and said, "But you have to release it."

He called in. We took lunch as takeout and drove north until the road ended, deep within the national forest. When we stopped, Aidan took the fisher out of the bed of the truck, stood behind the cage, and opened the door. At first, it stood still, evaluating the situation, until Aidan kicked its cage. It bolted and disappeared under the low sweeping branches of the fir trees, but Aidan kept right on kicking until the trap's sides were mangled and the cage door bent. Finally, he heaved the twisted hunk of metal into the woods with a furious yell and got back in the truck. An hour later, without having spoken a word, he dropped me off at my house and drove back toward the police station.

I can't say I wasn't frightened by his rage. The men I've known have all been expert at hurling hateful sarcasm or a cut-to-the-bone remark, but none ever raised a hand to me or punched a wall in my vicinity. Never before had I witnessed the visceral fury that comes from a strong man feeling powerless. I think Aidan would argue that it would have been better to let him kill the creature, and maybe it would have fulfilled some primal need for vengeance within him, but there has been too much blood spilled on the threshold of Wright Farm. If he ever wants it to return to the peaceful place it once was, there can be no more.

With a heavy heart,

Mimsy

Dear Gerald,

I haven't been inside the walls of my mom and dad's house in sixty-one years, but it remains essentially unchanged. Sure, the massive broiler-oven range is gone and the refrigerator is now a stainless-steel model. But despite the wallpaper being redone in a historically accurate 1920s vintage print, I am at home in it as I ever was. I caressed the oak banister I used to slide down, remembering the rush, and placed my fingertips reverently against the mirror where my father used to shave, making silly faces as he stretched his skin flat for the blade. Memories linger in material things.

Historical purist that she is, Batty hadn't made a single change to the façade or to the interior layout. She never replaced the old counter-weighted windows. The parlor is still for sitting only, no television. The library is still the library, shelves weighted down with her local and state history books instead of Dad's accounting texts. I found the scar in the woodwork I made when I was seven, swinging Daddy's hammer wildly while reciting a poem about John Henry, the steel-driving man. The natural linoleum, painted with lovely flower patterns that I used to trace when I was a child, is intact on the kitchen floor.

On my way out, I pulled the chain dangling from the dinner bell bolted to the porch ceiling. Listening to the clear sound, I wondered how many times Mom had desperately rung it trying to draw me home from whatever mischief you and I had cooked up, and how many times I'd ignored it, wanting just a few more wild minutes alone with you.

As we descended the steps, I couldn't resist mentioning how odd it was that the historic home plaque attached to a post in her front yard had not yet been amended to include the information that a famous rock star had spent her childhood here.

Do we always return to our beginnings before we meet our ends? The visit to my old house transported me through time today, Gerald. I had my childhood back there for a moment, even if it was only an illusion.

Wistfully yours,

Mimsy

Dear Gerald,

I'm not usually one for a sub at lunch, too messy and hard to control, but Booker asked me to meet him at the sandwich shop instead of Bay's today. I hadn't realized the establishment had a picture window at the back of the store that overlooks the White Mountains, a life-size work of art, quite the perk for a common chain restaurant. I went through the line and then snagged the most panoramic seats.

Booker waved when he came in and kept looking over his shoulder sheepishly as he chose his fixings. I was immediately on alert. You don't live to be eighty-one without learning the signs that bad news is coming. Booker deflected as long as possible. Filling his mouth with the giant sandwich creation so he couldn't speak at all, then asking about the band, requiring details about my current song that he couldn't possibly understand. He'd have asked "How's them Patriots?" to avoid saying what he had to say if he didn't know me to be a confirmed sports atheist. Spit it out, I kept thinking as he squirmed in his seat like a six-year-old child. And finally, I said it aloud, "Spit it out!"

The bad news was that during his stay in Menotomy, researching and writing about his genealogy, Booker fell in love with the Fessenden family, all of whom now live in the Pacific Northwest. And like in all cases of true love, he is drawn there. And the pull of living relatives is stronger than being in his father's hometown or near his father's old girlfriend, as gifted a storyteller as she might be. He's leaving us, Gerald. Going to live near those uncles and aunts and all those cousins.

My stomach soured. I thanked him for meeting me for lunch and fled before he could see me cry. There will be a proper goodbye, but I want to prepare for it so I won't be a sobbing mess when it happens. I want him to remember the fearless Mimsy Browning, not a bereft old Mrs. Bell.

Someone once said that old age is just a series of losses, but you don't expect to lose the young ones. I'm sorry I couldn't keep your son here, Gerald.

Mimsy

~~~

Dear Gerald,

Argh. Another ice storm last night. As beautiful as they are when it comes morning, every tree branch and twig encased in sun-catching ice, they bring life to a halt. Today I was looking forward to meeting up with the band at Burnt Meadow Music to rehearse for our show on Friday. But instead, I listen to the sound of tree limbs cracking like gunshots, see my beautiful birches bent to the ground, and wait fruitlessly for the sand truck to make it past my door.

Aran, who tries to make the best of every situation, offered to practice with me in the studio (what we used to call our dining room before he moved a soundboard, mics, amps, keyboard, drums, and two hundred guitars into it). But despite an earnest attempt, there was no way our duo could replace the full band.

Instead of fretting, I poured my creativity into composition. Been working on a new song, one inspired by a pair of screech owls romancing in our backyard. They whinny like horses and then trill like toads, not a screech to be heard. No great horned owls or barred owls joined the hootenanny last night, but if I work in some of their classic night sounds, I can legitimately label this one a nocturne.

Despite my earlier doubts, the road crew got the roads cleared by mid-afternoon and I was able to safely pilot Becks to meet everyone at the arts center. I was so happy to see the band, I hugged them all. Uncharacteristic? Yes, but lately my emotions have been getting away from me. Everything seems precarious and fragile. If I don't pay attention, my whole world could fall apart.

Maybe it's just age getting to me. Or maybe it's my community. Aran's going on tour. Aidan's close to a breakdown. Booker's moving away. My little Cécile is lost. Got to keep my band going, play the pain away. That's how I've always done it. I'll keep on doing it a little longer.

My stalwart love,

Mimsy

Dear Gerald,

Got rid of a fisher only to find a stoat. That's what Aran calls the tiny weasel we found in my kitchen cupboard! We heard some crinkling and crunching from the general direction of my stash of beef jerky, an unhealthy habit left over from my days on the road. Aran opened the cabinet door and saw nothing but a white blur. He decided it might be a rare albino mouse or somebody's lost pet, so we sat quietly in front of the cabinet, me kneeling (very painfully) and him cross-legged in a yoga pose, our ears perked, ready for the slightest sound. At the next rustle, I yanked the cabinet door open to find a pointy-faced predator. He looked at us without amusement before turning tail and plunging down a hole that mice—who now probably rest in peace in his stomach—had chewed in one corner.

The little guy is winter white with a black-tipped tail. I call him Frosty. The next day we tried to trap him, but the squirrel trap we rented at the hardware store had the tiniest bit of play in the door, no more than a quarter inch, and he miraculously weaseled out of it, the metal edge indenting his body to a remarkable degree as he slid underneath. But before taking advantage of his freedom, Frosty turned around at the edge of his escape hole and gave us the finger (metaphorically, of course). His disdain was clearly communicated, yet despite the weasel's contempt for us, every night before bed, Aran fills his little bowl of water and unwraps a stick of jerky. He wanted to make him a little bed out of one of my scarves, but I drew the line at a full-service weasel B&B.

Clearly, the man has a soft spot in his heart for feisty little creatures.

Mimsy

Dear Gerald,

Last night, Oswald knocked on my door at the most ungodly hour. It was closing in on midnight and I was already tucked into bed. Aran's response to the frantic banging was to snore even more loudly, so I rose, put on one of the truly-unattractive-but-very-warm, floor-length, flannel nightgowns that the natives wear, and responded to the summons. I greeted the minister with raised eyebrows, thinking I was making it clear that his timing was questionable, but he ignored my irritation and staggered right on through the door. He was so shaky I was afraid he might be having some kind of attack—heart, stroke, seizure—at our age, these are the go-to worries. But after I sat him down and gave him a cup of tea, I realized this was an emergency of a very different sort.

Though he had heard nothing about his ex-wife in all the decades since she left, the grapevine wasted not a second in communicating Mary's death. And the news did not come through a gentle phone call, but in an anonymous social media post. A cruel one at that. "Menotomy's homegrown Jezebel, Mary Martin, finally got her just deserts today, succumbing to sepsis in a Knoxville hospital. Care to wager on where that slut's going to spend eternity? I've got a hundred on somewhere down low." Oswald pushed the phone over to me with hands as lined as my own, the skin over his bones paper-thin and fragile as tissue.

He didn't speak. I could see he was struggling to swallow the vomit that was rising in his throat. The post was vile. I am pretty sure Oswald, as sheltered as he was, had never seen anything so hateful in his life. I turned the phone upside down. Then I reached across the table and put both my hands over his. They were stone cold. We sat quietly and still for a long time.

At first, I wondered why he'd come to me. But then I realized that I'd seen Oswald here and there about town, at the dump, doing errands, eating out, just like everyone else. But unlike the others, who did their chores with family or had drinks at the bar with friends, Oswald was always alone. You might not notice it at first, for on Sundays he was leading a crowd of one hundred and every evening there was an activity in the basement of the church. He did his rounds, checking in on the sick and the elderly. He was heartily greeted by fellow pedestrians, bank tellers, police officers, children, postmen, and crossing guards. But not once in the months I'd been back had I seen Oswald walking side-by-side in conversation or even sitting in companionable silence with another person. He rode his motorcycle alone even though there was a bikers' club in town. He ate at the smallest table by the window of the health food store alone. He went home to the parsonage alone. Despite being well-liked and well-known, Rev. Oswald Pingree Martin didn't have any friends. And now, when he'd found out the worst news in the worst way, there was no one he felt close to, so he came to me.

I am not unfamiliar with the pillory of the press, but Oswald has lived his whole life completely innocent of predatory media, of the foul things that circulate on the Internet. To learn of your ex-wife's death was shocking enough, but to learn of it in this manner was, frankly, dangerous for an octogenarian. I offered to call his doctor. He shook his head no, but I was ready to dial if he gave me any reason.

When he spoke, it was not with the booming voice of the pulpit; it was a choking whisper. "Why would anyone say something so horrible?"

"Doesn't matter why. We don't listen." I told him.

And we sat there, hand in hand, hearing no evil, until the break of dawn.

I don't have any answers,

Mimsy

Dear Gerald,

Cécile wrote to Aidan! He swung by during his break to show me the letter. It was only four sentences and a little bit spacey. Here is the text: "Dear Aidan, Thank you for writing letters to me about the farm. You don't have to, but some of them cheer me up. The one about the kitten getting into the maple syrup was funny. The doctors say hello. Bye, Cécile." Aidan was, of course, overjoyed and held on to the letter like it was treasure. I suppose any communication is a good sign, but the Cécile I knew was well-spoken and this sounded like it was written by a child. She might be on a lot of drugs or maybe the doctors she mentioned had a hand in pushing her to write it. I am not going to get my hopes up too high, unlike my friend Aidan, who was beaming when he left.

Booker's moving is weighing heavily on me. No more reliving Gerald and Mimsy stories for an appreciative audience. No more Tuesday brunches at Bay's. No more insider gossip about the historical society ladies and their schemes. No more book recommendations. No more help with my phone!

Booker was the second friend I made here, and because of his connection to you, he was just a hair shy of family. I suppose I am lucky that he favors his mother in looks, otherwise it would also mean the forever loss of your features animated in his face. And then there's the silent, maudlin bond between us, witnesses and participants in Mackey's death and Cécile's (temporary) rescue.

Of course, Booker still doesn't get along with Aran, and he goes a bit overboard with the rule-following, but he wouldn't be his fastidious, reserved, upstanding self if he didn't.

So first the daughter I feel like I adopted leaves the country and now my almost-stepson plans to move to the opposite coast. The implications are clear: the fabric of community I have woven over the past year has begun to unravel. The question is, can I keep any more threads from coming loose?

Standing fast,

Mimsy

Dear Gerald,

I drove Booker to the airport. I figured if I was looking straight ahead the whole time, not gazing at him, it would be easier. I had the vents directed toward my eyes, drying tears as soon as they emerged. We talked but we didn't say anything of substance, which angered me more than silence would have.

He spoke of how he'd rent a lake house for a week next visit. All I could think was by summer, I will be eighty-two years old or dead. A week's visit isn't exactly a consolation for telling me a few days in advance that he is moving away. He'll write, he says. What a joke! He's about as good a letter writer as you, and you have the excuse of being dead. Booker doesn't even answer texts.

He's donated his car to the historical society. He has some material on his grandfather's tour in Europe during WWI that he wants to turn into a book. He might get a dog. He will stay with his cousin (the one who looks like you) until he buys a house. He won't miss the mosquitoes. He ordered a really good raincoat. He didn't order it from Bean's, because Bean's isn't a thing out in the Pacific Northwest. He can't wait to see his aunt and uncle. He will probably have a hard time adjusting to a new time zone.

Was he just unable to say he cared for me? So emotionally reserved that the words were unattainable? And why couldn't I be the one to get the ball rolling? Tell him that I was lucky to have known him. That he was a most special and dear friend. That his father would be proud of him. That he brought back memories of you that I didn't even remember I had. That I hoped he would be happy all the rest of his days.

We said goodbye at the drop off like buddies, with a quick hug and a miss you. But there was so much more, and I knew I may never get a chance again. So, I shouted from the curb as he was about to enter the door, "Your father and I think you are wonderful!" And he looked over his shoulder, tears streaming down his face, gave me a bashful smile, and waved once again before disappearing.

On the way back from the airport I passed a sugar shack, light splintering through cracks in the board siding, evaporator steam rising from the chimney. It was set dead center in an open field. The gibbous moon hung low beside it, casting blue light and shadows over the snow. The tableau was so arresting, I had to stop the car.

There, encapsulated in a single moment was everything beautiful and magical about our home, Gerald. Booker didn't get the chance to grow up here. He's not connected to this place. His roots here are history notes and headstones. Those cousins, on the other hand, are real. They are his home. We have to let him go.

Mimsy

Dear Gerald,

Geneviève called today. She told me that Cécile is doing better, but she's still not well. We chatted for a good ten minutes about her mental state before Geneviève dropped a bomb. Cécile's sister, Helene, wants to take the baby.

It's astounding how casually Geneviève mentioned something so life changing. She expected me to be relieved, as if the baby was an orphan in need of placement. And now that she's found a home for it with other little kids, problem solved! Except the baby's father is right here. He's ready to take on the job, working daily to try to help the baby's mother come back to a peaceful place, eager to take care of his own family.

I gasped aloud when Geneviève broke the news. I know I wasn't particularly nice when I reminded her, firmly, that Aidan was the baby's father and perfectly capable of caring for his own child. Our conversation petered out after that. I think she truly expected me to be happy about Helene's decision. She knows I am a friend of Cécile's, but she has no idea how close I am to Aidan.

I don't know how I am going to tell him. His lawyer is prepared to petition the court for custody as soon as the baby is born, but now with Cécile's sister, a Canadian citizen, also seeking custody, things are going to get really messy. After hanging up with Geneviève, I cradled the phone in my hand for at least a half hour, trying to come up with the best way to tell him.

The best way apparently was a hysterically blurted tirade. Aidan had to puzzle out exactly what I was saying, because between the sobs and the high-pitched frustration, I was incoherent. After he asked enough questions to get everything straight, he told me he'd be over after work.

I prepared the war room by sweeping all my songwriting clutter off the kitchen table so I could make space for Chinese takeout. No need to strategize on an empty stomach. When he arrived, we went over every possible scenario. Most of them didn't end well and his discouragement was expressed in the deepening creases across his forehead. His lawyer had advised staying calm and letting the legal system handle this. But Aidan's gut was telling him that the deck was stacked against him.

I asked about the letters. Was he still writing them? Was Cécile still responding? Apparently, yes. He handed me the latest letter. In this one, Cécile sounded much more with it. "Dear Aidan, Thank you for your letter. I have been taking my medications and attending group. We even had an ice cream social afterward. Thank you for telling me about my hen. I am glad you took her to the vet and very glad her problem was only mites. Letting the fisher go in the woods was the right thing to do. I am glad it is far away from the farm. This baby is coming soon no matter what I think about that. The doctors are trying to help me cope, but it is just so hard. Cécile"

I passed the letter back to him. "Go," I said. "You have to be there when your baby is born." He smiled for the first time in ages, like an inmate given an unexpected pardon.

After Aidan left, I felt optimistic enough to put on my slicker and walk down to the river. There's some melting at the edge where the runoff from the storms has made an entryway. I am going to slip this one under the ice and let her carry it to you.

It's been a long time,

Mimsy

~~~

Dear Gerald,

Last night I dreamt I was in her rushing waters. The relentless press of millions of gallons against my chest crushed my lungs, stopped my breathing. I struggled, without any success, toward the surface. Then, by incredible chance, I reached up and touched the gunwale of the canoe. Dug my fingernails into the wood and pulled myself up. I looked for you. Saw you bob to the surface. You were struggling. Then you were swept against the boulder.

When I woke from the dream, the rushing didn't stop. In fact, it was louder. I shook my head to release myself from the nightmare. I could hear everything clearly. The tick of the clock, the sound of the ice maker, and the rushing waters. I went to the window and in the moonlight the river reflected broadly—three times her normal width. So close to the house, I felt her reaching for it. I stood frozen, charting her progress through the stand of birches in the yard, toward the walls that sheltered me.

The snow, the rain, the tiny tributaries and freshets that flow down the mountains, all were complicit in the crime, each one a co-conspirator. The snows, well, they piled more and more on top of already too much. The unseasonable rains, they pushed this mess into being, swelling the bosom of the river and bursting her skin of ice. But even with their help, the damage wrought is all her making. The town is awash with her excess. They call it a hundred-year flood, but it is so much more than that.

Touchingly, she saved all this devilry for your birthday.

Ice floes, ten inches thick, exploded from her frozen surface, crashed together and piled up along the riverbanks, in the forests, beside the road, on my lawn. One was left standing on its edge in my backyard, seven feet tall, looking like an angry giant had upended his dining room table. It stands there gleaming this morning, a sun-kissed monument to her outrageous power. The trunks of the trees behind the house are surrounded by slabs of ice, as if they grew five feet overnight and lifted up tablets of frozen ground with them. Their icy girdles relics of her high-water mark.

The graveyard fence that the nice men had painstakingly installed is missing. The family burial ground is now smaller by a third. She washed away the spot I was to be interred in, the place I planned to lay myself down to sleep. The gravesite is underwater; if there were a gravestone, it would be no more than a small ripple in her course.

Perhaps she didn't like me coming down to the banks to spy on her yesterday. Her response to my trespass, "You want to send those letters? Go ahead! I'll open up a channel. Damn it, I'll make ten new channels. I'll bring the river up to your goddamn door!"

Bert, the mailman, dropped by. He said there was a massive ice jam up by the bridge that backed up the water for miles. Roads are shut down, a bridge is out, three houses flooded. But the one house she wanted most still stands. Her floods tore away the ground, uprooted trees, moved stone. She takes earth and gives back silt and sand. But she can't undermine me.

Happy Birthday.

Love,

Mimsy

~~~~

Dear Gerald,

The floodwaters may have receded, but the roads on the north side of the river are closed until they can get some heavy machinery out there to move the ice floes. It may be a casual effort on her part to fling thousands of pounds of ice about, but it is certainly a mighty endeavor for us mortals to push it back.

Aidan postponed his departure a day to help deal with the mess. But he's headed north tomorrow. Maybe not to witness the birth of his baby, but definitely to be in the waiting room while it happens, perhaps to see the child through the nursery window. Not how it is supposed to be, but life sometimes requires us to improvise.

I got a call from Aran. They are playing sunny California for the next five days. Seventy degrees and sunshine. He asked me to fly out, this time prefacing it with "I know you don't have a gig until the twenty-ninth, so why not join me?" But I declined. I don't know what it is, but I feel like I must stand watch. She ripped away half my yard. She came within three feet of my house. I will not let her win this time.

The wheel of Karma turns,

Mimsy

Dear Gerald,

Young Jack came over after school. He was disappointed that he only got one day off because of the flood. He'd been hoping for two. After he set up his stuff in the studio, we jammed a bit. He has improved so much, both on the fiddle and the guitar. I would, of course, like to think that he was particularly gifted only with the fiddle, but Aran has certainly taught the boy a thing or two.

As we played, I kept thinking about the sound of rushing water. How it has defined my life. How it invades my dreams at night. Maybe I can capture it. Get it under my control. So, we spent the rest of the session working on replicating the sound. It is not an easy thing to mimic. Our instruments are more suited to chirps and heartbeats, deep reverberations and crashes. Young Jack was all for synthesizing the sound, but that's not how I groove. Music comes from the belly of the instrument, tickled by the hands of the musician. We played around with the bells and chimes, with no success. The electric guitar has a wide breadth of sound, but couldn't quite reach where I was looking to go. The drums weren't even touched. At the end of the day we agreed, if she's going to be tamed, it will be by fiddle but I'll have to push the instrument to her limits.

Composing,

Mimsy

Dear Gerald,

Postman Bert came to the door with a package from Aran this afternoon. He stuck around long enough for me to open it in case it contained juicy tidbits of gossip. I'd given my new husband the key to the storage bay where all the keepsakes from life with Lawrence were stored so he could retrieve a quilt my mother had made me. He'd called to say it was on its way last week, but mail takes a long time to get to Menotomy.

It was folded in tissue just as I had put it away. Wrapping it up this way seems a quintessentially feminine gesture. Tucking a treasure into a bed made of gauzy paper sheets, sighing, giving it a goodnight kiss, wishing it sweet dreams. A fantasy of protection and safety. And yet here it was, seven decades after its making, unblemished. The fabric of my dresses, flowery and sunny and fruity and nautical, patched together into an artifact of my history. There is the evidence of a third birthday party. Here the embroidered stitch of my mother sewing my name into the frock I wore on the first day of school. Along one edge, a strip of the Easter dress I loved, torn while climbing a tree. Disparate bits of time stitched together. A record of events that happened during the making of a real live girl.

The quilt no longer carries the scent I associated with home, a blend of wood smoke and anise. That faded quite some time ago. But the physical and emotional warmth remain. Just having it in my hands brought me right back to childhood days and play. Things I have found harder and harder to recapture as I age. I took the quilt and wrapped it around my shoulders. The afternoon sun spilled across it, melting the yellows and burnishing the blues. Then Bert pointed out an envelope at the bottom of the box.

Aran must have nosed around the storage bin for hours to find this. Inside the envelope was an old promotional photo of me on Aran's shoulders. We were draped in garlands of flowers, so many it hid the fact that neither of us had on a stitch of clothing. Bert's eyebrows lifted when he saw the image; he cleared his throat and immediately took his leave.

I remember the photo shoot. It was late in the afternoon in some prairie town, the hardpan of the earth stretching out in infinite flatness in all directions. Lawrence had fallen violently ill after his lunch date with two voluptuous bottles of tequila and was in no shape to be photo-graphed. Aran stood in for him. The photographer's assistant pinned rope after rope of tropical flowers to my hair. The cascade weighed me down so much I needed assistance climbing onto Aran's back. Once I was up, Aran wrapped his hands firmly around my thighs to steady me. While the photographer and his assistant fussed endlessly over the placement of the garlands, Aran sang "People Will Say We're in Love" from *Oklahoma!* Oh! I was so naïve a child then. There he was taking Lawrence's place again, for the hundredth time, and I had no idea he was singing about us.

I knew how much you loved me, Gerald. Every moment I could feel it. It was silent and unwavering and solid as the ground I walked on. I never doubted the strength of it. I just don't know how I could have been so blind to the same devotion in Aran. He was always there.

Always.
Mimsy

Dear Gerald,

My heart dropped when I read the first page of the Sunday paper this morning. "Biddeford Man Drowns When Snowmobile Breaks Through Rotten Ice." Unwillingly, I saw it unfold it in my mind's eye: The man's boss had been on his back all week, as he was every week, and so he lived for weekends like this one. Chasing the full moon through the pines and fir of the snowmobile club trails. Having the crystalline winter world all to himself, with no one to tell him when or where to go. After an hour he wound his way out of the woods, and emerged upon a moonlit field topped by a vault of stars where he tested the throttle. The sled rose and fell over the undulations of the ground like a boat flowing over waves. The speed was exhilarating and he felt like himself for the first time in days.

The boundary between the field and the river was seamless. Last year the farmer had bush-hogged the shoreline for a better view of the water. Last night six inches of new snow had fallen on the ground. There was nothing to indicate a transition between icy land and snowy water. At the speed his sled was moving, you'd think he'd have made it across on velocity alone. But snowmobiles weigh over four hundred pounds, and late January sunshine rots solid ice. So deceptive was she that he didn't realize he was on the river until her cold, delicate skin began to break beneath the weight of his sled. There was a sharp crack. His heart thudded in his chest. He tried to accelerate, to outrun the inevitable, but the ice fractured in all directions around him and the snowmobile tipped backward, fell through the widening hole, and sank.

The water, only a degree warmer than the ice, soaked his clothes and filled his boots. Cold-stunned and breathless, he couldn't fight the weight of them pulling him downward. Her current took care of the rest, dragging his body a hundred yards down the river under the ice, so that it would take rescuers hours to find and retrieve it.

Your mistress is starved, Gerald, her want bottomless.

Distraught,

Mimsy

***

Dear Gerald,

The Maple Keys album is selling! Not just a handful to my friends, but thousands of copies! I am sure its popularity has something to do with Aran's name lending cachet to the project, but I am not ashamed of that. Burnt Meadow Music uploaded it to an online music marketplace, it was reviewed on NPR, and now we're making money. Aran and I are donating our cuts to Burnt Meadow Music, and the other musicians are getting paid for their share. And just like that Young Jack goes from high school student to professional musician! He was so excited when I handed him the check that he took a selfie with it to impress his new girlfriend.

For my part, I feel… I feel floaty, in a state of happiness that is almost unreal. Gerald, I really worked hard with Lawrence's band. I perfected my craft as much as I could. But the success was never mine. In fact, I often felt Lawrence succeeded in spite of me. Oh, how I drained that man's energy. A storm cloud, he called me on more than one occasion. The cloudbursts were frequent and the downpours unrelenting, requiring his constant clean up. The Maple Keys are different. With them I am normal, no fights, no breakdowns, no drinking, no hookups. A mature, professional musician surrounded by other mature musicians pursuing the perfect sound. No longer a wild, starry-eyed youth orchestrating her own destruction.

Gerald, the river has iced back up after that deadly warm spell, but it's almost February, and so there is hope you might get this tall stack of letters delivered eventually. As much as I hate her, she actually looked beautiful the other day after the snow, like a frosted cake glittering with sugar crystals. I took a photo and sent it to Aran. His evil goddess all dressed up in diamonds.

Popular recording artist,

Mimsy Bell

❧

Dear Gerald,

Drove into town late this afternoon. Batty was standing out in the cold, wrapped in a wool shawl, amidst the garlands which decorated the doors throughout the holiday season. Bert, finished with his route, careened into the post office parking lot, hopped out of his mail truck, and disappeared inside. Dana, the barber, flipped over his closed sign and carried a bulging money bag down the street to the bank's night depository. Noticing that the Pequawket Land Trust was still open, I pulled in, and spoke to that smart young woman, Lillian, who runs it.

I've been over and over it in my mind, with my lawyer, and with Aran. I feel confident my land will be protected by the land trust, and this one has a thirty-year history of managing preserves. And I didn't just take Lillian's initial word for it. I tracked down some land donors and asked them. Fourteen were filled with praise. James Roberts was the only one with a complaint, and it is well known that complaints are all you'll get from James. After a long discussion with Lillian who explained every detail, I decided to have the lawyers draw up papers for the transfer of the wildflower preserve upon my death.

There are so many loose ends to tie up, Gerald. Your threads were cut cleanly. You didn't have to make any preparations or decisions. You didn't have to think about people left behind, of legacies, property, or possessions. Of course, you were so young, you didn't have many to be concerned about. But at my advanced age, I want everything to be left just right so I can pass on without regret and with a tidy sense of completion.

Which makes me think of a huge oversight on my part. I am going to have to hire someone to go through the storage unit. All that band memorabilia should be properly housed, maybe in a museum or at Berklee, Lawrence's alma mater. I don't know where he would most like it to end up, but I know he wouldn't be pleased if I didn't take care of it before I died and it got auctioned off to the highest bidder on a reality show. But a trip to Cambridge to oversee the work seems daunting now with all the snow. Perhaps in the early spring when the ice goes out. Your river will clear out the deadweight holding her back and I will start pushing aside mine.

I hope you are resting peacefully. That's what I hope for myself. To rest peacefully by your side once again, under the pines, in the old fields, and on the sandy beaches of this old, cursed river.

Love,
Mimsy

Dear Gerald,

The days have begun to get longer. For a while there, after the end of daylight savings time, it was full-on dark just minutes after 4 p.m. Now we've got until 5:29 to get our daytime chores done. It was hard to have such a long stretch of darkness ahead of me every evening for months on end, and especially now when I'm so alone. With Young Jack AWOL, off with his girlfriend every afternoon, I've been rattling around the house, trapped indoors by the cold and by the darkness I can no longer safely drive in. Some of those hours have been productive. The rest have been nerve-wracking.

I've finished another piece for my album. This one was inspired by the Geminid meteor shower back in December. I swear I can hear those things sizzle as they burn up across the sky, so I decided to put their music on record. It took a lot of innovating with metal tines and springs and zippers to replicate the sound—Aran tried to convince me to record the sound of frying bacon—but I captured the magic without resorting to pork.

But once night falls, if I'm not busy writing music or playing the fiddle, the cozy little cottage I bought transforms into a cavernous haunted house. And I react to every little creak with a shudder and every outdoor noise with dread. While I always felt safe before, I suddenly feel vulnerable. Maybe the vulnerability is a manifestation of age. This year I will be eighty-two. Sounds even more risky than eighty-one, doesn't it? I know I will feel better once Aran gets home. He fills the house with light whether the sun is up or down.

The phone rang and I nearly jumped out of my skin. It was the land line—which almost never rings—an old Bell telephone which hangs on the wall and has a cord and a dial. Somehow Batty got my number. Her shrill greeting did not settle my nerves. She started right in begging for money for the Congregational raiment and vestments fund. I think she forgets that I am not a member of the church. Just because I helped out the choir once and the food pantry many times does not mean I want to fund all their enterprises. Oswald needed a favor and people need to eat. That's the extent of my responsibility. The good Reverend's stole and collar are fancy enough and a half a cup of bleach would brighten up those old choir robes. It took some verbal dexterity, but I managed to get off the phone with the same number of dollars in the bank as I had when she started her pitch, so I consider that a win.

I can't see the river; the moon is covered with clouds and no light reflects from her surface. But you know more of her daily moods than I do. You've had sixty-one years of learning to be at home with a river. And, yes, I begrudge her every one.

Love,
Mimsy

Dear Gerald,

Doing what you love, they say that's the way to go, right?

Onstage, in the rain, in front of hundreds of fans, that's how Aran

Sky did it.

I got a call at midnight two days ago. "I'm so sorry to tell you this, Mimsy, but Aran passed away during the concert this evening."

I heard Aran's lawyer say that. Then I didn't hear anything else. I imagine his next words were explanation, condolences, but all I heard was the blood pounding in my ears.

I had time to prepare when Lawrence was sick. Prepare for the inevitability of death. Not that preparedness made his absence easier, it didn't. I still felt the agonizing loss coursing through my veins just like I did when I lost you. But preparation spares you from the body's stunned response to an out-of-nowhere blow.

I'm still in shock, days later. I stayed up all night the first night. Lit the patchouli candles Aran left behind in the studio and watched the light flicker across the glossy finish of a Les Paul, the Stratocaster, his favorite Gibson. I didn't move a muscle for hours. I was afraid to break the spell. The spell where the sun rises and Aran rises and a few moments later the music rises up from this studio to my bedroom where I am sleeping.

But at dawn the first day, the sun rose, my bed was empty, and there was only silence. I heard knocking, but it went away. By the time it came again, I was asleep on the studio floor. At some point the banging was relentless, but I had lain so long on the ground, I couldn't have gotten up if I'd wanted to. I was on the carpet Aran brought back from India, the one with elephant parades and palaces. We made love on that carpet once. I would have wrapped myself in it if I could, but it was huge and heavy and I had no strength.

I dreamed of the worst fights I'd had with Lawrence, the ones with Aran directly in the middle, standing arms outstretched between us, begging us to stop. The dreams were realistic, savage. I'd wake on occasion, with my heart racing, Aran's name caught in my dry throat, then I'd drift off again, right back into the nightmares.

Sometime late on the second day, a female police officer broke through the front door. I opened my eyes when I heard the crash. First thing I saw was Young Jack pushing past her, reaching for me.

The boy saved my life, but I am not sure he did me a favor. I'd rather stay in the land of nightmares and dreams, at least in there Aran is still alive.

Mimsy

Dear Gerald,

I was in the hospital overnight. They gave me fluids. I know this because there are bruises on the back of my hand. What else they did, I have no recollection. The time spent at the hospital was like time spent under-water, all sound muffled and visions distorted. I didn't want to be there. As soon as I felt a little better, I insisted on going home.

Instead, I am at Young Jack's house in the guestroom. I do not want to be here either. But he wouldn't let me go home. I long to see Aidan. I need his strength. But he's still in Canada.

Young Jack is distraught. He can't even look at me without crying. Which is upsetting, because I haven't cried yet and don't know when I will. He told me Aran died of a heart attack in the middle of a song—a run-of-the-mill fate for a highly original man. I almost asked what song, but that knowledge suddenly seemed dangerous. One day I might hear that song and go insane, or worse, hate something that Aran loved.

Despite the saying about dying doing what you love, I know Aran would rather have died with me. We talked about it when arguing about the family burial ground. He wanted to go first and to go quietly while cradled in my arms, just like his best friend Lawrence had in that hospital bed six years ago. Aran's and my favorite place was under the covers in bed, arms and legs entangled. He even wanted us to be buried that way. I hope he wasn't disappointed when he died. I hope it happened too quick for him to notice that his love was not holding him like she'd promised to.

Aran's lawyer keeps calling my cell. I won't answer it. I can't.

Mimsy

Dear Gerald,

Young Jack answered the lawyer's call while I was sleeping. Now Jack Senior is planning our trip down to Boston. The funeral is on Saturday. I keep telling him I don't want to go. But he's ignored me and booked hotel rooms anyway. He gently whispered that I have to go, that I'll regret it if I don't, and then followed up with some claptrap and psychobabble about funerals bringing closure. But we all know that isn't true.

The phone is full of voicemails: Batty, Oswald, Booker, Aidan. I don't know if Aidan found out Aran died or he's called to announce the birth of his baby. And I can't bring myself to check. I can't listen to the sorrow in their voices. My veil of denial is thin. Sympathy will tear right through it.

Mimsy

Dear Gerald,

I am not used to being in the back seat. The loss of control is grating. I watch the world pass in a blur. We are approaching our destination too quickly and I'm not ready. It is kind of Young Jack's father to drive me. I know I have to attend. But the moment we arrive it will be real, and I cannot bear it.

I was lolling about in the back, car sick and heartsick, when I glimpsed something rising between the trees. I am not unfamiliar with mountains. At home, I've got Washington and the Presidentials on one horizon and Mt. Tom and Pleasant Mountain on the other. But this is something else, something alive, waiting within the deep solidity of stone. I see a sign for Mt. Chocorua. I demand a stop. In the rearview mirror, I see Jack Sr. roll his eyes. We've barely begun the trip.

Aran would have felt the spirit of this mountain in his bones. He would have danced for it, offered it a devotion. He would have thrown aside the limitations of his eighty-five years and climbed it. Stood upon its highest point, arms upstretched, then lay down upon its cold stone in supplication.

I could insist on staying right here in front of this mountain until spring. Hold my own funeral when the snow melts. Pray for Aran by skipping rocks across the image of the mountain that will be mirrored in the lake when the ice melts. Burn sweetfern, weep, and sing. But Jack and his father were showing their impatience. So, I stood with my toes at the water's frozen edge looking up at the granite crags under caps of snow and blew Aran's spirit a kiss.

No sooner did the door of the car open for me than we were driving sixty miles an hour past an infinitely forgettable landscape. The end of the mountains marking the clear transition between home and the outside world. A journey with a cemetery at the end of the road.

Mimsy

Dear Gerald,

They say you don't have to wear black to funerals anymore and only two mourners were so outfitted, myself and Glimmer Linkletter from the band. One look at her and I realized some of my trepidation about attending the funeral had to do with seeing them again. And there they were, band members old and new, clustered together. Glimmer front and center, directly opposite me. As annoyed as I had been about their insistence on driving, I was glad to have both Jack and his dad on either side of me now, shielding me.

The Sky-Garfinkel family plot was iron-gated and well-appointed with monoliths rising from stony, shrub-landscaped paths. In contrast to the foot of snow at home in Menotomy or the deep snowbanks of Chocorua, there was only a light dusting of snow on the ground. I felt somewhat sad that Aran wouldn't be tucked in under a white blanket. But he was probably dancing across Elysian Fields or basking in the glow of Nirvana, so snow or no snow in Massachusetts would make no difference.

Aran's service hadn't even begun yet, but I could see already that Lawrence's burial was to have been the easier of the two. I'd planned that one myself and felt in control. Here I was a spectator. Everything had been planned long before I was in the picture. The flowers, blue delphiniums and pink heathers massed in front of the tall green stems of his favorite, seven-pointed, star-shaped weed. The coffin was carved with spiritual symbols from all over the world as Aran had directed. The rabbi had his script. I don't expect Aran intended for Glimmer to be boring holes through me with her eyes during the opening poem, but chaos can lie beneath even the most carefully choreographed event.

There was an interlude provided for those who wished to get up and speak. Several people went before me. The rabbi had cautioned before the ceremony that I should go last. I'd prepared a little piece for Aran, a few words and some music. I touched the fiddle case at my feet for comfort. And soon after the others praised and mourned him, the rabbi invited me to stand, introducing me as Mimsy Sky, Aran's wife. Hearing the words, Glimmer let out an uncontrolled gasp.

Aran had kept his promise to keep my life secret. I was pleased by this but I swayed as I rose from my chair. My friends did not let me stumble. I held on to them and straightened my shoulders. My husband had just died and I was going up there to say fine and beautiful things about him and no acid-tongued, staring ex-best friend could stop me.

What I said about Aran was that he was joy incarnate. He was Pan. He was Shakespeare's Puck. He was Dionysus. A merry lad at play. A spark of light in the darkness. Dancing, laughing, honoring, praying, loving. Quite honestly, I said, if all the people of Earth were granted one tenth of Aran's ability to love, the world's problems would be solved in a single day.

I hadn't intended to include anything about our wedding, but from Glimmer's exclamation earlier, I felt compelled to tell the story about our reconnection on top of Mt. Washington, the proposal in front of the fireworks, our cozy home in Maine, and how he was the one who brought out the best music in me.

And then I played. In front of the people who never thought I was good enough. And like at the fairgrounds after your death, I played away my sorrow and I was good, really good. As if by magic, the members of the band were transported, probably against their will, but their faces showed they were moved all the same.

And with that testimony I buried my husband.

Mimsy Sky

Dear Gerald,

I tossed and turned, deep into the night. I should have been recalling sweet memories of Aran or crying inconsolably, but once again my emotions have been hijacked by the band and instead of being a good wife, I am reliving all the indignities Glimmer perpetrated upon me during the last two years we played together. The constant retakes when I'd play in the recording studio. The albums with my fiddle tracks mysteriously absent from the final cut. The tone she'd used with me at the end, as if addressing a child. Making my temporary replacement permanent. Smiling with satisfaction as she dismissed me from the band.

Maybe she'd felt this way all along. Maybe Lawrence's presence had kept her venom in check, but after he died every rehearsal had its pile-on-Mimsy portion. Overnight she turned on me and the rest of the band went along with her. Aran and I were still friendly. He was so clueless and happy-go-lucky, I am sure he didn't notice the active ostracism. And even if he had, Aran was just not the type of person to hate someone on another person's behalf. If he'd known, he'd have gone to great lengths to get us to make up.

Maybe I should have gone to see Aran play when he asked. Staked my claim. I would have loved to see the look on Glimmer's face if we'd shown up hand-in-hand. But I worked so hard to build a real community for myself and I was pursuing my music at home, I couldn't just interrupt it all to tag along after him. And he supported me in that. I can't be making up regrets now for choices I made then.

Tomorrow I'll be home.

Mimsy

Dear Gerald,

The house is hollow. The emptiness reminds me of the blank spaces left behind in your home after your brothers died in Korea. I didn't feel it as much in the house down in Cambridge after Lawrence died. He gave me free rein when we moved in and the place was all mine. Lawrence had his studio, but we lived our day-to-day lives in rooms I had created, rooms his hand had never touched.

Aran was only here a short time, but his touch is everywhere. Guitars leaning against walls, sofas, the bathtub. There's even one on top of the refrigerator. His pockets were always full of treasure—stones, acorns, shiny slips of paper—and they're deposited in tiny piles all over the house. An altar he set up in an east-facing window with half-burned candles and the scent of jasmine incense lingering in the air. He's got an open bottle of that stinky kombucha in the fridge. He never folded and put away the extra blankets like I asked him to; they are still tangled in the laundry basket at the foot of the stairs.

How am I going to be able to live here with all these reminders? Was remaining on Wright Farm what pushed Cécile over the edge? Everywhere ghosts. The same space in a different time. He used to walk through this door. He used to sit at this table. He used to sing. I don't know if Mackey sang, but he did plant flowers, perennials that surround the farmhouse where he and Cécile lived, all of which have outlived him. Aran won't sing again, but his voice lives on in recordings. The question is when will I be ready to listen?

Even if I banished all his things from the house, the ghosts would remain in the low doorframe where he always bumped his head, the creaky board he always failed to avoid when sneaking quietly downstairs at dawn, the coffee cup rings on the windowsill by his chair. I can't say that the new floorboards in the living room of Cécile's house and the fresh paint covering the walls were any less painful to see than the bloodstains. Tiny bandages over weeping wounds. I could raise the ceiling, fix the squeak, and refinish the windowsill, but I couldn't erase the traces of what had been. And I know what had been will always be on my mind. It's where my thoughts rest when I'm not busy making music.

I'm always reliving rather than living. Running through the scenarios, wondering how different decisions would have changed my path. I could have saved you. I could have made Lawrence's life better instead of so very hard. I could have… well, you know what… for once, I may have done it right. Aran and I were so good together. I don't think there was a do-over I could have done better in the past six months and still been true to him or to me. Aran's time came after eighty-five joyful rides around the sun. I know he had no regrets, nothing left unappreciated or undone. I know he loved me. Now, if only I could learn from his example. Untie my inner knots. Set aside the past. Live the rest of my life like Aran Sky lived his. As you lived yours. In the present.

Mimsy

Dear Gerald,

All the knocking has got to stop. I am not answering the door.

I am counting now. Whoever it is has knocked one hundred times. He or she is slowing, no longer a rat-a-tat-tat but a thunk, wait, thunk, wait, thunk. The knocker's energy must be flagging. Maybe his or her knuckles are sore, and if the knocking doesn't stop soon, those knuckles will soon be cracked and bleeding, an appropriate punishment for disturbing my mourning.

Argh! One hundred forty-nine! I can't stand it. I am going to drag myself out of bed and peek out the window, take a look at the car, figure out who it is so I know who to hate.

No car. This highly annoying person must have walked from town.

I must have made a noise while opening the blinds because the incessant knocker backed up into the driveway and lifted his gaze up to my window. Shit, Oswald! I ducked and hid, but not quickly enough.

He saw me and began knocking with renewed vigor. Knockity-knock-knock-knock-knock-knock-knock-knock-knock-knock-knock-knock-knock.

Christ, I give in. Talk to you later, Gerald. I have to deal with Pious-the-well-wisher or I'll never get any sleep.

Love,
Mimsy

Dear Gerald,

Know that after I went downstairs, I opened the door and immediately returned to my bedroom where I am going to stay, probably forever. He hemmed and hawed but eventually followed me upstairs. I just let him stand there awkwardly while I pulled the covers up to my chin. His condolences were effusive: My sympathies are with you. I am so sorry for your loss. Aran was such a good man, gone too soon. Blah blah blah. Why do people use such milquetoast language when talking about death? Why not the truth? Something like: Well, this is totally fucking horrible. Goddamn, your life is going to suck now. Or how about: You lost two husbands and a boyfriend? What the hell were you thinking exposing your heart to that kind of pain over and over again?

I didn't reply to his platitudes so he wandered around the room, reading the titles of the books on the bookshelves, reverently touching the sitar in the corner, and giving the hanging plant a twirl. I still had nothing to say. He took a second tour around the room, this time lifting a book from the shelf. "Shall I read to you?" he asked. I didn't agree. I didn't object. He pulled up a chair and opened to the first poem, Jane Kenyon's "Evening Sun." I must have fallen asleep soon after, because when I woke it was dark and he was gone.

I kind of wish he'd brought food along with his sympathy. It is a long way back down to the kitchen and I don't have the strength to make the trip twice in one day.

Mimsy

Dear Gerald,

The man is like a bad penny, always turning up where he's least wanted. But this time Oswald brought soup and bread, a thoughtful gesture which I am sure he didn't come up with on his own. Probably the church secretary's doing. She even sent one of those breakfast-in-bed trays, which—though I had thought myself too upset to care about such things—pleased me. Even in my current state of despair, I am tired of balancing my dinner plate on my knees.

Oswald updated me on the town gossip as I ate. Apparently, I missed a lot over the past few days. The tourism shack is getting new siding this week. Batty has offered to pay to have the church tapestries professionally cleaned. A huge granite boulder appeared mysteriously on the corner of Doctor Brower's property. Then the next day the boulder was gone. There was excited talk of aliens and Bermuda triangles and parting the Red Sea, but turns out the landscaper just reversed the numbers and delivered it to the wrong address. At the town meeting, the selectmen got to hear an earful about how unfair it was for Penny, just outside the village line, to be able to keep chickens in her backyard, while her next-door neighbor, Janyce, the first house within village limits, could not. And last but not least, for the first time ever, the Flag Day committee did not request any extra funds for patriotic cupcakes. This sparked a wave of protest throughout the town. The committee chairwoman could not be reached for clarification as she is wintering in Boca Raton, so the issue remains unresolved.

I made noncommittal noises after he finished each uneventful story. He seemed encouraged by my response and picked up Jane Kenyon's book again. I waved it away explaining that listening would just put me to sleep, and at this point I was tired of sleep. He took a deck of cards out of his jacket pocket and started dealing. Five-card draw? That was interesting. I guess the minister has graduated from bingo. Since I had nothing better to do, I played nine hands and won seven times.

Pay up, pastor.

Mimsy

Dear Gerald,

Well, he seems intent on ruining my sleep every single day. Plus, today he went nuts and started in on deep topics when I can barely handle local news. He started it by talking about irrevocable moments. Moments that cannot be undone. Little decisions like turning to look at your phone when your eyes should be on the road. And bigger decisions, like those choices made in relationships when you are too young and too inexperienced to know better.

He apologized for crossing the line gossiping about us dating a few months back. He said he had a strong reaction to the news I was getting married. He had found it comforting that in the end we ended up in the same place. Both single, both in Menotomy, both feeling the effect of age in our bones, both having experienced a great loss. But then Aran asked me to marry him, and I pulled ahead in the race again. And as soon as he heard the news, Oswald started reliving that moment in high school when we kissed. Wondering if he'd reacted more maturely, we might have gone steady, married.

He suggested I would have been a more loyal wife than Mary. I responded that he shouldn't paint a romanticized picture of me. I was a drug addict. I cheated on Lawrence and slept with more men than I could remember, and some women, but mostly I spent my time in my husband's best friend's bed. Oswald looked shocked by this—I was surprised that the slutty gossip hadn't made it through the church doors—but he recovered. He cleared his throat, and continued his thought experiment, arguing that he remembered me as a sweet girl who would never have been tempted by drugs if I hadn't been thrown into such an immoral environment.

Oswald pressed on. He argued that if he had handled our first kiss better, hadn't been so brainwashed by his parents' fire-and-brimstone lectures about girls and sex, you, Gerald, wouldn't have died. That I would have been with him throughout high school. You wouldn't have dated me. And as a result, you never would have been in that ill-fated canoe. Your mother would have still have had one living son. Booker would have had a father. I would not have had such an unsettled, drug-crazed life. Finally—and I realized, most importantly—he and Mary would never have gotten together and therefore she would never have left him.

The guilt and sorrow on his face was heartbreaking, Gerald. It was as if he believed he had had the power to make everyone safe and happy simply by changing a single moment, and he had failed.

I know what it is to live with guilt, and I have seen it play out around me all my life. I had my irrevocable moment on the river. Aidan had his, losing his partner in the same cursed waters. Cécile had hers in the living room of Wright Farm.

Compassion washed over me. I didn't even counter with the fact that we couldn't know what other fates would have been triggered by changing the past. Might we both have been killed in a plane crash? Would I still have met Lawrence at the county fair and left with him, abandoning Oswald? Would we have been exposed to measles or a bad flu and died in the prime of our lives? Or, most likely, would I have gone wild under the constraints of being the minister's wife and run away, just like Mary?

But his story wasn't really about me or his idea of an irrevocable moment. It was about Mary. The same way I lay here chastising myself for falling in love over and over only to experience death again and again, Oswald wishes he never met the woman who broke his heart. But no matter what fantasies we cooked up in our heads, neither of us could have chosen otherwise. We composed our own tragedies.

By the time he left, we both felt worse. We really should have stuck with reading Kenyon's poetry. The results were better. But, once again, we can't change the past. Not even the most recent hours can be undone.

Mimsy

Dear Gerald,

Oswald was nowhere to be seen today. I was restless, so I checked my messages. Aidan called to say that the baby had been born and was a seven-pound, ten-ounce beautiful boy. Cécile was spending a short, supervised time with him every day, but Aidan got him the rest of the time. I texted back that I was overjoyed to hear it, which intellectually I was, but emotionally it didn't register. The next message was from Batty, who declared that it wasn't good for me to mope around the house and I should get up and help her repair the bindings on some old hymnals at the church. The last message was from Booker, who had just found out about Aran's death, through the internet. He chastised me for not calling him and offered condolences and asked if there was anything he could do. As there is literally nothing he can do, I texted him that I was sad, but fine. Which is not true, but probably made him feel better.

After all the messages, my nerves felt jangled and I couldn't get back to sleep. Kenyon's volume of poetry still lay at the foot of my bed, but when I tried to read it my mind couldn't wrap around the words. Finally, I dragged myself to the shower, because I was just now noticing my ripe smell. The water fell from a wide panel, a rainfall showerhead Aran had had installed. He was also behind the veritable jungle inhabiting the bathroom. As the rain fell and the mist rose and the gardenia soap—that man did love his tropical flowers—scented the air, my body finally relaxed. And then I started crying.

Still haven't stopped.

Mimsy

Dear Gerald,

Aidan called me this morning from Canada. Distracted me from my tears with his baby drama. He explained that until yesterday Cécile refused to nurse their new baby. Now, Aidan had read all the baby books that Cécile was uninterested in, which definitively say breast is best, and had become the biggest breastfeeding advocate around. He was kicking himself that his tiny child was not getting what he needed. But Cécile just couldn't. She wasn't well enough, her remaining strength sapped by the birth itself. She needed to tend to herself more than the baby needed mother's milk.

Under relentless pressure from Aidan, the hospital nurses and lactation consultant did finally cajole Cécile into pumping milk for the baby. It relieved the pain of engorgement and released some calming hormones so she stuck with it after a successful first try. But she still would not hold the baby or nurse him. Aidan did all the holding and bottle feeding. He brought the baby into her room during their visits and fed him there. Aidan got her to look at the baby each time he visited and she watched him talk to the baby and smile at the baby. Her counselors were right by her side when she was ready hold the baby for the first time. Gradually they increased their supervised one-on-one time together.

Then one day, the baby's mewing and rooting at her breast triggered some deep instinct within and Cécile asked for help to try nursing. The lactation consultant was overjoyed. Aidan was so relieved he cried. The baby, who had been restless since birth, calmed instantly. Aidan and the nurses and counselors had been ready to stop the experiment if Cécile became distraught. But even though she was not what anyone could call enthusiastic, Cécile continued to nurse dutifully after that. And Aidan and the doctors began discussing a plan for discharge.

Guardedly optimistic,
Mimsy

Dear Gerald,

All I wanted to do was finally send you this stack of letters. I needed you to know what happened to Aran. But what happened instead was Bert, the postman, got a second opportunity to rescue a damsel in distress.

It has been warmer, even at night, and the river finally gave up some of her ice. I could see from the house that a channel by the bank was open and I rushed out the door to get this stack of letters out to you straight away. Who needs boots or a hat or mittens on a sunny fifty-degree day? I held your letters to my chest and went out in my slippers like a child excited by the first day of spring.

I slipped on some leaf-covered ice and fell forward, ending up on my hands and knees in the shallows. The water was excruciatingly cold. My limbs went completely numb in an instant. I couldn't even engage them to crawl backwards out of the water. I just stayed there in shock, freezing. I started yelling for help, not thinking anyone would hear. But seconds later the sound of the squeaky brakes of the mail truck inspired me to scream louder. Thank goodness for Bert. If he hadn't come along there would have been no more letters for you. I heard the smush, smush, smush of his boots in the slush as he approached. When he picked me up, he was beaming with pride. I started to say I was fine and insist he bring me indoors, but he carried me to the mail truck and drove me right to the hospital.

They didn't keep me long. I wasn't hurt and I wasn't hypothermic. When we got back, I thanked him from the bottom of my heart for saving me, gave him a kiss on the cheek, and called him my hero. You'd think his face would crack, his smile was so wide. Telling this story is going keep him going for decades.

As glad as I was to have been rescued, I was as upset at myself for being so careless. I am not a young girl who can run about wildly on a whim. I am elderly, and I have to be cautious. Something as small as a patch of ice can not only bring me down at this point in my life, it could kill me. Believe me, after I was snuggled on the couch under my mother's quilt, I spent long hours berating myself for my stupidity. I will try to see it doesn't happen again. But sometimes—especially when I am thinking of you—I act seventeen again.

I can't believe I put myself within her reach,

Mimsy

Dear Gerald,

Oh, good God! Oswald heard about my fall and came over to check up on me. I know it is part of his job to visit shut-ins, but I think widows who purposely remain in bed do not come under that category. At least this time he called ahead instead of showing up in my dooryard. Gave me just enough time to slink back upstairs. I'd come down to the kitchen to make myself a cup of tea for the first time in weeks, but I am not going let him see me outside of my bedroom and somehow get the idea that I am ready to go out, restart my music, or socialize with more than one person a day, because I am not.

Unfortunately, he noticed the steam rising from the cup by my bedside and said, with annoying enthusiasm, "Oh! You've been up and about today!" I responded that the tea was delivery. He lifted his hairy caterpillar eyebrows at that, knowing full well that no one in town delivers tea in pink and white china cups. I tried to distract him, redirecting his thoughts to church business. Why was Batty constantly asking me to help her over at the church? Why was she always working around the property? Was she his new assistant or something? Oswald admitted he had no clue why she was being so beneficent, though he really appreciated the help.

Then, out of nowhere, casually brushing my distraction aside, he cleared his throat and accused me of not having made peace with the river. I guess he was parroting my early hope that this reunification would be a possible outcome. He then explained in a most ecclesiastical tone, "Hating a river is like being angry at God. It cripples you. It doesn't hurt God."

I was surprised he hadn't started in with the God-talk earlier. Now that I'm almost eighty-two, lying in bed, practically on death's doorstep, I must look like an easy mark, but trust me, I am not. Jesusing me won't get him anywhere. I only believe in the little gods: art, wildflowers, music, rivers. Oswald isn't going to collect my soul. It's already spoken for. But when I complained about his word choice, he claimed that religious conversion was not his objective. He was just concerned that I was using up all my strength fighting an imaginary enemy.

The river. An imaginary enemy! That's rich.

The river has killed at least three people a year since the curse began and who knows how many before that. She is conscious of our being and completely unconcerned for our welfare. There is no placating her, no offerings we could give, no supplication she would accept. Our belief or disbelief in her is immaterial. She is movement and violence and power and death. And I know I planned to make peace when I came here, but she has rejected every overture. And not only that, in less than ten months she's tried to kill me not once, but twice.

So much for the advice of the kindly pastor when presented with things way beyond his ken.

Love,

Mimsy

Dear Gerald,

Postman Bert met me at the door with an envelope from Aran's lawyer today. I wasn't expecting a letter. It felt hot to the touch, as if the contents might burn my skin. I brought it in the house and turned the envelope over and over in my hands. I set it down on the counter and picked it up, and dropped it on the coffee table and picked it up, and tucked it in the basket with the bills and picked it up. It was inescapable.

By the time I opened it, it had become an object of great weight. The paper, heavy linen. The printing, dark and fine-edged. The words, weighty and solemn. I sat in Aran's chair, the wingback he preferred because it fit his tall frame best. His lawyer's words assaulted my eyes, concerned as they were with property and its distribution. As Aran had told me, the bulk of his estate went to marijuana legalization efforts in the more "backward" states. He'd left his band memorabilia to a rock-and-roll museum. His possessions at our house were mine, except that I was to invite Young Jack to choose four guitars. Not nearly enough, he said, but the rest had to be earned. I was to choose one for myself; only one, and only after Jack, because he knew I was just going to get all sentimental about it and never pick it up to play, and guitars live to be played. The remaining guitars were to be given to the music department at the academy with a codicil that they couldn't be sold for fundraising. They had to be used by the students there. All these details and the rest of the lawyer's letter were nothing more than housekeeping, the tidying up of a glorious life's loose ends.

There was another envelope within the letter, smaller, with my name in Aran's handwriting on the outside. So here was where the heat was coming from, I thought. Strangely, when I opened it, my mind went to the grocery list. I think because that is the only place I ever saw Aran's handwriting. It wasn't a long letter, despite the long years we held each other safe. Aran always had been more comfortable with penning lyrics than paragraphs. I copy it word-for-word by hand here for you, because upon reading it, I felt a great weight disappear from my shoulders.

God, I loved that man.

Mimsy

❋ ❋ ❋

Dear Mimsy,

I know you will have a hard time believing this. Just promise me you will think about my words and remember that I've always told you the truth and I have no reason to lie now.

You are a truly gifted musician. It has come to my attention that you don't believe this, but you belonged in the band and, no, you were not there just because you were married to Lawrence. You were there because your sound was whimsical and fresh and your talent was raw and full. I saw your bandmates, the same ones who were your detractors, transfixed every time your turn came to cross the stage mid-set, the sound from your fiddle and bow reaching their hearts. But you never saw that. You were in the music. Unaware of its effect on other people.

I have had the privilege of playing with you for months now and I think you know that I know what I'm talking about when it comes to music. You are the real thing, Mimsy. Your new direction into composing proves it. Those songs you've written are enchanting.

So, I beg you, let go of the band, let go of your self-doubt. You are a fine musician. Finish your album, start another, play with the Maple Keys, and live the music. Never stop playing.

Of course, you are also beautiful and lovable and spritely,
and that is why I loved you from the moment I saw you and
never stopped, not for a single breath.

Forever,
Aran

Dear Gerald,

Oswald and I really delved into the deep dark secrets of life today. He should consider a second career as an interrogator, because when he pressed, I cracked wide open and admitted that the story I have been telling him and everyone else, including myself, for decades is not entirely true. The conversation started when he mentioned he wished he'd been able to ask Mary for forgiveness for not giving her what she needed, for not making her happy. Then he asked me if I felt there was anything I wanted forgiveness for in this life. I explained that there was something for which there could be no forgiveness. That on the day you died, the river made a play for you, and I handed you right over.

I told him that we'd spent half our lives in boats, on the lake or in the river, paddling from one friend's camp to another, delivering groceries to the summer houses on the island, chasing herons downstream, fishing for hours, practicing our whitewater skills on Walker's Rip. We knew full well what was safe and what was not. But we thought of ourselves as invincible. Beings to whom the rules of fate did not apply.

A line of thunderstorms had passed through to the north of town that night. We could still hear the distant rumble when we threw our gear into the bottom of the canoe and set out under partly cloudy skies. I told Oswald we had intended to meander down the river, stopping to swim in the deep pools and to fish in the secret fishing holes and to find a spot for a picnic and a cuddle.

What we actually did was stop halfway along our route and make love on a thick bed of pine needles along the shore. When it happened, I thought it was the first time for both of us, but the existence of Booker has subsequently proved that untrue. Still, it was my first time and a magical one. I was feeling high and giddy and full of life. Which translated to foolish and reckless once we were back on the water.

We heard the thunderclaps get louder and closer, but they had been background noise all day so we paid them little mind. We were pretty loud ourselves, joking and fooling around, engaged in one dramatic play after another, entertaining ourselves with our own cleverness.

In terms of a day together it could not have been more perfect. But the river must have resented our joyfulness, and as her bile rose so did her waters. The runoff from the storms up north in the mountains had traveled downhill and downstream, collecting in the basin that was her slender body, bloating it beyond its margins, expanding her reach into the forest on either side.

The current swiftened and we were exhilarated by the speed. When the rain came it came as a wall of water. We challenged it with shouts and screams of defiance and brandished our paddles and pumped our fists in the air. I told Oswald you assumed the voice of Neptune, god of the sea, commanding the river to rise.

Carried away by your zest, I stood up in the bow of the canoe. The water was rough beneath us. The cold rain hit my face like tiny stones. I could feel the thunderclaps resonate in my chest cavity. And I defied the gods. I lifted my paddle, holding it in one hand. A wind gust caught it, threatening to pull it from my grasp. I proclaimed myself Queen Neptune as if I were on stage in a high school play and not in the middle of a river roaring past flood stage.

I explained to Oswald that while I was fooling around, you suddenly woke up to the danger. You were losing your struggle with your paddle in the tumultuous water, using all your strength to try to control the canoe. I heard you yell, "Sit down! It's getting worse." When I turned to flash a sassy smile over my shoulder, my weight shifted to the left. The canoe dipped treacherously. At that moment a wave hit us broadside. The gunwale disappeared beneath the surface and the canoe gulped water. I described how you threw your weight toward the right side to counterbalance my mistake. I explained that I tried to recover, but what I'd done couldn't be undone. The canoe flipped with me and we were both in the cold, raging water.

We were close. I could see the terror in your eyes and saw you reach out for me. But the canoe bumped my shoulder and I reached for it. You were trying to get to me, but the power of the river was too great. By the time I was safe, you were out of reach.

And then you hit the rock. I swear I heard the impact, but in reality, I probably couldn't have heard anything over the pounding rain and the rushing water and the thunder filling my ears. You were still then, no longer calling for me, no longer struggling. Your eyes were empty. The canoe got caught up on a snag. The river carried you away. And we never saw one another again.

I told Oswald I've tried to obliterate the memory, erase the shame by overwriting the truth with tales in which the river is solely to blame. But in the end, I was the one that tipped that canoe over. I was the one who killed you.

When I finished telling the story, Oswald looked at me with a look of such deep compassion, the like of which I have never seen before from another living being. He reached out to hold my bony hand as I had held his when he found out about Mary's death. There was some comfort in that and some in the telling. But I have been drowning in that river for sixty-one years, and at this point there is no way out.

I am sorry,

Mimsy

Dear Gerald,

Oswald felt so bad for me, he decided to take me on a field trip to the woodland I'd been trying to buy from him for months. We made our way very slowly down an old lane, past old cellar holes, the foundation stones heaved out of place by the freezing and thawing of the ground over the past hundred-and-fifty years. Oswald's ancestors had lived here once, farmed fields bound by the stone walls that now ran like belts through stands of trees. The land had rebounded from its agricultural past. Though here and there stood a relic apple tree or a strand of rusted barbed wire, the fields were forest now and the ground was covered with wild red trillium and lady's slipper, whose balloony flowers nodded welcome as we passed.

The family members in this burial plot died too long ago for Oswald to have met them. But Oswald's parents told him their histories. He said that as he got older they came to mind again, drifting into and out of his memory at odd times. And that now that he is ancient, the ancestors have taken up permanent residence in his head. He fancies they are calling him, the last in a long line, to sleep forever in the family fold.

Oswald led me to a headstone and said this was the person he wanted me to meet, Caroline Pingree. She was wife to his great-great-great uncle Truman Pingree, but her maiden name was Browning, just like mine.

"I know Fight Brook Burial Ground is out of room. You said the little graveyard at Wright Farm was out of the question. I know your private burial ground was washed away in the flood. And you told me that modern, flat-stone-plastic-flower cemeteries turn your stomach. I'd rather you were in the churchyard where I could look after you, but I know you'd rather look after your forest and flowers. And since I am adding these two hundred acres to your preserve, I'd like to offer you a place to rest here, beside kinfolk, just like you hoped, and inside your sanctuary where you will be safe."

Put that in your will, old man. I told him.

It's already there, he promised.

I looked around at the old fir trees and tall pines and shiny-barked beech and white sentinel birch shading the worn slate and granite head-stones, and for the first time, in a long time, felt at home.

Oswald Pingree Martin, the answer to my prayers. Will wonders never cease?

Mimsy

Dear Gerald,

Batty brought over some buttered fiddleheads she'd gathered and pan fried. "Harvested from your preserve," she said excitedly as she served them. I refrained from mentioning that inherent in the word "preserve" is the notion that it refers to a place where you do not pick the ferns. But since I hadn't had a plate of fiddleheads in sixty-one years, I wasn't going to pass on them now no matter how ill-gotten. They tasted like spring, a tightly wound package of sunshine and dew.

The fiddleheads were apparently an attempt to mitigate what she had to say. And she said something I'd never have expected to come from her lips. That she loved Oswald Martin and that she wrote the post about his wife's death.

I wanted to wring her neck. Honestly, lording her perfection around town, keeping me from my ancestral home, playing one game at church and another behind closed doors at home on the internet. But she braved my furious look and continued.

She told me she loved him since ninth grade when he was a senior in high school and she was a freshman, but he never noticed her. She finished high school, pining for him every day, and waited for him to return from divinity school. But just as soon as he returned, he was engaged.

Many years later, when Mary left Oswald in that very public cuck-olding, Batty came to his defense. She tried to put down the rumors before they spread. But it was impossible. Batty came to his side to comfort him, but he'd locked his heart away, too damaged and ruined by Mary to trust anyone again.

So, when the word of Mary's death reached Batty's ears, she went crazy with the idea that vengeance had finally been delivered, and she let spew all the feelings she'd kept inside for decades, posting them anony-mously on a local gossip page. In some bizarre way, she thought she was being supportive of Oswald. But her victory dance was short. Oswald had been hurt by Mary, but that did not mean he'd stopped loving her. And if he heard about it, the act of spitting on Mary's grave would make Batty the last person on earth Oswald would ever want in his life.

Yesterday, one of the ladies in the historical society had found out.

Why she was coming to me, I had no idea. Suddenly I was every-one's best friend and confidante. This was not exactly what I envisioned when I came home to Menotomy. But, since I was no angel myself, and like her secret love, she appeared to have no friends, I decided not to throttle her.

Besides, it is very hard to watch a frail old woman weep without feeling some sympathy, even when she's guilty. And I do have decades of experience of doing things that made my lovers angry with me. One can't have spent eighty-one years living the way I did without garnering some insight into the ways of men. They will forgive you, but not lightly, and only on their own terms.

When she quieted, I pointed out two birds that were facing one another on a branch just outside the window, chirping at each other vigorously, their heads bobbing with the effort of their vocalizations. I explained they were either fighting or falling in love, which I have often found to be one and the same. Either way there is tension and it is about to erupt. I mentioned Batty had decades of tension wound up within her like a spring. Unrequited love, jealousy, judgment. I wouldn't have been able to keep it inside a week, much less for years, and I praised her for her restraint.

I did not go on about how all of this could have been avoided, because it would be hypocritical. I never avoided a stupid fight in my life. I stuck my foot in my mouth daily. I lashed out at everyone when I was hurting. As a result, I did learn something about patches and stitches and glue applied in the nick of time to make my relationships last one more hour, one more day, or sometimes, another year. Patching things up generally has nothing to do with begging for forgiveness. It has to do with make-up sex and brutal honesty.

As sex was likely out of the question for Batty and Oswald, I suggested she was going to have to lay it all on the table from high school crush to social media attack to the acts of service she'd just completed at the church. She looked down as if I'd just ripped out her intestines and they were spilled on the floor between us, but I think I was a better friend to her today than I've ever been.

The river is low tonight, Gerald, only the center carrying water. A collage of random rocks and boulders frames the channel. The river has the ability to strip away all artifice and to reveal the underlying truth of the land. The soil and all its pretty contours and decorations last only until the river washes them away. The naked bones of bedrock, the shattered, weathered stones are all that remain.

The truth is often ugly,

Mimsy

Dear Gerald,

Young Jack and I were playing by the river this evening when he noticed the first patch of trout lilies, sunny bells with orange pollen, their leaves speckled like a brook trout's back. I lay down, eye level with the flowers, looking at them for quite some time, watching as they trembled in the spring breeze, until I found myself a little dizzy. I recently read that flowers can sense the frequency of their pollinators' wings and they ramp up their nectar production when they hear them coming. If that is the case, we have definitely underestimated them.

As it got closer to dusk, we heard the oddest sounds from across the river. A "beep," pause, "beep," reminiscent of the call of that old cartoon roadrunner. The last beep was followed by a "whooshing" noise, then some electronic babble. Young Jack looked it up on his phone and discovered the songster was a woodcock (also referred to as a timber-doodle by those who blush easily). Well, this little bird auditioned his crazy little heart out, and I've decided he's getting a part in my album!

After Young Jack dropped me off, I worked in the studio late into the night. Aran's synthesizer sat in the corner mocking me the whole time. In about an hour I could have had a fair rendition of the woodcock's song on that thing. Gosh, I could have just recorded it on my phone and enhanced it on Aran's computer. But I am old-fashioned when it comes to work and have never been comfortable with shortcuts. I believe it is going to take woodwind and brass to get this bird off the ground. Better make some calls in the morning to see what new musical talent the Maple Keys can flush out of the White Mountains.

When I slipped outside at midnight to mail this letter to you, the night shift that began with the woodcock was in full force. Spring peepers and their sleigh-bell chorus, coyotes with their cacophonous kittering, barred owls asking "Who cooks for you?" What a place this is where the wilderness comes alive with song! I did appreciate it as a child, but I appreciate it more as an elderly woman. Reverence. That is what I have learned in all my travels, all my relationships, all my music. If you don't feel awe in the presence of beauty, your work will never reflect it.

The river, her work tonight is stillness, mirroring the stars,

Mimsy

Dear Gerald,

It didn't take long to find some new talent to help out on my next album. The Maple Keys scoured the hills and brought forward a couple of talented hermits, lured from their dens by the promise of playing with Mimsy Bell. Shocking how little it takes to lure out a hermit these days. I guess the band members talked me up or made up stories or promised them something, I am not sure which. Regardless of the bargains made to get them here, the new musicians brought a coronet, a flute, an oboe, and a box full of whistles, some turkey feathers, bird calls, and a paper fan, and we worked for several hours to match the sounds of the woodcock. I think we came up with a fair approximation and called the initial session a success with plans to practice after I get the entire composition down on paper.

I guess I spent too long sitting in one position while we worked. When it was time to leave, I stood up and I was so dizzy I had to sit right back down again. It was embarrassing and the attention I received made it worse. Everyone asking what they could do, if I wanted some water, if I was too hot or too cold. Then they "Aran-ed" me to death, insisting that Aran wouldn't have wanted me to drive, be alone, or ignore this. And that he definitely would have wanted me to go directly to the hospital. Unfortunately, the vertigo didn't resolve right away. Everyone waited around until I committed to leaving my car behind and letting Young Jack drive me to the hospital. Now the newbies have a sorry tidbit to add to their story of meeting the "Great" Mimsy Bell. Might as well diminish their expectations right from the start because the real me can't hold a candle to my press.

Dizziness, Gerald, is a dreadful thing. You can't control the direction your head is spinning in, much less stop it spinning in the first place. So much of what we take for granted in our own bodies disappears as we age. It is one thing to lose control over events and plans in your life; you can choose smaller goals. It is quite another to lose control over your own body; you only have one. Well, I hope this is not the first symptom of a new condition. I think at my age, creeping up on eighty-two, I have enough to contend with.

In the hospital, my heart sank when the nurse on duty recognized me instantly. I have been here far too many times. Unlike a bar, the ER is not a place where you want to be on a first-name basis with the staff. When the time comes, is this room going to be where I spend the last moments of my life? In a hospital gown on a gurney? Just like the last quiet, ignoble days of Lawrence Bell. No raging rivers or heart attacks on stage. Just IVs and pulse oximeters and catheters until I flatline and they wheel me down to the morgue.

Well, luckily tonight wasn't the night for my personal end-of-times scenario. The doctor ordered some tests, but he thinks my blood pressure medicine, which my internist recently changed, is playing havoc with my ability to stand up. So, a new prescription and I get to live a while longer, I can leave the hospital on my own two feet, and that hospital bed is not going to be my boat over the river Styx.

Because, believe you me, I am going to do death differently,

Mimsy

Dear Gerald,

I think I have made it quite clear I don't think much of surprises. However, today's surprise was more than welcome; it was celebrated. Aidan with his baby boy in his arms! I have never been much interested in babies and I am not one to coo or make funny faces around them, but I found myself warbling away to get this precious infant's attention. His little eyes! So dark and serious. Clearly, he's seen a lot in his first months, but now he's home and there are better days ahead. Mama Cécile was in the truck. I moved as if to go see her, but Aidan held me back. "Give her time," he said, and I settled for waving joyfully and getting a brief smile in response.

Aidan stopped by before they got to the farm because he'd heard (you don't even need to stop the car to hear the gossip in this town) that I was taken to the emergency room last night. He was already caught up on all the medical details and simply chastised me for not calling him, explaining that now that he was back, help was but minutes away. I resisted the urge to "Yes, Dad" him, because I was so relieved to see them home. Tension I didn't even know I was holding was released from my shoulders the moment I saw his face.

Aidan and me, we might be unlikely best friends, but we share a tendency toward dark pragmatism, him from his encounters in law enforcement and me from my crazy years on the road. There isn't much that surprises us, especially the fact that things, more often than not, go badly. And we have in common the ability to read other people's emotions better than our own, so we take on the responsibility of looking out for each other, because neither of us has been that great at figuring out how to take care of ourselves.

The river, dark and snaky today, is unconcerned about Aidan's arrival; she's already taken a chunk of his heart. Too bad she doesn't have the same feelings about me; I sense very keenly that she believes I still have more to give.

Tell her she can forget it,

Mimsy

Dear Gerald,

The emergency call that came after dark was not from me to Aidan. Cécile freaked out about being at the farm in the middle of the night and Aidan bundled up the whole family and brought them over to my house. I gave the three of them my room. I slept on the couch downstairs and didn't hear a peep from them until the little guy started crying at six in the morning. I got up and put on some coffee.

Aidan said that he was going out to reserve a suite at the Hobblebush Inn and check in at the police station and that I should keep Cécile and the baby occupied until he got back. Accepting my assignment, I lured Cécile into the kitchen by telling her how hopeless I was at cooking oatmeal. I heard a sigh, but she picked up the baby in his carrier and followed me into the kitchen where I had arrayed some microwavable packets on the counter. "Mon Dieu!" she cried out seeing the blasphemy spread out before her. "Non! Que fais-tu." Aidan had told me she'd reverted to her native French in the hospital in Québec. I was hard pressed, but pulled enough high school French vocabulary from the cobwebby corners of my memory to understand that invoking God to understand my bad choices was her reflexive response to the sight of processed food.

Seeing a kitchen about to be defiled. Cécile perked up and swept the packets into the trash. "Tu devez avoir autre chose," she cried out as she rifled through my cupboards and refrigerator. In truth, I didn't have much else. I haven't been eating regularly or with any sort of culinary curiosity. But she did find buckwheat and white flour, baking powder, and salt, and with the addition of hot water, she whisked up some batter for ploves. Way back in the freezer she discovered some sausage links that she defrosted in the microwave while waiting for the batter to begin to bubble. By the time Aidan was back, with a wink and a thumbs up—mission accomplished, our breakfast was on the table. The baby nursed under a receiving blanket while we dug in. Aidan was openly staring as Cécile downed an amazing amount of food; he was clearly pleased by her appetite. I assumed she hadn't been eating much in the hospital.

I watched as they interacted, awkwardly, and hoped things could work for Cécile here. I am very concerned after last night's incident. On the phone last night, Aidan said Cécile refused to go into the living room (which one has to cross through to get from the kitchen to the rest of the house) and had slipped outside and walked around the house in the dark to avoid it. He hadn't seen her leave and tore through the house looking for her only to have her emerge through the side door with the explanation that of course she went around, the room was haunted.

Ever since the day I had to take her to the ER, I have wondered if there was far more than the pre-partum depression going on. Mackey's suicide must still weigh heavily on her heart. Burying a trauma under a new life does not make it go away; it festers, and boils rise to the surface. This I know firsthand. Nobody knew how to help me when you died, Gerald. Now, I have to figure out a way to help her.

Worried. Very worried.

Mimsy

Dear Gerald,

Lillian from the Pequawket Land Trust called to invite me to look at a property last night. Apparently, they are pitted against a developer for a massive piece of land that has been in the same family for two hundred years. The elder of the family passed away and the heirs have no interest in it beyond putting it on the market so they can split the proceeds. The land trust has had their eye on this piece for a decade but so has Glenview, the local developer who specializes in turning forests into lawns interrupted by poorly constructed McMansions. They've already got a proposal. They're calling it "Birch Grove." Naming your development is tacky, and naming it after what you cut down, bulldoze or burn is a sure sign you are in league with the devil. Glenview's work is so out of touch with the character of the region that you can spot their developments on the satellite map like open sores across a child's downy skin. It is as if they were trying to make Maine into a tacky suburb of New Jersey and are proud of it. Lillian hates them and now that I know about them, I hate them too.

Yes, we rich people are privileged and out of touch, but we do have our uses. There is no way Pequawket Land Trust could mobilize its regular donors fast enough to save this property; Glenview already has its first bid in. When a nonprofit needs funds, and needs them now, they turn to those of us who have no other use for our hoard of cash. And I, for one, definitely have no better use for my money than to help the land trust protect wildflowers and trees. So, it was with great excitement I met Lillian there this morning.

The property hasn't been lived on since the farmhouse and barn were lost in a fire decades ago. The stone foundations have filled in with plants and trees, but can still be seen as twin depressions on the hilltop. There once were sheep here, and stone walls run through what was their pasturage. Carriage trails remain; the real estate company had them mowed so prospective buyers could inspect the property. We walked along one, past the foundations, over the hill, through the tame but stately wood, and then I saw a sparkling glint between the trees. The carriage trail turned to parallel the riverbank, and we continued along it with just a thin row of trees between us and her rapidly moving water.

With one glance, I knew exactly where I was. I knew that straight-away. I knew those boulders. I saw your face.

I sat down abruptly, unable to stand under the weight of memory. Lillian sat down beside me saying a rest would be good, probably mistaking my anguish for a senior moment. Lillian was like a bird in a distant tree, chirping, giving her spiel. She talked about the increased flooding if the developer were allowed to cut the hillside to give the houses river views. The herbicide and pesticide runoff from the lawns that would pollute the waters. The house lights that would dazzle and trap the aquatic insects the fish relied on. The good soil that would erode into the river bed. The increase in water temperature where the shoreline trees were removed would disrupt aquatic habitat. But I paid her just as much mind as I would a distant bird.

You probably noticed me on the riverbank among the cinnamon ferns. I was held only by the thinnest thread to the here and now. Time seemed to collapse around me. I was simultaneously on the bank and in the river, seeing, hearing, feeling all the same things I did the day you died. The water so hateful and loud. My young heart beating like a fearful wild creature. Your voice, rising in fear from its usual confident baritone to a frantic higher pitch. The pelting rain and the deafening explosion of lightning hitting nearby. The slow unbalancing, the fatal tip, and the final plunge into the cold, deadly maelstrom. The boulders unmoving as we flew by them. Your gentle flesh against their absolute solidity. Your body, its life drained from it, disappearing downstream.

A belted kingfisher shot blue across the river and landed in a tree beside Lillian and me. The noise startled me back into the present. I turned to Lillian and apologized. I struggled to get up and then stumbled back to the car. She followed me, asking if she should drive me home. But I brushed her off and somehow made it back, although I have no memory of the road.

For decades, I have looked at your loss from odd angles, backwards and sideways, but never once head-on.

I am so sorry,

Mimsy

Dear Gerald,

Aidan and Cécile are at my house a lot, considering she owns her own home and they have a room at the inn. I watch the baby while she naps or goes to therapy and Aidan joins us after work. Trying to evaluate their situation without being too obvious, I inquired about the chickens. Aidan explained that a while back a farmer he knew had moved the hens over to his house and they'd assimilated surprisingly well into his flock. Cécile thought it best the hens stay in their new home. Both Aidan and Cécile seemed pretty nonchalant about giving up hens that they'd built a military fortress to protect a couple months back. But, of course, they have a baby to fill their time with now. Despite that new reality, something tells me that it's going to be a long time before the family takes up residence at Wright Farm and that the tab at the inn is going to get pretty high before they do.

But I am not complaining about having company. The house is so empty without Aran. Instead of dwelling on his loss, I get to play with baby Remi, who never tires of staring awestruck at the colorful toys I dangle in front of him. Aidan reads the back issues of The Jockey Cap Tattler, making sure he is up to speed on everything that went down in town when he was gone. And Cécile cooks supper, singing while she stirs. And I am happy to be around the living—and to have something besides oyster crackers and grapes for supper.

The river has a bit of an edge to her today. The wind has riffled up her waves. The air brings her cold up to soak my bones.

Love,

Mimsy

Dear Gerald,

Aidan pulled into the driveway two hours late. Cécile had been checking the window every fifteen minutes, more worried every time a set of headlights passed by without turning in the drive. I knew something was wrong as soon as I saw him. He was looking down at my feet instead of into my eyes. Aidan took a deep, shuddering breath, and then told me as calmly as he could that Oswald lost control of his motorcycle on the bridge. He struck the guardrail. The bike remained on the tarmac. Oswald's body was thrown over the rail. A truck driver found him on the riverbank.

Oswald was probably taking advantage of the nice weather, Gerald.

The first ride of spring. I am sure he zipped up the same roads that he took me on last year when we went to the White Mountain National Forest. He seemed to know them like the back of his hand. Maybe he decided to add on an extra loop of road to take in one more mountain view before calling it a day. The diversion took more time than he reckoned it would; he wouldn't make it home before dark. After sunset a fog rose, then the temperature dropped to thirty-two, and a thin layer of water froze on the cold surface of the bridge. Oswald wouldn't have anticipated that. The main roads had been safe and dry. So, when he hit the black ice at speed, he lost his steering, his brakes; the wheels went out from under him. The bike continued its course at forty miles per hour. How he must have struggled to regain control, but the bridge is narrow, the guardrails firm, and inertia cannot be overcome by prayer.

Don't think for a moment that I don't know she took him too. The accident may have happened above her reach, but the bridge is within her jurisdiction. This is punishment for walking away from the potential land trust property the other day. She could not convince me to save her, so she took one of my own.

Taking to my bed again, all too soon after escaping it,

Mimsy

Dear Gerald,

Sometimes the only reason to get out of bed with the dead is because the living need you more. Young Jack was visiting, writing a homage to Oswald for The Jockey Cap Tattler. He got Oswald's basic data down, when he was born, where he went to school, a polite bit about his short marriage to Mary. But when he tried to go deeper, Jack quickly found that while everyone in town liked and respected the minister, no one really knew him.

I didn't know what to say either, but I knew it was important to do this right. Jack and I wrestled with the words for hours. I would say something. He'd type it into the computer. He'd read it back to me. I would tell him to delete it.

I was at my wits' end. Here was a man who had given his whole life to Menotomy. Someone I'd seen at his most vulnerable and his most generous, but the things I knew to be true about him, the things that made up his innermost self, were secret and private. The portrait I would paint, as gentle and touching as it was, would not be something Oswald would want exposed. So, as much as I didn't have the strength for it, I knew we had to ask Batty for help.

Like me, Batty had shut herself in her bedroom, seeking refuge in response to the news of Oswald's death. Young Jack waited in the yard. I entered my childhood home and headed up the staircase. When the tattle-tale stair creaked with my step, I heard my mother's voice questioning why I was home so late. But the sound trailed off to a whisper by the end of her sentence and did not repeat. Entering Batty's room, decorated with her pretty things, brought me right back to the present, severing the momentary connection I had made.

Batty was, as I had expected, sick with regret. She hadn't had the spill-your-guts-on-the-table heart-to-heart with Oswald I'd suggested. And now he was dead. It is amazing how dead people inspire regret, when at the same time, if they were alive you wouldn't be doing the thing you now regret not doing. There is a reason you're not doing it, probably because it is too hard or too embarrassing or too honest or too forward. My mentioning this would not improve Batty's emotional state, so instead I offered her the option of memorializing the man she loved through a written tribute. I explained that it was only fitting that she did it, because she knew him best, plus the positive words she spoke now would balance out the negative ones of the past.

I was expecting her to be reluctant, but she leapt at the opportunity. I called in Young Jack and let them work, excusing myself and sitting on the porch for an hour until Jack was able to craft his article. I gave it a quick read before he submitted it to the paper. The quotes from Batty portrayed Oswald, with his pure heart and hands always willing to serve, perfectly.

Amends have been made.

Let her be free from guilt for the rest of her days.

Love,

Mimsy

Dear Gerald,

I think the guilt transferred to me, for when Young Jack dropped me off at home, I was mortified to see Lillian on my doorstep. With Oswald's death I had completely forgotten about the property, but there she was, in a panic. She told me that the heirs don't really care to whom they sell the acreage, but the listing agent is a friend of hers and he convinced them to give us an extra day to get an offer in. But that day is today and then it goes to Glenview.

I offered dizziness as an excuse for the "spell" I had at the river. I told her vertigo seems to come along unexpectedly these days. Her smile was as tight as a drumskin, her sympathy low. I realized I probably had a number of urgent messages from her, unheard on my phone. There was nothing on her mind but saving that plot of land. She didn't know my good friend died two days ago. She didn't know that my lover drowned sixty-one years ago in the exact spot she wants me to protect.

So, I told her. That the recently deceased Rev. Oswald Martin had been my friend and that the largest boulder in the center of the river was the one that had ended my first love's life. She looked so abashed that I almost thought to take it back! Her professional demeanor crumbled, and her apologies tumbled one over another. I let her prattle on, trying to work out in my head what would be best.

The preserve is the location of my nightmares, Gerald. My God, the river took you right there. And now I have the power to hurt her back. Maybe not a killing blow, but if I don't back the land trust purchase, she will be choked by sediment and poisoned by lawn chemicals. Her pretty shade trees will be gone and a mile-long stretch of her shore left naked.

As much as I want retribution, Lillian, who helped me with the wild-flower sanctuary, just wants to save more trees from the axe. And she's right; the trees don't want to be clear-cut to please Glenview's buyers. The meadow flowers don't want to be plowed under. The soil shouldn't erode and the nights should be dark. And though I didn't see them, I am sure there are bluets and wild geranium and bird-on-the-wing sheltering in the forest that can't survive being smothered by sod or poisoned by herbicide. And as much as I'd like to spite the river, there are lives at stake: the trees, flowers, grasses, and ferns and all the animals of the forest, field, and water. And if the river benefits from my gift to them, so be it. I will think only of the fates of the little flying insects and the shining fish and the toads and the friendly kingfisher.

When Lillian finished asking for forgiveness for being so brusque when I was obviously grieving, I told her I would happily give the land trust the money to outbid the developers, but only if they let me name it the Gerald R. Fessenden Sanctuary. I told Lillian not to forget the middle initial on the sign. There have been a few other Gerald Fessendens born in this region in the past two hundred years, and I don't want any of them taking credit for dying in such a beautiful place.

Let the river know she owes me,

Mimsy

Dear Gerald,

I am not doing well dealing with my friend's death, and I think that's why Cécile stayed with me all day. She started using English again, probably in an effort to get me to stop staring blankly at the ceiling and respond to her efforts to get me to eat. But no matter how delicious the scent of the treats she brought me, I pushed them away. Nothing will stay down. My loathing for the river has turned to physical sickness. More than once today, Cécile had to hold my hair as I puked in the toilet. Unwelcome flashbacks of Glimmer doing the same after parties on the tour bus flashed through my mind.

Poor old Oswald. He was an innocent. Probably the last of them. Not that the river cares about innocence. That is a totally human construct. What she cares about is how deep she can dig her banks and the speed at which her waters pass between them. She cares about rocks and how she will move them or if they won't move, how she will wear them away, and she cares about the heat of the days and the nights and whether the temperature is high enough to keep her water moving or if she will be stopped in her tracks by ice. The river is flow. She is time. Every second she is changing. She builds and unbuilds the world. Compared to her, we are mayflies—living a few months underwater and a day above it, and she cares for us as much as she cares for the mayfly nymphs clinging to the stones on her riverbed. Aware of us in aggregate, not as individuals.

Knowing that if some perish, as long as her waters run clean, more will come, people and mayflies.

Oswald said I think sloppily, conflating mindlessness with animus when I cast blame on the river. That the river has no mind to guide it, no mind to be directed by a curse, no mind to pick and choose victims. Just because something is dangerous doesn't mean it is hateful. Oswald was certain of this. That every single death on the river had been the result of carelessness or inexperience or being in the wrong place at the wrong time.

I know Oswald would not like my attributing his death to the river. In fact, he'd be insulted. He was a man who knew about mistakes, and behind the closed doors of his office, he spent many hours consoling people who made them. He would blame bad luck, maybe, or pure chance, his inability to see well in the dark, unusual weather, being rusty after not riding all winter, and the extra miles-per-hour above the speed limit he was traveling. He would never blame the river.

Maybe that's why when I thought I heard knocking at the door this morning, I expected it to be Oswald, there to set me straight. And I was ready to admit, this time he might be right.

But he wasn't there to tell,

Mimsy

Dear Gerald,

I've taken to sitting long hours by your river, just thinking the things that need to be thought. Bert, the postman, comes by in the morning and I enlist his aid with getting down to the water. He's not one to think elderly people shouldn't be left alone outdoors all day near treacherous rivers, even ones they've had to be rescued from, so he carries my picnic basket, my fiddle case, and my letter-writing materials. He deposits me like an old stone beside the water. Fills my ears with what gossip he's discovered along his route, hands me my mail, and heads off to parts well-known.

The river is quiet today. There's a little bit of activity here at the edge, several small caddisflies crawling across the stones, hauling their houses made of pebbles. A few minutes ago, I caught a glimpse of a great blue heron upstream, coming around the bend in the river and landing in the shallows, cocking one eye toward the water, intent on spearing a fish. After it captured its prey, it flew awkwardly away, leaving me and the river alone together. When I witness scenes like this, I can almost believe she is like any other river.

I do have some news. My album has been released. I have never been so proud in all my life. It already has a couple of good reviews, and I am happy now that I made something that will live on after me. I have access to it on my phone and can play it for you, if you'd like. The phone speakers are a bit tinny. A live performance would give you a better sense of the work, but I haven't been able to pull everyone away from their day jobs to play a concert for a dead man, so you are just going to have to be satisfied with what comes out when I press play.

Listen up!

Mimsy

Dear Gerald,

Cécile is doing much better with the baby, Gerald. When she touched him in the past it used to be incidental, involved with daily care: diapering, dressing, laying down to bed. Now her touches are intentional. She's holding the baby a lot more, sometimes brushes her fingers over his downy head. I even saw her kiss the baby's feet and count his toes, and I tell you, the relief that flooded through me when I saw that was magnificent. The therapy and the medication and Aidan's devotion to making sure he takes over baby care as soon as he gets home so she can get enough rest, they are all working. Their little family is being reborn.

Your son called to offer his condolences on Oswald's death. Booker's a little quicker at receiving news than he was back when Aran died. Maybe it's that online subscription to The Jockey Cap Tattler I got him. He is planning on vacationing at a lake house for two weeks in July, and he's bringing his new girlfriend! She's a data miner, whatever that is. There are jobs now, Gerald, with computers and the internet that are mysterious and seemingly impossible to understand the point of, but they certainly pay well. Anyway, whether she mines data or diamonds, I am happy for him. I'll bring them down to the river so you can meet her. Hopefully, I'll be in a better state for company by then. Wouldn't want my new "daughter-in-law" to find me a morose, bitter old woman and make alternative vacation plans for next summer.

Your river is still and full this afternoon. Pale green ovals tint her surface, a reflection of the new spring leaves overhead, creating the impression of a verdant pool. A couple of fish leap after some small flying insects that whirl together in a vortex over her surface. I kind of like her when she's like this. I can almost hear Oswald expounding her virtues.

Love you.

Mimsy

Dear Gerald,

You heard it here first. Mimsy Bell, composer, and the most excellent band in the world, The Maple Keys, have a seven-venue tour booked in the Northeast! The Burnt Meadow Music director heard through the music industry grapevine that a new folk band out of Tennessee just lost their opening act in the middle of a fully booked tour. Once they had a listen to our album, they were ready to sign us up! We are going to hit Portland, Portsmouth, Boston, Northampton, Hartford, New Haven, and Providence. Small, intimate, artsy concert halls. I know we're just the opening act, but since we weren't planning on touring at all, this is a great gift. Aran would be over the moon!

It's taken a lot of juggling to get the tour organized so quickly. Some of The Maple Keys have jobs and had to take time off. The retired ones needed the okay of their spouses. Young Jack got permission to do online school, so he's on his first tour. Since it starts right away there's no time for my nerves to get the best of me. Cécile is helping me choose outfits at the boutique later today (no, I am not digging out the 1960s costumes) and tomorrow we rent a bus and head south. The Maple Keys on the road for their debut show!

I'll write again when I get back. Aidan and Cécile are watching the house. Don't worry about me. With fifty-five years of experience on the road, I'll be in my element.

Love,

Mimsy

❧

Dear Gerald,

I'm back! I have the baby in my lap. He's a big fan of the mallard ducks swimming at the edge of the river and squeals with delight whenever they dart around or turn in circles. Mommy Cécile is inside, busy with the real estate agent. She's decided to sell the farm. Sometimes the only way to move on is to let go.

For the time being, Aidan and Cécile and the baby are going to live with me, just until they find something new. They've agreed to wait until something in the village comes on the market. As soon as I heard they were selling, I contacted Lillian from the land trust. She offered a conservation easement to Cécile. This would allow the land to remain intact as a working farm and nature preserve through any property transfers. Cécile was certain Mackey would have wanted his family's property, with its beautiful fields and forests, protected forever, so she worked with Lillian to draw up the paperwork before the house went on the market. Wright Farm will never be developed.

Aidan told me privately that he is a little disappointed about the sale. He enjoyed the chickens, even defending them from predators, and before everything happened, he'd been planning on getting goats and sheep and a couple of horses. But he's a realist. There isn't any extra energy in the family right now. Every bit of strength has to be concentrated on the child and on Cécile's recovery.

I suppose you are dying to hear about the tour. There is too much to tell, so I'll stick to the highlights. For a surprise, whirlwind tour, it went seamlessly. And despite my fears, it was nothing at all like being on the road with the band. Nobody drank, everyone went to bed in their own room at a reasonable hour, there were no fights, and all the plates and dishes in the tour bus kitchenette remained intact.

Knowing we had only twenty minutes to warm up the crowd, we

spent most of our time on the ride down selecting songs. There was no arguing about this. Nobody felt slighted that their top choice wasn't picked. It went so smoothly I began to wonder if back on the road with the band we'd purposefully tried to complicate things. This week, I braced myself for conflict so intensely that I had to force myself to relax when there was none. It was like unlearning my whole way of being, which is very hard to do when you are eighty-one.

Going to sleep for a week,

Mimsy

Dear Gerald,

Bert dropped off a parcel today along with the mail. I was expecting it. The personal organizers I hired to sort out the storage unit down in Cambridge sent it up. I'd asked them to send only items of a personal nature, private stuff that might be mixed in with all the albums, equipment, posters, notebooks, memorabilia, and thousands of pages of music that were being donated to Lawrence's alma mater. What was left fit in a medium-sized rectangular box. I let the box sit on the table overnight, worried about what I might find inside.

I hadn't wanted to wake any bad memories just before bed. But by morning I felt strong enough to deal with what was inside. I figured the residual calm left behind by Aran's spirit would make the process easier, so I brought it into the studio and opened it there. On the top of the package was an envelope. Inside was a curl of my brown hair and one of Lawrence's blond locks tied together with a blue ribbon.

I had completely forgotten this moment, a sweet one among the many sour. We were sitting beside the road waiting for a flat tire to be fixed. Lawrence was high on mushrooms and was playing with my hair, mesmerized by the sunlit highlights. He was going to keep my beauty forever, he said, and I let him snip off a tendril. Then I playfully took my due from his honeyed head. He gently untied the ribbon I'd used to hold back my hair and bound our locks together. He must have hidden these away, for I never saw them again. Holding them now, the intermingled curls reminded me of how we'd wake up every morning, our heads close together, our hair flowing, two-toned, spilling across the bedsheets like a braided river.

Beneath the envelope was a photo album. An old one with sticky pages holding the prints in place. In here were all the candid photos the band members took of each other. Nothing slick and promotional about these, just real-life moments backstage, on the bus, outdoors, in the hotels. I braced myself before opening the cover.

And I was greeted by the smiles of children. We were just babies, Gerald, when we started the band. Naïve, impertinent, awkward kids with great talent, carried to stardom through hard work and hubris. Inside the album were images from our first year on tour. There were photos of us eating raspberries off each other's fingertips, of all of us in a pig pile on the bed. One where Glimmer was being swung round and round in the air by her arms by the piano player. Another of Aran Sky taking a ride on the back bumper of a passing car. A black-and-white image of Lawrence Bell doing a handstand on the hood of the tour bus. And there I was, arm and arm with Glimmer Linkletter, dandelion crowns on our heads, unclothed, charging headlong into the Pacific Ocean.

None of us had any idea what we were doing. We should be forgiven for what we became.

Mimsy

Dear Gerald,

There was a bit of confusion this morning, which I caused by hearing voices, then wandering outside looking for their source, getting dizzy, and falling in the driveway. Thank goodness it was Young Jack who found me. Aidan would have had me in the ambulance in a millisecond. I was able to convince the kid I had tripped. Up until now, I've explained away the other dizzy spells as exhaustion or grief, but now as I sit at the breakfast table, still muddle-headed and shaky, I know it is more than that. I can't let Cécile and Aidan know just how bad it is. They'd bubble wrap me.

It won't be long. The veil between the worlds has begun to part,

Gerald. For a few moments each day, the present gets fuzzy, the music garbled, the edges wavy. I get dizzy. One eye dims. My head hurts. Time flows. I hear you calling me to go on an adventure, but when I reply, you do not answer. Other times I hear Aran play, but when I go downstairs the guitars are in their places, the dust undisturbed by his fingers. I even heard Lawrence once, popping a bottle of champagne, making a toast, but I keep no wine bottles here. Oswald knocks at the door from time to time, but when I turn the knob the knocking stops. My father's garden hoe, I hear it out in the vegetable patch, pinging as it hits stones, but he never gardened in this backyard. My mother's singing drifts out through the kitchen window.

Time's coiled in upon itself and my whole life is playing out in the present time.

Soon,

Mimsy

Dear Gerald,

There is thunder in the north, somewhere up past Mt. Washington, and sheet lightning. Here, where the sky is still bright, four turkey vultures circle overhead. Their giant wingspans tipped with widely separated feathers, like fingers. Their heads are bald and red, the skin wrinkled. Their patience as they spiral above me is justified. They're not wrong to watch me and wait.

Bert set me up on my riverbank perch. It's no longer the peaceful, solitary overlook it was. Boating season has started early this year with several eighty-degree days in a row. I've counted sixteen tourists riding inner tubes, nine kayakers, and five canoes already this morning. The riverbank is covered with red-sparked spires of cardinal flower. The dizziness and confusion continue. Time in my vicinity is no longer stable. Sometimes it repeats itself in loops. Sometimes it skips ahead.

The sun was so intense, I made my way down to the riverbank and dipped my feet in the water to cool off. I noticed something luminescent among the stones, a pink and green tourmaline projecting from a weathered bit of pegmatite. Obviously, an early birthday gift from you.

I reached into the water and picked it up, turning it in the sunlight. It has come a long way from the mountains where it was formed. I am using it as a paperweight now as I write. The wind is picking up. Storm's moving closer. I wonder if this weather has caused a change in the barometric pressure, because I have the worst headache all of a sudden.

Well, this is unexpected. There's an empty canoe drifting down the river towards me. At first, I assumed its paddler was reclining, sunbathing, letting the current direct the course, but there is no one inside. Without my glasses, from a distance, it looked like a new fiberglass canoe, but now I can see it is an original canvas and wood boat with a gold and black geometric design just below the gunwale. It looks just like the ones we used to borrow from empty camps along the river whenever we wanted to go for a paddle.

When I first spotted it coming around the bend, the canoe was gliding along the far shore. But as I watched—or perhaps when it spotted me—it changed course. Now it has come to rest at my feet, nosing against the shore. The canvas is in excellent condition. The strips of cedar inside are burnished to a glow. There are two paddles on the floor.

Oswald might say it is happenstance, but I know an invitation when I see one.

Why not one more adventure, Gerald?

See you soon,

Mimsy

THE

JOCKEY

CAP

TATTLER

—

May 24, 2018

LOCAL ROCK STAR'S LAST RIDE

By Jack Bourgeois Jr.

MENOTOMY–Among the mountains and lakes of her hometown, Margaret "Mimsy" Bell, née Browning, passed away from a stroke at eighty-one years of age while taking one last ride on the river that claimed her boyfriend's life sixty-one years ago. Although there were no witnesses, it has been determined that Ms. Bell got into a vintage canoe that had been reported stolen from a dock upstream. Mimsy Bell paddled some distance, past the village, farms, and woods, before succumbing to a stroke. Her body was recovered from the canoe by Officer Aidan Ward of the Menotomy Police Department, who was also acquainted with Ms. Bell. When asked for comment, Officer Ward said, "Mimsy was my best friend. She was talented and determined and precious to my family."

Mimsy Bell spent her formative years in Menotomy, going to school at the academy and spending time with her first love, Gerald Fessenden. Mimsy, an accomplished fiddle player, later married Lawrence Bell, principal member of the internationally famous, Grammy winning, multiple gold record band, Bell's Sky. Ms. Bell played fiddle and toured with Bell's Sky for fifty-five years. After Mr. Bell's death, Mimsy returned to her hometown to "find a patch of ground to rest my bones." During her search, she discovered friendships; established her own band, The Maple Keys; created a wildflower sanctuary; and composed an album. She also married long-time friend and bandmate, noted guitarist, Aran Sky, and the two made the most of their few months together living life joyously.

Mimsy Bell will be interred in a private burial ground where she will rest in peace next to her great-great aunt, Caroline Browning Pingree. Engraved on her headstone will be some of the lyrics from her recent album, *Tourmaline*. In keeping with her support of music education and wildflower protection, she bequeathed substantial portions of her estate to Burnt Meadow Music and the Pequawket Land Trust.

Ms. Bell is survived by her chosen family, Aidan Ward, Cécile Wright, and their baby Remi Ward, Robert Booker Thompson, Jack Bourgeois Sr. and Jack Bourgeois Jr., Belva "Batty" Holt, and Postman Bert Glidden. One close friend, Rev. Oswald Martin, predeceased her by several weeks. Donations in Ms. Bell's memory may be made to the Pequawket Land Trust for the continued upkeep of the Browning Bell Wildflower Sanctuary and the Gerald R. Fessenden Preserve.

Acknowledgements

Thank you to my parents for having
a house full of books and instilling in me
a love of reading. This book was made
immeasurably better by the intense support
of Hope Worthington and Joshua Brodersen
of my Rochester writers' group and
the encouragement of my wise readers
Kate Coffin, Dale Potter-Clark, Elaine Abel,
Colleen White, Ben Paris, and Douglas
Morrione. Thanks as well to Avery Hunt
who got me started on the search
for a publisher. To Agnes Bushell who kindly
read my manuscript and became my editor
and publisher, I am deeply grateful
for the opportunity and honored
by your enthusiasm. I could not have
done it without all of you. Finally, sincere
appreciation to two people who are no longer
with us. Thank you to my English teacher
Lee Sharkey for letting me grow artistically
in her wildly creative classroom. And thanks
to the man I credit with getting my seat
in the chair and this book finished, brilliant
essayist, writer, and friend Gary Socquet.